THE
SAWMAN

RONNIE HEWITT

THE
SAWMAN

THOROGOOD

Thorogood Publishing Ltd
10-12 Rivington Street
London EC2A 3DU

Telephone: 020 7749 4748
Fax: 020 7729 6110
Email: info@thorogoodpublishing.co.uk
Web: www.thorogoodpublishing.co.uk

A CIP catalogue record for this book is available
from the British Library.

PB: ISBN 1 85418 362 1 / 978-185418362-0

Cover and book designed and typeset
in the UK by Driftdesign

Printed in the UK by Ashford Colour Press

To Anne, David and Judith

1. The primary source

Monday 16th September – Day one

It is quiet, a few bottles and some food wrappings are all that are left from the partying by late night revellers now silent in sleep. He is alone on the streets. A tight knitted black cap pulled over his ears sits high on the upturned collar of his long dark coat that flaps its rear vents as he walks. His hands are buried deep in his pockets. From a distance the outline and posture of his body resembles that of a rook – dull, black and wary. The yellow streetlights follow his progress, like theatre spotlights they track him as he passes from one to the next, until finally he steps off stage into the dark and is gone.

In the blackness of the shadows his eyes peer forward as if staring into a dark underground tunnel, in the centre a rectangular shape: black upon black like the colours of a despairing Rothko painting. After a few seconds, his eyes adjust to the gloom and the darkness lifts. Ahead, the shape of the narrow alley's perspective is defined. At the far end and about nine feet from the ground is the fire escape ladder that was added as a planning condition when the four-storey house was an old people's home before it was converted into flats. Above he sees the window, no light just the murky darkness of months of unwashed grime. He walks slowly and silently down the lane.

His dark clothes cloak him from the street and his shape shrinks to no more than the weakest of traces as he walks on.

After eight, cushioned, but purposeful strides he is under the ladder. He looks up, draws out the extending pole from inside his coat, slides it to its full length, reaches up and clasps the end rung with its hooked finger. A sharp tug and the ladder jerks free. Supported by the pole it lowers gently to the ground like a flag from its mast. Then he telescopes the shaft into a short stick and slips it back into its pocket. It is the detail that matters and the detail is, as always, perfect. As he climbs like a trapeze artist, smoothly and silently skywards, his soft shoes make no sound. When he reaches the landing he rolls down his knitted cap, which instantly becomes a mask: a black Balaclava with three tiny slits. He takes off his coat and lays it down gently on the metal grill at his feet. From a pocket deep inside he withdraws a long thin bar. He guides the thin metal flange effortlessly between the top and bottom window frames and then with the smallest leverage releases the aged worn catch easily. After an audible intake of breath he pushes the window open in one easy movement. A knee on the sill, a little spring and he is up and in. He starts to close the window behind him, but when it is halfway down it squeaks so he stops pushing. A little extra pressure is applied in the right place and it closes without a sound. He raises his hands in the air, smoothes each of the wrists of his black latex gauntlets and listens. It is deathly quiet apart from the sound of his muffled breathing and his pumping heart. As his eyes adjust to the light from the neon brightness that spills under the door, he scans the room. He sees the outline of a bed and a desk with a computer VDU; its screen is blank, dull and idle. He is ready.

In the gloomy darkness he takes four paces and he is there. His legs slide apart as his right hand grabs the door handle, next he turns the round wooden knob slowly until there is a faint click from the old brass latch as it frees itself from the jamb and then he stops. His fingers move from the handle to his side and flick up the leather retaining-strap, a second later the hunting knife's long steel blade is drawn clear of its holder. As if pulled by a magnet, the chink of light from under the door strikes the blade at its sharp tip and travels along its steel shaft like a strip of smooth silk, flashing as it traces its edge; a ridge of constant peaks, each sharper than a razor. He lifts the blade to his face and with a flick, like the blurred fingers of a poker card player, the blade and handle are reversed. The blade between his fingers picks up the whites of his eyes as he draws the grip up to the slit under his nose and breathes in deep. The embalmed leather handgrip secretes a pungent sour smell of salt and musky sweat. His first snort is like the rush from a line of coke, addictively stimulating, the second floods his senses as if it has been injected straight into his vein; he shivers once, throws his head back and then is deadly calm. A few seconds later he grips the door handle in his left hand and with the other lowers the knife to waist height.

He presses his shoulder flat against the wall, listens and then eases the door open just enough to scan the hallway with his right eye. All he can see is a small table with a lamp burning bright – it is clear. He puts his ear to the space and listens again – nothing. He takes another look along the corridor and then he slides his head into the space and checks both ways. He crosses the passageway and turns off the lamp. This takes away the bright glare, but there is still dusky light from the street through the window at the end of the corridor.

He makes his way to the first door, stops and listens. He switches the knife to his left hand and turns the door handle with his right. The door opens – the sitting room – he closes it again. Another few steps and then he follows the same procedure; he listens carefully *for the sound of breathing. All is quiet so he opens the door just enough to identify the room – it is the kitchen. Along and across the hallway to another door, he stops and listens – this is the one he is looking for.*

The nasal draws of breath and the slow expelling snores confirm that there is someone in there. He puts his hand in his trouser pocket and takes out the newspaper cutting. In the gloomy light he can still make out the face of the man in the newspaper picture. Ernst Muche is smiling. In the black and white photograph his gold front teeth look like dark cavities. The head, frozen by the camera, shows a shiny bald pate with strands of hair standing straight up in the wind. He nods and puts the cutting back in his pocket.

As he opens the door wide the faint light sweeps across the dark room until the widening beam stops over the snorer's face. It is an ugly face with piggy eyes, a wide twisted nose and a walrus moustache. Long wisps of hair drape over the pillow, their follicles rising from the side of an otherwise shiny bald head. "The photo flatters you Mr Muche," he muses. "The next one will suit you better."

He walks right up to the bed and leans over to within a few inches of his face and smells him. Muche is heavily scented. It smells of the sea, biting and sharp, but sweeter. "Davidoff Cool Water," he whispers to himself. The scent blends uneasily with Muche's over-powering and foul smelling body odour. He lifts a magazine off the bed. It is pornographic with pictures of a man having anal sex with a woman who is tied to a bed while another man is whacking her with a studded belt. He lays it on the table at the side of the bed with many others, each of which display depraved sexual acts. He places the razor edge of the blade about an eighth of an inch from Muche's skin and traces it down one cheek, under his chin, around the swell of his Adam's apple, then up his other cheek, and stops just below his right eye. He holds it there as he closely studies the mottled skin, its little blemishes, lines and folds. "What is in this face that tells us that you are a beast?" he asks himself. "Is it your thick nose hair with their long and springy thin strands of steel or is it your sparse and patchy eyebrows like stubble?" He wonders if these are clues.

It is so easy now; the meticulous planning from somewhere deep in his subconscious takes over. He knows exactly what to do. He is no Jack Ruby. This isn't a one off: for Muche is number three. He is a ghost with no identity and he knows that there will be more.

He focuses on the eyelids and watches the fine blue veins dance as Muche's eyes roll from side to side. He wonders if he is reliving the rape of Miss Joyce Walters, a librarian, spinster, and virgin until Muche had got hold of her, dragged her to an alley and plundered her. There is a smile now on Muche's face, a kind of smirk.

"You knew she couldn't make you; corpses don't talk or point, you made sure she couldn't. You were lucky the prosecution was pathetic, but your luck has just run out." Muche's eyes, still closed, are even more active now. "Does your fantasy have more than one Miss Walters?" The black and white picture of Muche grinning flashes across his mind. "You, may have loved it rapist, but you don't deserve to be admired or loved even by scum like you." He traces the knifepoint down the cotton cover sheathing Muche's bloated body and stops at the pronounced bump of his penis. He draws around it. "Such a pathetically small salami for such evil hurting and degrading. Si mangiore," he whispers. Muche's body shifts, then settles.

He looks around in the gloomy light and sees what he is looking for. He leaves his sleeping victim and walks quietly to the chest of drawers. He slides the deepest drawer at the bottom and immediately the camphor fills his nostrils and his receptors identify it immediately – Eucalyptol. With one hand he empties the clothes

11

onto the floor. He picks up the glossy photographs that were hidden by the clothes. These are of battered and bruised women; each picture defaced – the eyes have been removed. His stomach churns and he throws the photographs down where they slide across the floor. He runs his hand along the inside of the drawer and then returns to the bed. He has work to do.

The invading grating sound of a bin lorry's rising arms as they swallowed the contents of wheelie bins ten floors below drew me out of my sleep. When I opened my eyes the bright light from my reading lamp momentarily blinded me. I drew back too quickly and pain shot from my neck through my body. The blood supply to most of my joints had been cut off by my unintentional yoga position on the sofa. My head throbbed and my swollen tongue pushed hard against my teeth, clawing for water. I could have been surfacing from one of my late night sessions in The Horseshoe bar, but I had been home all night. I was still dressed in my painting clothes – T-shirt and underpants. I felt like shit. It all flooded back, the whole fucking goodbye scene welled up in my head. I had been on my own for only two days since Liz walked out on me and I was already living like a 'dosser'. She warned me that I was heading for another one and she was probably right. That's the problem with mental illness you don't recognise it sneaking up on you and when it does it's too late to save yourself. Just then I never gave it a minute's thought: I had a job to do and that was all that mattered.

I levered my body into a sitting position and as I swivelled around I clocked the painting through the opened sliding door to the studio. I covered my eyes and groaned at yet another fuck up. The person that I had been trying to paint had a lot to do with my wife Liz leaving. When her patience eventually ran out she was standing among the prints that had spilled: a collage of his butchery; his not for human consumption grisly handiwork surrounding her like a rug speckled with red, brown and black, releasing the dam of anger that she had been holding back for days. Thanks to him in my trance-like existence, however, I had been unaware of it building. I tensed and cursed myself for being so dumb. I sat where I was for a few minutes and stared out the window. Our apartment, on the corner of the top floor of a converted office block, had wonderful views south across Glasgow's city centre to the river and east over the M8 to the hills beyond. I could tell from the traffic, what time it was and if I was to catch the 8.45 BA flight I needed to get up so I slung my legs around and rested my naked feet on the smooth beech flooring. Just then the BBC's Breakfast television theme blared out from my plasma screen in the sitting room – 7.30 and my wake up call. Reluctantly, I got up.

I checked the phone – no messages; nothing from Liz. 'Fuck it' filled the air. I lumbered to the bathroom and squatted on the loo. I sat there with my head resting in my hands, elbows on my puny knees and unloaded last night's carryout pizza. Was this as bad as it could get I asked myself. I knew the answer was no. At least some of the crap from the past few days got flushed away. I dared to look in the mirror. The enervated face reflected how I felt. The heavy sunken eyes matched the growth of stubble that covered my chin – black and dull. I instinctively stuck out my tongue; its grey furry coat resembled something ejected from Iian Mellis' cheese shop. I pulled the disgusting organ back inside.

I hauled off my paint-splattered T-shirt, spun the taps until the sink was full and then plunged my head into the water. The shock blasted me into the here and now and there was no going back. As I towelled my face half-dry the echoing familiar voice of the newsreader only accentuated the emptiness of the place. It felt different – vacant and bare. My few bits and pieces looked pathetic on the bottom shelf of the stand that used to stock our toiletries. The upper two glass shelves cleared of the creams, hair products, brushes and cotton wool pads. Even the electric Braun toothbrush had been taken – in the ceramic cup in which we had kept our 'his' and 'hers' there was only my little white brush head, with its lonely blue ring.

I only realised that Liz had had enough when she gave me a clear and simple ultimatum; to give up my work and save my sanity and our marriage. But how could I? I had to go on. I had to help them because he had to be found, had to be stopped; and I was their last hope.

I slicked my hair back, squeezed out some foam, lathered my face and then erased the stubble with a few scrapes of my razor. I went back to the kitchen and switched on the coffee and blanked the TV.

It was at times like these that I could have stayed in the shower for hours, but I only had time to wash off the night's sweat before I had to head for the airport and Manchester to find 'The Sawman'.

I finished the shower, dried off and then rubbed my teeth and tongue with the tiny plastic lifeless stump of a brush to get rid of some of the stink of nicotine and stale whisky. I don't know why I bothered as I was about to gargle with the previous night's stewed coffee. A mug later, drunk in a oner; black and no sugar, I was dressing fast. The final act completed when I slipped my portable computer into its case. I was ready for another day. I ignored the mess, threw my jacket over my shoulder and was out the door and on my way.

If I was to shake off my body's reluctance to wake up I needed to get a lung full of fresh air. I took the lift to the ground floor and snaked through the crowd of office workers who were waiting to fill my vacated space ten times over before they ascended to floors one and two that still functioned as offices.

I exchanged insomniac nods with Alec our security man, who was rooted to his desk as usual; his face as grey as the pictures on his monitors and indeed as the day itself. I went straight to the front doors.

When I pushed the glass doors open I was blasted by the trill of Glasgow's vocal commuters and the throb from buses that trundled passed. Another few steps and I felt the full effect of Renfrew Street. Even at that time in the morning the place was in full swing, it was like plugging yourself into a socket and everywhere you looked the attitude of Glaswegians was on full display – brash and unapologetic and just then I was happy to be one of them. I could feel my mood lift, helped by a hole in the rain clouds that promised the hope of a beautiful bright day. The painter in me took the time to appreciate the view that the watery sun's beam of light framed. Buildings nearby were transformed. Their void and colourless glass windows changed into solid shimmering orange mirrors and their flat concrete greyness into hollow silhouettes. It drew my eyes to the workers dangling from safety harnesses above the Glasgow Film Theatre, somehow invisible until then. I loved Glasgow and I was lucky enough to live in the heart of the city, the main shopping streets of Buchanan, Argyle and Sauchiehall Street were just a minute's walk away as were cinemas, bookshops, galleries, the concert hall, restaurants, pubs and clubs – fantastic.

I went back inside and took the door to our communal garage. The sound of its voluminous air-conditioning filled the enormous cavern. Parking places were like gold in Glasgow but my dark blue Mk III Healey deserved every carat.

Like every other city in Britain the traffic at that time in the morning was nose to tail and I crawled along bumper to bumper in the queue for the Kingston Bridge and the M8 motorway – Glasgow's gateway to everywhere. The planners had bulldozed right through the city to enable drivers to get from Greenock to Edinburgh without a traffic light. Why anyone would want to go to Greenock I don't know, anyway in their wisdom they created one of the best commuter roads to serve a city airport, although at that time of day the normal ten minutes that it took to get there were extended to half an hour. I didn't care. I had time and my old classic's three-litre burble was providing my morning fix. The Healey took my mind off Liz and I enjoyed the drive over the Clyde with its grandstand view of Glasgow's new skyline.

It didn't take long to get over the bridge and the traffic wasn't too bad all the way to the airport. It was my lucky day, I found a space only two minutes walk away from Departures. I parked up and joined the other commuters at the gate. By then I was on automatic pilot.

The flight was uneventful, although my nap from take-off to landing made sure of that. Isn't it odd that you toss and turn in bed for hours before sleep comes yet when smiling stewardesses get ready for their safety demonstration you fall asleep instantly.

I was to meet Inspector Ron Naylor from Greater Manchester Police at Arrivals. I had never met him before, but it turned out he was easy to find. He was the one wearing the uniform and holding the sign bearing my name, Dr Ahearn. Even without the uniform it wouldn't have been difficult to guess that Naylor was a long time policeman. He had that straight-backed, thick-waisted, big footed and hard-nosed look. His size underlined GMP's slogan, 'The force against crime just got bigger'. I introduced myself and we walked briskly to his car.

Naylor was to take me to Chester House, GMP's Headquarters in Manchester where I was to meet Assistant Chief Constable Robert Ulis responsible for Major Incidents, Crime Investigations and the Special Branch. Naylor never asked why I was there, I was glad because it would have led to "What is it that you do?" and I wasn't ready for that. Instead, we spoke of nothing important; just the rain in our two hometowns, which we measured in feet and United's likelihood of winning the European Cup as well as the Premier. In truth, I wasn't interested in football, but you don't grow up in Glasgow without being well versed in the country's national game.

The traffic was heavy and I spent the time looking at the other drivers. They all blanked us as we passed as though we weren't there. I've been there and done that you just hope that the uniform doesn't glance your way. We were still on the M56 when Naylor's new digital radio kicked into gear. The message was short. Naylor was to take me to Deansgate and the scene of 'Sawman's' previous night's handiwork. He put on his flashing blue lights, hit the siren and I was pushed back into my seat.

It was about 10.30 when we got to the old brick apartments and the place was swarming with activity. It looked like the media people outnumbered the crowd and that was saying something because at that time of the day those streets were teaming with shoppers. I clocked the black Jaguar and guessed that Naylor's boss was already there. We double parked next to Traffic cars and nodded to the two beat policemen who were attempting to keep the crowd back from the blue and white tape. The constable at the steps told us the top floor and I looked up the abused decorative banister and the ladder of worn dark brown stairs and sighed.

As I climbed the last few stairs to the top I was met by the odour. Death has a smell all of its own; a clogging rancid stench that is like no other and just then the air was full of it.

The door was open and I walked along its dingy corridor to the bedroom – the crime scene, and Assistant Chief Constable, Bob Ulis.

"Excuse me sir, this is Dr Ahearn," Naylor said.

"Good. Dr Ahearn," said a long face with an ingratiating smile that meant everything and nothing. He looked intelligent but maybe that was just because of his receding hairline. He shook my hand.

"Nice timing," he said with a booming voice that gave him presence and he knew it.

I weighed him up. He hadn't said much, but I detected a slight West Country accent that made him sound genuine, which from what I had heard about him I doubted.

"I'll introduce you to Detective Chief Superintendent Geoff Wheaton; he's leading the investigation. You'll know Chief Superintendent Wood from the Met Office." Ulis gestured towards a tall deep-set man with a crooked smile.

"Yes." I said and nodded to Woods.

Bert Woods was a secondee from the Serious Crime Squad at the Met, someone I knew well, a crafty politician who I didn't like.

Ulis was tall, slim and immaculate in contrast to the man he next introduced.

"Geoff, this is Dr Rob Ahearn."

"I've heard a great deal about you," said Wheaton. He was short and a little crumpled looking. A moustache hid some of his flushed face. I had never met him before, but from his body language and expression he looked a decent enough guy.

"I hope it wasn't all bad. The name's Robbie, or Rob, by the way," I said.

"I understand from our colleagues in the Home Office that Dr Ahearn might be able to help profile our serial killer gentlemen," said Ulis, addressing the other two.

"I hope so," I responded.

"Have you familiarised yourself with the background?" Ulis asked me. "I've read the Conran file. I was looking forward to seeing the house where the Sawman killed his last victim, but looks like I'm in it," I replied.

"I'm afraid you are right – our man's been busy. This is Ernst Muche." Ulis nodded towards the bed. "The important part is in the drawer." He directed me to the bottom drawer of the oak chest of drawers, which was open. I could see that a large head crowded the space. The eyes were destroyed and his face was bloated. And there was something stuffed in his wide mouth that filled his fat lips – it was like a wrinkled cock-tail sausage though that one hadn't come from the local deli, no it was strictly Muche's own brand. Not to my taste, but it was difficult to shift my gaze from the frozen penis.

"Surprisingly small for someone his size," I commented.

"Haven't you heard Rob, it's not size that counts." It was Bert Wood.

"Yeah, yeah it's the tobacco." I lit up a Marlboro.

"I thought that you kicked that filthy habit," Wood said. He sounded like Liz. She had said that my excessive smoking was one of the signs I was slipping away again, the smoking, the heavy drinking a precursor to becoming more morose and withdrawn – I was already there.

"Ernst Muche was a bit of an unsavoury character; he has a record of indecent assault, rape and sodomy of a minor and it should have been longer. Last month he got off of a charge of rape and murder – insufficient evidence they said. I'd prefer you not to smoke here and if you are going to look around I'd prefer you to be suited up," Wheaton muttered. I put out my cigarette.

"Okay." Naylor's hand came around my side holding a plastic suit. I scrambled into the oversized 'baby-grow'.

"Hmm." Muche had the face of a scumbag. "The eyes got a makeover." I said.

"Sulphuric acid probably," said an attractive looking woman with short blonde hair.

"Dr Ahearn, this is Doctor Jane Warren from the coroner's office." Geoff said.

She had a nice pair of legs, not quite as shapely as Liz's, but they came close. She had the beginnings of laughter lines around her eyes, had to be in her late 30s. I thought that I'd better keep my mind on the job, so I asked Jane for some answers to a load of questions that popped into my head.

"When was the time of death?"

"Around midnight I guess. I won't know for sure until we've conducted the post mortem."

In each of the previous murders, Sawman had carved something religious on the torso and had doused their abdominal area and eyes with sulphuric acid. Not to hurt them for they were sure as hell dead by then.

"I suppose the MO was the same?" I asked.

"Looks like a hunting knife was the murder weapon and the head was removed by a saw. A surgical I would say, but I need to check it in the lab."

"Is it his?" I pointed to the penis.

"Definitely."

That had finished that line of questioning. I returned to the head and begun to speculate how the killer had carried the head to the drawer. I could feel one of my crazy moments coming on. I'm not sure what else to call them. I got these crazy thoughts at times like these and still do. Maybe they were signs that things weren't quite right in my frontal lobe area, but I never noticed at the time. Just then I wondered whether The Sawman had put a finger deep into each of Muche's ears and made a weightlifter's snatch. I settled for his index finger being inserted into the orifices, his thumbs placed just above each ear with his pinkies positioned under his cheekbones for balance. That was it, his index fingers penetrated as far as the Eustachian tubes and when he unplugged them he collected the wax and moulded a miniature head for his collection; all tanned and shiny. "And it is my privilege to present the National Academy of Design award to Sawman."

I turned to Ulis.

"Hmm. Did anyone hear anything?" I enquired, as I studied the head.

"Nothing so far, but we're still taking statements from the neighbours," Wheaton answered.

"Who reported it?"

"A friend of his, a Mr Leon Melnar. Let himself in with his own key. Found him just like this. Melnar is next door with Steve Cale one of my detectives. You can't miss Melnar, he looks like a pimp." Wheaton said.

I checked out what was left of the rest of Muche's body. It was anchored to the bed end like a gruesome crucifixion; pretty tasteless neckties bound the hands, but then Mr Muche wasn't too bothered about that. The pillows were black and scarlet from the throat cutting and the carving. His chest was drenched in blood.

"Do we know what it says?" I asked as I stared at the grisly markings between his nipples.

"Steve says it's 'Gomorrah'. He might be right, but it is hard to make out. The message on the wall is clear though," Wheaton said. His eyes arrived at the back wall just ahead of mine.

I read out the scrawled writings. "'*Those, who have not done penance and have not known you, will never know you.*' Is it his blood?" I asked as I gestured towards Muche.

"I don't know." Jane responded.

"You can be sure it is. The person who did this is too tidy to drip any of his own." Geoff said confidently. And he was probably right. On Saturday when I read the report of his first murder last May I knew that there was something about the neatness of the murders that would make finding the killer difficult. There was an obvious attention to detail and the murders had been carefully planned suggesting that he was obsessive and likely to be well above average intelligence. The selection of his victims too had pointed to a complex character on a personal crusade. I was certain that he would do more and Muche was proof that we had a serial killer on our hands.

I scanned the bed and the surrounding area; I wasn't sure what I was looking for, but I'd know it when I saw it.

"Anything been moved?"

"No, nothing."

"Good." I looked at the bed. "Our killer must have looked pretty gruesome." I said to no one in particular and got no reply for my trouble. It probably wasn't so certain because apart from the writing on the wall and the bed, which looked like it had been marinating in pomodoro sauce – the sheets glued together with the congealed blood – the room was remarkably free of the stuff.

I followed a light trail of blood to the chest of drawers and noticed the photographs scattered on the floor.

"Has your photographer got these?" I asked Wheaton.

"Of course, he's in the back bedroom."

"Is that where he came in?"

"That was the entry," Wood interrupted. There was always the hint of sarcasm in his voice. I knew he didn't agree with my methods, I didn't hold that against him, but he was always trying to get one over on me. I returned to the photographs. Those were of battered and bruised women. Some of their faces almost obliterated with swellings that made them look like footballs, a patchwork of black and blue. Each picture was also defaced so that the women's eyes looked as though they had been gouged out. Just looking at them made me feel nauseous, but I was numbed too, which seemed to at least freeze the feeling of nausea. I had seen scores of dead bodies before, many had been women including some beaten to a pulp, but there was something in those pictures that was worse than anything that my mind recalled. It was the scratched out eyes. The faces were strangely naked without them. The eyes were always the first things that I noticed when I met a woman. Liz's hypnotised me when I first saw hers. They had been very special and still were: wide, staring and defiant. They sparkled and glowed, snatching the light and beaming it back. They were also my last memory of her when she walked out on me, full of disappointment and sadness. What kind of man could have inflicted such horror? In Liz's case it had, of course, been me, but the damage to the women in these photographs must have been by some perverted fucker. Of course I already knew that it was someone like Ernst Muche. I looked again at the gruesome pictures. The Sawman had made him pay for the suffering that he had inflicted and a whole lot of me wanted to pat him on the back.

"A bit of a misogynist Mr Muche. 'The Sawman' could have done us a favour," I said to Ulis.

"It is as well that you're not answerable for the violent crime statistics," he replied looking more than a little depressed. "Dr Ahearn, I believe people think you quirky. Well we don't do quirky here. I would like you to remain focused on the job in hand. What is it you do anyway?"

And there it was; that question that always led to suspicion and misunderstandings.

24

"I am a forensic psychologist, a profiler. I quite literally paint out the profiles of murderers from the imprint of their inhuman acts."

I could have said I have a PhD in clinical psychology, but I was the first to admit that was where the similarity with other profilers ended. My methods were unconventional and distrusted, but my results were compelling.

"He's not like other profilers, " Wood interjected. "Dr Ahearn is a kind of clairvoyant."

"No I'm not."

"But you have the second sight I believe," Wheaton retorted.

"I've heard people call it the second sight or a sixth sense, but I don't. I just accept that I have a unique insight that enables me to visualise a crime through the eyes of both the victim and the perpetrator. As well as drawing up a personality and behaviour profile I'm usually able to paint his likeness. My reluctant employers at the Home Office send me as a last resort. I make them stop."

"And how does this insight work?" Ulis asked.

"I have no explanation for it scientific or otherwise." I wasn't trying to be evasive, I simply didn't know how.

"What happens?" Ulis asked.

"When I visit a murder scene my subconscious 'captures' a copy of what happened. Sometimes part of it is revealed to me there and then, at the scene, but mostly it comes later when I paint. The paint seems to transcribe the buried images usually revealing a profile of the serial killer."

I could have added that those paintings weren't for the squeamish for they tended to reflect the ghoulish images from my morbid imagination, hellish visions that so far have accurately portrayed the people that I was after.

"With Dr Ahearn's input we hope that we can help your officers achieve a quick arrest Sir," Wood said.

"Provided we arrest the right person," I sneered at Wood and then turned to face Ulis.

"I hope so. We need to stop him before we've another Muche on our hands."

"I doubt that the good citizens of Manchester give a shit about what happened to this guy. If anything, they'll be hailing his murderer a hero," I said.

"You're probably right and the last thing we need is for a few crackpots to set up vigilante forces to hand out their own justice. We have a psycho on the loose in my territory of responsibility, and the Home Office believes that you have something to contribute. If so I would like to see it sooner rather than later. I'll see you in Chester Street when you are finished here." The look that he gave me was a well-practised one, but I didn't scare easily. "Are you coming?" Ulis said to Wood.

"Make sure I am copied in on your report," Wood said to me.

"A pleasure." I replied and with that he turned and left with Ulis.

I breathed an inaudible sigh of relief. Ulis was right though about the mood of the public. The media would use the Sawman case to highlight the police's failure to lock up depraved bastards like Muche, even though they knew the real culprit was the Crown Prosecution Service. I was just glad that the Sawman had rid us of some of the scum that stalked our women and children.

If Wheaton was sceptical about my contribution he hid it behind a very polite facade. I could see though that he was happier doing what he did best, detection and I was relieved that he left me to my own devices.

I knew that with all the activity going on I wasn't going to relive Sawman's experience; I would have to come back later, but the exploration was useful background material that would help seed the detail. So I spent the next ten minutes studying the place. I made my way to a wardrobe, waltzing around the impedimenta of the Scene of Crime Officers who were crawling all over the place in their oversized suits. I opened it and registered the clothes that hung on the rail; most were dated, but they had been expensive. There were more ties, just as tasteless as those used as restraints.

The bedroom, like the house before it had been converted, had once been very grand, but that had been a long time ago, probably before Muche. Only the ornamental plaster, now with pieces missing, and the wide-board pine floors remained of what must have been a beautiful room. The ceiling was high, but sagged from water damage. The décor was dilapidated mottled by black and green mould and the new graffiti hadn't improved it. The walls were covered in maroon wallpaper, which had lifted here and there because of the damp. It hadn't been painted for some time; the woodwork and around the light switch at the door were covered in greasy filth. The rugs were pretty grubby too; they had probably never been vacuumed in ten years or more. The detritus of a sloth was also evident on the bedside tables. There was an ashtray full of butts; old tissues; shot glasses and what looked like the remnants of a pizza – artichoke and chorizo, if I wasn't mistaken – not one of my favourites, but protruding from that lot were

27

two expensive gold ornate art deco lamps. I could see that the tables themselves were also art deco and valuable.

I checked out the corridor, opened each of the doors, viewed the rooms and got a feel for what the 'Sawman' had confronted in his search. Each room seemed gloomier than the one before. The general ambience was definitely seedy, particularly the bathroom, which looked like it had been raided by the Vice Squad. The place was strewn with unlaundered towels and sex aids. An old brown plastic bucket was half full of water and stuffed with dildos of all shapes, colours and sizes – most were extra large or, I should say, gargantuan. I felt a pang of inadequacy. I wondered what the Sawman would have made of these if he had seen them because that place gave me the creeps, but I could tell that he hadn't been in there. The atmosphere throughout the house at night must have been pretty eerie, but I knew already that The Sawman wouldn't have been bothered by it. From the forensic reports that I had read I had gleaned that he was a cool customer. They had combed the previous two murder scenes and, despite the skin and hair samples recovered, none of his were identified, not even the slightest trace of his sweat or body oil, so I didn't expect any DNA samples of the Sawman to be found.

As I looked around I had the feeling that, even before the previous night, Muche's apartment had witnessed some horrible scenes. There was a lingering rancid smell, not from the body, but from the walls. I opened the lounge door and saw another of GMP's detectives. We introduced ourselves. She was called Dawn Burns. I recalled her insightful input to the reports that I had read.

"Anything interesting?" I asked.

"Nothing so far. I don't think he was in here."

I closed my eyes. Dawn was right, he hadn't been in that room. I was at college when I first discovered that I had an ability to visualise crimes of murder or significant violence. It was all a bit weird at first, but I have grown to accept it as a gift of an extra sense.

"It's a strange looking room," I said. And it was. One wall was stripped of paper down to the plaster and had been left unpainted. The floor had no carpet and there was very little furniture.

I left her bagging and tagging and headed next door to the back bedroom where a photographer and a forensic investigator were working. I introduced myself. The photographer was called Jim Sloan, a big man, tall and fat. The investigator was called Andy Cooper, black and handsome with broad shoulders and bright eyes. He was dusting for prints and acknowledged my greeting with only the slightest of movements of his head, his eyes glued to the patch that he was brushing.

"Anything?" I asked as I watched Andy's wrists flick the brush along the window frame like a conductor encouraging his first violin. Andy shook his head. I surveyed the room and settled on the wall beside the door, certain that he had stood just there. "Can you check this area out thoroughly?" Andy nodded.

"I've already told him to check that out." It was Wheaton again.

"Any fresh ideas on this?" I asked.

"Fucking mental case, but I can't say I'm weeping any tears for Muche. Any idea what that smell is?" He asked me.

"Mothballs" I replied.

"Not that. You any idea Andy?" Geoff asked.

"What?"

"That sort of herb smell," he said. There wasn't much of a trace that I could sniff other than the general rancid smell of the flat.

"Can't say that I can smell it over the stench of shit and spunk Chief," Andy replied without turning his head.

"It smells familiar, but it doesn't feel as though it belongs here. Can you detect anything Jim?"

"No Chief, don't think I do. Could be my sandwiches though."

"What's in them?" I asked.

"I never know, but they always smell like cheese," Jim laughed. He had a belly like a sack of gravel that hung over his belt, and when he laughed it jiggled up and down.

"Very witty Jim, but I think this smell is too upmarket for your sandwich. Hmm, there's something here." Wheaton sniffed the air theatrically and wafted his hands under his nose, but I had the feeling that he already wished that he had never mentioned it. I crossed to the window.

"Did you check around these light switches?" I asked.

"Not yet, but I will," Andy replied.

I instinctively looked at my wrist again.

"Are you looking for the time?" Jim asked me.

"Just habit, my watch is broken. I rely on the clocks on microwaves and cookers and passers by."

"Have you been over the fire escape?" Geoff said to me.

"No not yet. Has it been checked?"

Andy chipped in, "I've been up and down there. It was definitely the way he came in. The bottom ladder has been down recently, but there's no sign of him anywhere, no footprints, nothing."

"I'll take a look," I said and left them to it.

I looked out the window and down the fire escape. I put my hand on the safety railing and ran my fingers along the rough rusted metal. It was hard to believe that Andy hadn't found any forensic evidence there. It was time for a cigarette so I stepped out onto the grating and took out my Zippo. I shook it and opened the top with its reassuring clink. A solid thumb and the fresh air helped it fire first time. I leaned against the wall with my Marlboro. The nicotine penetrated deep. I thought about going down the steps, but I didn't want to spoil the moment, so I just leaned over and looked down.

The view through the diamond holes reminded me of when I used to spend a lot time up trees. When I was a boy I would camp out in the bluebell woods near my home to hide from friends and watch them search the bushes below. Sometimes in the summer I would spend most of the night in my tree hideaways. I used to take a thin blanket with me, just thick enough to smooth out the jagged bits and I would lie belly down on it, hang my head over the top of my makeshift bed and stare through the branches to the ground below. I even slept up there and once I saw the O'Neil boy have sex right below me. Even now I'd swear that the girl had been smiling up at me as her lover pumped his bare arse up and down like a piston. I guess she had never said anything to him or I wouldn't still be walking around today.

"Rob?" It was Geoff at the window. I should have known that those few seconds were too good to last.

"Steve's in the kitchen drinking coffee with the person who found Muche. I'm going to interview him; want to join me?"

I threw my pleasure over the safety barrier and climbed back inside.

"The pizza – find out where it came from and if it was delivered," Geoff ordered Andy as we passed him in the hall. I suppose the delivery boy could have seen someone lurking around, but it was a long shot.

"Introduce us," Geoff said to Steve.

Like the prosopographer that I was, I scrutinised the small thin agitated man that was antsing on the edge of the chair next to the table. His skin was olive and waxy like a new tin of boot-polish. His shirt was loud and he was wearing a lot of gold; on his wrist, his neck and most of his fingers, but it was the shoes that were a dead give away. They were snake-skin with silver buckles; the ubiquitous footwear of a pimp.

"This is Leon Melnar. Mr Melnar found Mr Muche," Steve said.

"Detective Chief Superintendent Geoff Wheaton."

"Rob Ahearn Forensics." I looked straight into his eyes the whole story was there, liar, cheat and fucking scumbag; a murderer, probably, but not Muche's. I could also see that Wheaton was thinking that Sawman would have done him another favour if he had bumped into this guy.

"Must have been a bit of a shock Mr…" Geoff said.

"Melnar, Leon Melnar. This is weird shit man I'm freaked ok. What mental case could have done that." The whites of his eyes flashed as they flicked towards the bedroom.

"I was hoping you might help us work that out," Geoff said as he narrowed his eyes.

"I don't know anything about this crazy stuff man. I told your guy everything I know. I don't know any mad mother-fucker that could do something like this."

"When did you get here?" Geoff asked slowly.

"About half past seven," he fired back.

Geoff paused and then asked: "Where had you come from?"

"From my home man, of course."

Leon Melnar showed signs of anxiety and a little aggression crept into his melodic voice.

Geoff paused again. I could see that he planned to frustrate Melnar a little more. I was certain that Geoff knew instinctively that Melnar wasn't the murderer, but you could tell that he thought the sleezebag was involved in some way and he seemed determined to find out what it was.

"And where is home?"

"I already said."

"I'm sorry, but not to me. You must have said it to Detective Cale."

"Salford, I've got a loft in the Quays," he said smugly. The Quays was the new fashionable place where old warehouses had been developed into lofts and it was rising fast in the trendy stakes.

"How's living among the upper classes?" Wheaton said sarcastically.

"I'm comfortable in anybody's hood."

"Did you get here in your own car?" He asked ponderously.

"Sure man, my BMW, crimson red. Why?"

"I ask the questions," Geoff retorted.

I watched Melnar's eyes get smaller and his mouth tighten.

"So you left home when?"

"I don't know 7.10, 15 whatever."

"And you let yourself in with a key?"

33

"Yeah, I had a business meeting with Ernst." He was trying to play the role of a responsible businessman – as an actor he was a Hollywood BA (failed).

"What kind of business meeting was that Mr eh?"

"Melnar, Leon Melnar. It was just business, man, you know stuff."

'Stuff' the language of the inarticulate, crooks and liars.

"No I don't know Mr Melnar what stuff?" Wheaton asked with emphasis.

"I was here to make some arrangements man about some entertainment for Ernst." He used the word 'entertainment' like an uptown business consultant uses made up words to bewilder clients.

"What kind of entertainment?"

"Hey what is this? I just found the man, okay."

"I am sorry to bother you Mr eh."

"Melnar man Melnar."

"Well Mr Melnar we have a very nasty murder here and I am sure you want to help us find the person that did this to your friend." Geoff's slow speech cried out for an interruption and he didn't have to wait long.

"Hey he's just an acquaintance man, someone I know, right."

Geoff didn't believe him, but the moment called for patience.

"An acquaintance who gives you a key to his apartment, as I was saying, if you prefer to answer my questions at our Headquarters we can go there now, but I thought that you wanted to co-operate."

"I am co-operating man, go on ask me your dumb questions I don't care."

I took out my cigarette pack and offered one to Melnar, neither Geoff nor Steve smoked. He took it eagerly. Geoff waited patiently until my trusty Zippo lit us both then said:

"Right. Can I ask you again what kind of entertainment are you both involved in?"

"You know, girls man. I run an escort agency and Ernst was one of my clients."

"An Escort Agency and Ernst was one of your clients," he replayed back.

"Yeah man."

"Yours is a legitimate business yes?"

"Sure man."

"Had Ernst used your services before?"

"Sure many times."

"Maybe you could furnish my colleague with receipts confirming dates and times." Leon almost spoke out but instead tightened his lips around his teeth. I was glad because his flashing gold caps were irritating my sense of good taste. Geoff carried on.

"Do you usually have keys to your clients' apartments?"

"Some. What is this? I had nothing to do with this fucking shit"

"So you have told me. Someone took a serious dislike to Mr Muche."

"Some mad fucker you mean," he interrupted again.

"Maybe. You'll understand that if Mr Muche had enemies we would want to know about them. Did he have any enemies?"

"I don't know man. The truth is that Ernst was a peaceful man, but everybody's got strange dudes that would like to shit on them man, I don't know anything about his murder. As far as I know there was never no reason for nobody to have drama with him. Anyway I wasn't a friend, just a business associate."

"Oh he was a business associate I thought that you said he was a client."

Just then Melnar had an unfortunate accident. It happens to all smokers at some time. The filter had stuck to his lip, well I suppose he had good reason to be dry in the mouth, and his fingers had travelled down the length of the cigarette until they gripped the tip. In case you don't know, a cigarette burns at 700°C at the tip and right then Mr Leon Melnar was playing with fire.

"Oh shit, shit." He jumped to his feet.

"Are you okay?" Steve said.

I was just sorry that it didn't melt those gold teeth.

"Yeah fuck; cigarette shit."

I offered him another light, but his cigarette was still burning.

Geoff carried on with his pointless questioning. "You just said that he was a business associate I thought that you said he was a client."

"Hey it's just words man. He was client, a good client. He sometimes slept late and his hearing was dull man so he gave me a key to let myself in."

"Tell me about how you found him. Did you ring the bell?"

"No I just let myself in and shouted on Ernst." His voice wavered and almost shifted up a key.

"Did you go straight through when he didn't reply?"

"No I went to the kitchen and switched on the coffee."

"And when he didn't come?"

"I went to his room to get him up." Melnar's hands twitched constantly.

"And then."

"And then I ran like hell."

"Where? Down the hall? Down the stairs?"

"No I went back to the kitchen."

"Oh the coffee."

"No man I was ready to throw up."

I didn't believe him. He wasn't the squeamish type.

"Hmn, right the pizza," Geoff said. Melnar looked bamboozled. "Never mind. Then what?"

"I called you."

"From the phone in the kitchen?"

"No man on my mobile."

"Why didn't you call from the kitchen phone?"

"It was easier man to use this." Melnar held up his mobile, which sparkled like his gold teeth. What a sad character he was and useless with it. I was warming to The Sawman.

"When you went into his room did you touch anything?"

"No nothin' man."

"Are you sure?"

"Like I said, nothin'."

"How did you know it was him?"

"What do you mean?"

"Well it wasn't as if you recognised his grin was it."

"I just knew."

"So you didn't see his head in the drawer."

"What?"

"Mr Muche's head. His head was placed in an open drawer beside some intriguing photographs. What do you know about the photographs?"

"What photographs?"

"The ones showing women's beat up faces."

"I don't know anything about them man, I ain't never seen no photographs." Melnar had begun to sweat profusely. I knew from his face that he was lying.

"Did you make any other calls Mr ..." Geoff was at it again.

"Hey man, what is it with you? I told you a hundred times its Melnar, Leon Melnar okay. And no, I haven't used the phone since I called you."

"Well Mr Melnar you have been very co-operative. We'll want to speak to you again I'm sure, do we have your mobile number?"

"Yeah can I go now?"

"Well I'm sure my colleague will just want a few more details then you are free to go. Detective Cale will get you a lift to your next appointment."

"I don't need a lift."

"Oh yes you have a BMW outside waiting for you, a bright red one License LM 100."

"Sure."

Geoff smiled, turned away and walked out. As I was leaving I heard him ask: "Hey how do you know about my BMW?"

Geoff carried on walking as Steve replied.

"He knows a great deal about you Leon. A great deal."

I bumped into Andy who was brushing the light switches.

"Anything yet?" I asked. He shook his head.

"Andy can you check Melnar's records and fingerprints. He's done time for a series of sexual offences. And see if there are any matches on the photographs next door," Geoff said. Andy nodded.

"You know this guy?" I asked Geoff.

"Sure we go way back. He doesn't remember, but I do. What do you make of all this?"

"It's too busy here for me to get much. There's just too much disturbance. I'll come back later when everyone's gone, maybe after the post-mortem. If you don't mind, I'd like to take a look at Conran's place."

"Sure, Ron will take you there. I'll get him."

Geoff returned with Naylor.

"Ron will take you to the Conran flat and when you're finished there he'll take you to Chester House. There's an office for you there, Ron will show you where and give you a quick tour of our communication centre where we have our major incident room. We can meet up at the autopsy."

"Okay I'll see …" I was interrupted by a shout from Dawn Burns.

"Chief!"

I followed Geoff through the door to the lounge and could hardly believe my eyes; it was as though I had stepped through the door of a tardis into a different world. Dawn was standing in a photographic studio. The walls and ceiling were mirrored and there were cameras everywhere, both still and cine. I'd only ever seen that much equipment in a television studio.

"I found it behind that back wall. The room seemed too narrow, so I had a closer look and when I slipped off the strip that covered the join, the wall parted easily. If the filming was against that wall," she pointed to the greyish matt finished wall, "you wouldn't be able to tell the location." Dawn was very good at her job, but was clearly one for the obvious too.

"I want prints of everything here and call up the Vice Squad and tell them to get someone here fast," Geoff responded.

Dawn got on her mobile and I mooched around. Judging by the number of new and used videotapes that lay around it was a highly prolific studio. There was a hook on the ceiling and the floor was scratched and worn directly below. I shut my eyes.

I could see the woman with the dyed blonde hair in the photograph, her struggling hands were tied at the wrists and pulled high above her head by a pulley attached to a chain that was hooked to the ceiling. Her mouth was gagged tight, binding her desolate screams and forcing the blood and mucus to flee from her nostrils. Her pointed toes scraped the floor as she performed involuntary pirouettes. As she tried desperately to anchor herself to something solid and familiar, Muche beat her senseless and her eyes, full of anguish and fear, searched for mercy as Melnar pawed her spinning body. I opened my eyes and shivered. I wasn't sure whether the videos and the studio had anything directly to do with the case, but I was sure that they had everything to do with Leon Melnar.

"It was the blonde in the photographs. Muche and Melnar."

Geoff looked surprised, but I could tell that his thoughts about Melnar had been close enough to give my statement credence. "Bastards." He said and was gone. I stayed behind, but I could hear his shouts from the kitchen:

"Right Mr Leon fucking Melnar enough fucking bullshit you're coming with me." A few seconds later Geoff came back dragging Melnar by his jacket lapel and threw him into the middle of the studio.

"I want to make a phone call."

"Listen you fucked up asshole I want to know what you had to do with this and I want to know now." Geoff grabbed

Melnar's golden cellphone almost before it was out of his pocket and whacked him over the head with it, smashing it into tiny pieces.

"Wait," I shouted and stepped between them.

"Rob keep out of this, okay?" Geoff spat at me.

"You better come clean scumbag or you'll be pulling cell-phones out of your arsehole for months."

"Geoff hadn't you better stop?" I intervened.

"Hadn't you better get going?" His eyes were ablaze with anger.

"Dr Ahearn leave this to us," Steve Cale said apologetically.

I left them to it. I went back through to the bedroom where I met Jane.

"Sounds like trouble," Jane said.

"Apparently, Geoff's on top of it." I answered sarcastically.

"Well I'm all done here," she said.

"When will you have the results?" I asked.

"After the autopsy; it should be underway about two. Are you attending?"

"Don't see that I've any choice. Will you be doing it?"

"No, I am on the road today. Do you need a lift?"

"No. Ron is looking after me. Thanks anyway."

"Okay, well it was nice meeting you."

I found Naylor outside the secret film studio and we left for Moss Side.

2. It's a dirty job but someone's got to do it

It took less time than I thought it would to reach Moss Side. It was the kind of place that typified old Manchester: rows of back-to-back houses with small backyards opening onto narrow passageways. Some had been knocked down and replaced with more modern social housing, but there was still a feeling of decay about the place, despite the efforts of some of its residents with their neat gardens. I could see that the Council was also trying to improve things with new leisure facilities and new housing, but the sprawling housing scheme that we drove into suggested that it wasn't enough. It was bleak with burnt out cars and rubbish strewn everywhere. I knew of its reputation for drugs and gangs and I couldn't help wondering how the Sawman had got there. It was hard to believe that anyone would park his car anywhere near and he wouldn't have come by taxi. It also explained why Naylor had arranged for a couple of community policeman to be there for our arrival.

I nodded to the policemen from the panda car and was glad of their escort up the stairs to Conran's flat, but I left them outside the door when I crossed the tape. I needed to be on my own.

It had been his second murder, yet the entry had been the work of a professional; no housebreaker could have done a neater job. His quarry had been taken completely unawares just like the first and Muche. I closed my eyes and waited. The air was chilly, the silence only broken by the noise of blue-bottles trying to escape or die. The atmosphere was one of a narcotic undertow and I got the impression of pervasive depravity with every wave that moved through me. A lot had happened there even before The Sawman's visit.

I closed my eyes. It seemed like a long time before I picked up my first real vibration. I traced the sound like a stetho-scope and with my eyes still clenched tight I followed the gentle rhythm of the pulsating baritone pump. When I opened my eyes I was staring at a closed bedroom door. I pushed it wide. The room had been cleared. Only the skeleton bed frame remained in the dingy room, the bedding taken for forensic examination. An inspection that I had read revealed nothing except the missing fluid from Conran's vacated body. I sensed that those last exaggerated heartbeats had pumped his blood from his arteries at speed. Only when his life had gone would the pressure have slowed the flood to a dribble, eventually clogging the ends of the sluice pipes. The Sawman had used some of the excess to scrawl the simplest of sentences on the cheap wallpaper above the bed end. It read 'Sinner'.

I closed my eyes again and immediately my head throbbed. I could feel that I was being tied into our collec-tive perception. My brain was being squashed in a vice, tightening with every intake of breath. When I could take no more it suddenly eased and I saw The Sawman's hand clasping the saw.

I watched the rapid movement of the saw as it jostled the head free then the wrist was captured in freeze frame. The thin latex gauntlet drew the flesh tight accentuating the trape-zium and trapezoid. The thin wrist connected a perfect hand, every carpal and metacarpal chiselled and moulded like a Rodin sculpture and the phalanges were exquisitely formed creating elongated fingers like those of a concert pianist. The crushing pain in my head returned and I opened my eyes and it was gone.

I felt anger, not mine his, not rage more controlled, but deeply wounded. And disgust; the smell of blood and torn flesh was overpowering. I gagged and my stomach heaved. I rushed out and found the bathroom. My insides blew out. I wracked and heaved until the bile was expelled.

My head throbbed, there was nothing more for me to do there but flee. I turned and left, glad to be out of that chilling hell. I raced past the two policemen standing guard and dashed down the stairs. When I reached the open air I tilted my head back and gulped it in. It felt intoxicating, clean and pure. I walked quickly to Naylor's car and got in, relieved to be away from that horrible flat.

I had recovered by the time we got to Chester House. The scale of the building was reassuring. An enormous glass edifice standing on pillars with the look of a 70s converted office block built, it was not unlike the building that housed my loft apartment. The throwing up episode had left me with a thumping headache no doubt exacerbated by the sediment of the previous night's drinking. I didn't feel like working but I knew I had to get on with it. Naylor made no mention of the tour and took me to my office. I guess he knew that I wasn't ready to face the social niceties; anyway, the computer and communication centre was a no smoking building and just then I couldn't have coped with that.

I was shown to an office the size of a large walk-in cupboard that was probably an unused interview room. The windows were sealed and it had no air conditioning. Its tight white walls would have given me claustrophobia if it hadn't been for the reassuring yellow and brown nicotine glaze that tainted every surface. Importantly, it had an ashtray. It was probably the only place in the building where you could smoke. The lingering smell was evidence that someone had taken advantage of its unique status. The vinyl chair behind the desk had smoker's acne on the arms with little eruptions like mini volcanoes where hot ash had lingered too long. It was kind of inviting, so I plopped myself down and flicked open my Zippo. That first deep inhale makes you see things differently. The room might not have been much, but it had everything I needed: a PC, although old fashioned, dull grey and grubby, it worked; a telephone, a desk with two drawers made of chipboard, the swivel chair and my ashtray. And with every puff my headache eased. Anyway, I had to get on with it; I had to write down what I saw at Conran's. But first it was time for George. I should explain. At one of my previous investigations the desk that I used had a bottle of malt in one of its drawers with a note that said 'Take of this freely, you'll need it, George.' Ever since then I always took a half-bottle of malt with me. I kept it in my case and popped it in the drawer of my workstation wherever it happened to be. Before I put it in the drawer I took a deep swig.

I opened my bag and took out my notes and stuck them on the wall. They were short and read:

5 May, Time: 1.00am. Victim: Alexi Zochten. Place: Salford.
12 September, Time: 2.00am. Victim: John Conran. Place: Moss Side

I sketched out the hand. It was no Rodin, but it was a fair representation. I didn't have fingerprints, but that slender wrist alone cut down the choice of candidates significantly. There was the saw, not a joiner's, something much shinier, a fine tool capable of cutting through bone. I realised that the nausea I felt in Moss Side was all mine, The Sawman went about his task like a professional. I was making progress, slow but progress nevertheless.

When I had finished sketching I scanned the front pages of the morning newspapers, not for facts, but to get a feel for what the serial murderer might be thinking after reading about his handiwork. And there was plenty to read. Since the second killing he had been big news. Judging by its liberal use, his nickname, The Sawman, had captured both the headlines and fired the imagination. Our man was competing for the front pages with the story about two young 14 year old girls who had been kidnapped whilst returning from school. They were still missing but thankfully at that time homicide hadn't been called in. Theirs was a story of fear and worry while his was about rapists and butchery and from what I could see he had come out on top.

It was easy to see how The Sawman's ritualistic executions had captured the media and the public's attention and that had guaranteed him the lead columns. The papers correctly portrayed the murders as executions: premeditated, with great organisation and planning. The reporting was graphic – you wouldn't have seen more had you been sitting in a ringside seat at the crime scenes.

I pulled out the drawer, took out George and topped up my coffee with a double shot. I was the son of a policeman, the grandson of a detective and the nephew of three policemen.

I could appreciate that a little nip might prevent you from beating arseholes like Melnar to pulp, but of course, might just encourage you too. I wondered how the interview with Melnar terminated, whether Geoff had sent him to the cells or the hospital. Geoff's treatment of Melnar didn't seem right, but that was just the liberal streak in me poking itself where it wasn't wanted the rest of me was thinking Melnar had it coming. I had come across a few arseholes, weirdos and crazies in my line of work. I could forgive the crazies, but shits like Melnar I wanted locked up; he was a piece of dog crap and, in truth, I would have toasted The Sawman if he had made it a double.

I turned to the PC, but as I tapped in my first command, Jim Sloan interrupted me.

"I thought that you might want these."

"Ah, some snapshots of your weekend," I said with a wry smile. My stomach was already preparing itself for the spin cycle.

"Hmm that smells good, make it yourself?" He said looking at my special Gaelic coffee. I nodded.

"Would you like one?" I asked.

"No I am still rough from last night. I was with the guys in Baker's Bar. I was fine until I met this old lady crossing the road."

"Doing a good turn?" I asked naively.

"No I met her at the crossing. It was okay until we got to the other side then she stood on my fingers." Jim smiled.

"As bad as that was it."

"Thankfully I don't remember the rest." We both laughed. "Are you staying here tonight?" Jim asked.

"Yeah, I think I'm booked in at the Royal."

"Fancy a drink when you get settled?"

"Thanks for the offer, but I'll be busy on this tonight."

"Okay." He turned and left.

I didn't want another hangover. The majority of eyes around there suggested those heavy drinking sessions were a common pastime. Anyway drinking in bars with cops for company wasn't my scene; too much cop-shop talk for my liking.

"Hey did you hear the one about the lawyer whose client is on death row."

It was Jim again.

"No." And I didn't want to hear it, but Jim was not a reader of body language.

"He says to his client, 'I've got good news, and bad news. His client says, Okay. What's the bad news?' He said, 'The bad news is that the Home Office won't issue a stay of your execution.' The prisoner says, 'Oh that's bad. What's the good news? And his lawyer says, 'The good news is I've got your voltage reduced!'

"Very good, but no more." I said.

"Is that today's?" He asked pointing to my newspaper.

"Yeah."

"Can I borrow it?"

"Sure." I passed it to him.

"I just want the sport." He removed the sports section and returned the rest to me.

"Thanks." I dropped it in the bin.

Most cops were like Jim: their interests tended to be football, wrestling or drinking. They preferred newspapers and comics to serious literature. My 'pops' was the same. I preferred to get my information from the primary source – the murder scene. Maybe that was part of my problem – I needed to lighten up. I took out another cigarette. It was time to look at Muche's photographs. I slotted in the CD containing the digital images which were crystal clear. Too sharp for my liking.

Muche was ugly and the acid mascara hadn't helped. His walrus moustache was draped around his clamped prick. There was enough gold there to give some dentist a decent retirement. And those ridiculous long wisps of hair – his head looked like some botched up Halloween mask.

I blew smoke out of the corner of my mouth and looked up his criminal records on my computer:

Sex: Male.

Race: White Alias: 'Pinkie'. I looked at the photograph of the head again. "Mm. Pinkie, that figures." I said to myself.

Height: 5' 10".

Weight: 230lbs.

D.O.B.: 27/4/62 he looked late fifties.

Hair: Bald.

Eyes: Brown – not now.

Distinguishing Features: None – correction by then there were quite a few.

Charges: 1979 Indecent assault – two years, 1985 punched, bit and raped a female victim – ten years. 1995 Sodomy of Minor Male – freed insufficient evidence.

Last Charge: Charged with the rape and murder of Miss Joyce Walters. Freed on August 20th due to insufficient evidence. Sawman had done us all a favour. If the Crown Prosecution had done their job properly Miss Walters would have still been dispensing books in the library. I made up my summary, printed it out and pinned it next to the others:

15 September, Time: 1.30am. Victim; Ernst Muche, Place: Deansgate – Three murders.

An e-mail message flashed up on screen. It was a copy of a memo to Geoff from Vice. I opened it. The message confirmed that the videos found in Muche's apartment were pornographic and contained obscene and explicit depravity and sadism. They had charged Melnor. I closed it down.

My stomach had settled but I had reached a low so it was time to eat something and get a shot of caffeine. I went down to the restaurant and grabbed a tuna sandwich and an expresso. The restaurant was a smart place – if it had had sockets and you had been allowed to smoke, I would have set up office there. I met Ron. He wanted to give me that guided tour, but for once I was glad that I was due at the autopsy.

I joined Geoff and Steve Cale at the morgue. I had only been there a few minutes when I regretted the tuna. My stomach started to churn when they took him out of the body bags; his head had its own hatbox. It was horrible. Just an hour before, I had been inspecting Muche pretty closely, and pretty gruesome he was too, but the weird thing was, there in the autopsy room he looked even more grisly and shocking. It wasn't just the spilled flesh and trailing innards, the phlegmatic coldness of the operation aggravated my revulsion. Not an eyelid blinked, as they cut him open. I felt odd, part of me expected the doctor and his assistant to piece Muche back together, which was ridiculous because I knew they were intent on taking him apart, except for the head – well there was no need was there. These conditioned meat packers were colder than Muche and he had iced up by then. Geoff had clearly got his morgue legs because he was untroubled. Steve on the other hand had already turned green. Steve must have seen many dead bodies, but he looked as though it was his first. I remember my first, the body was there, you wanted to look, but you couldn't, and then you took a quick glance and then looked away, well that was Steve.

James Wilby the pathologist, a towering figure, probably six foot seven, but built like a bean pole, was talking into a dictaphone. He looked bored; weariness and apathy characterised his every movement throughout the whole proceedings. In stark contrast his assistant, a little dark haired bundle of energy went about his task with enthusiasm. He seemed to be doing most of the work with consummate ease, as though he was carving the Sunday roast.

Dr Wilby was uncommunicative, but I got the gist of what was going on from his dictated record of whatever his assistant showed him. And there were no surprises. He agreed with Dr Warren's stated time of death – "about midnight" and confirmed the cause was a single slash with a very sharp knife that had a serrated edge. And that the same instrument was used to detach the penis, which I had already guessed. My mind was filled with a picture of Lorena Bobbitt's midnight attack on her husband's genitals and I considered myself lucky that Liz had just walked out. Apparently, Muche had been killed before his penis was removed and the sulphuric acid applied to his abdomen. His corneas had also been damaged after his head was removed. The one new thing that I found out was that The Sawman needn't have gone to the trouble of killing him because Muche was all but dead anyway: his oesophagus was riddled with cancer and so were his lungs.

I was fascinated by the attendant who was a butcher one minute, next a tailor measuring the body and then a shop-keeper weighing the head minus the penis on shiny scales. His industry was to be applauded, but when he started to bag the head I decided it was the perfect moment to leave and so did Geoff, so we left it to Steve and exited the autopsy room. We walked along the corridor to forensic where Geoff had arranged for us to meet with Alan Pinder, the Chief Medical Examiner and apparently a doyen of academic respectability.

"Dr Pinder," Geoff said to the back of a shabby pin striped suit.

"Oh Geoff," a man with a round smiley face in half moon specs replied.

"Dr Pinder can I introduce you to Rob Ahearn from the Home Office."

"Dr Ahearn, good to meet you. I've heard all about you. You know a good friend of mine, Professor Stanley Cohen?"

"Stanley, yes we've worked together a couple of times."

"Well, welcome to Manchester."

"Thanks."

"You will have come from the autopsy?"

"Yes, there wasn't much to help us. I'm hoping your team have unearthed something."

"Not much yet I'm afraid, but they are still working on it." He was a nice old guy, his voice was rich and deep, but with the soft and gentleness too of a real old timer.

"What have they found?" Geoff asked.

"The chemical used on the penis and the eyes was refrig-erated sulphuric acid. It is a strong corrosive chemical substance, which has a great affinity to water. It will literally attack water wherever it finds it and, as a result, produces lots of heat. The acid penetrated deep in the groin area, causing tissue damage similar to frostbite. It kills everything as it goes – no pain, no burns, but in a few hours the skin simply slides off leaving raw, exposed, muscle tissue as in this case. In the eyes, the sulphuric acid caused tissue freezing and cryogenic burns

The reaction and liberation of heat can be, and usually is, violent. It can be explosive and could result in drenching the person applying the acid in hot concentrated sulphuric acid. From the absence of burns to the cotton sheets that surrounded the body, I would say that the person who handled this knew what he was doing."

Here endeth the science lesson, I thought. The brief notion that James Wilby might have been enjoying some moonlighting came and went.

"Anything else?" Geoff said as though Doc Pinder was allowed one last wish.

"Yes, we found this." He held up a tiny plastic bag. It looked empty – no goldfish that I could see.

"It's a thread of black synthetic fibre. There was nothing else like it in the apartment so it might be from the murderer."

"Where did you find it?" Geoff asked.

"Now let's see." He looked at his file turning the page real slow. "It was above the light switch near the door exiting the room where we believe he got in."

"Precisely where?" I asked. Alan gave Geoff a photograph of the area and a note with the exact measurements from the floor, ceiling and the doorframe. Geoff passed it to me.

"Thanks. Can I keep this?" I asked Geoff

"I'll get you a copy. Thanks Dr Pinder that's a bit of a break-through."

"It's a pleasure my dear boy, but I'm afraid it is very common fabric used extensively in the cheap manufacture of wool substitute."

I looked closely at the thin fibre, squinting to see it.

"It's not much, but it's a start," Geoff commented to me and then, turning to Dr Pinder asked, "What about outside?"

"Nothing I'm afraid," he replied with a patient smile.

We were just about to leave and then I remembered that I had a question for the Doc.

"Dr Pinder, doesn't it strike you as strange that your boys haven't found one single trace of evidence on any of the three bodies?"

"Perhaps, then again he might just be very careful."

"There hasn't been a single hair or fibre," I said. He gave me a questioning look. "Until this one, not a drop of sweat, nothing."

"As I said, he's probably very careful. And anyway if murderers left clues all over the place we wouldn't need you would we?"

"No I don't suppose you would. See you."

"Oh, pass on my regards to Stanley when you next meet him."

"Will do."

The fibre find gave Geoff a lift, but he wasn't for cele-brating. I needed a cigarette, but it was too far to the sanctuary that was my office so I waved goodbye to non-smoking Geoff and headed for the back door where I intended to have at least one cigarette. When I got there a few die-hard members of the club were huddled guiltily around the back steps next to the wheelie bins, hiding from those goody goodies who blamed them for everything from making their clothes smell like ashtrays to giving them bronchial pneumonia. I would rather get a whiff of good old Virginia than some cheap after-shave any day. As I looked at their faces I felt I should roll up my trouser leg and give them a funny handshake to express my solidarity. We knew the risks and it wasn't as if we were having sex with a baby seal well not exclusively. Anyway, being banished to the basement drew us together and after only a few seconds I was having a joke and a laugh with my fellow lepers. Was it me or were the only people having fun smokers?

I enjoyed my cigarette as others came and went. We were sheltered by a large, dense, spreading mulberry tree, about 40 feet high. Its heart-shaped serrated leaves drew our smoke like living filters, removing our pollution from the air adding our nicotine to its coarse texture. I wondered how many it had smoked in its life and if the roughened longitudinal and diagonal splits and peeling on its dark greyish-brown bark were the scars of our loitering. Our grey haze rolled over the zigzag branches; stout, smooth, glossy, greenish-brown tinged with red. Despite our nicotine the leaves were still dark green, except for a few that were already spotted with the dull yellow of our advancing autumn. In truth it looked as though it was thriving on the stuff or at least that's what I hoped.

I caught a taxi back to Headquarters. I was beginning to find my way around the place, I got myself a coffee from the vending machine, poured half into the slop tray and when I got back to my office topped it up with a little pick me up from George. When I had finished the coffee I went to Geoff's office to collect my copy of the positioning of the fibre. When I got there Geoff was detailing a couple of his officers to investigate another murder; a small time mobster was found with his throat cut next to his car in an alley near the city centre – it seemed like Manchester was a dangerous place if you were a villain. I got my copy and returned to my office where I sat at my desk and studied Doc Pinder's note.

I'd investigated three serial killings before. The first two had been straightforward; in the first his murders of young gay men only came to light after his suicide. The second was eager to confess to his crimes when I confronted him with the evidence in his drains. Both of them had hung out in seedy places and selected, as their victims, innocent people who were unlikely to be missed, like hitchhikers, prostitutes, and the forgotten. Sociopaths didn't play by society's rules, they killed without hesitation or remorse. Both had been consciously sadistic, sometimes even resuscitating their victims just before death so they could inflict more torture. Their sexual deviancy was also extreme, but I found no evidence of such behaviour in The Sawman, unlike the people whom he murdered. There was plenty of evidence in their crime sheets that they sought perverse pleasure in torturing women and children. He was different although I believed that he would have some of the traits of the third serial killer I had investigated. When I found him, they had all said that it couldn't be true. Each had volunteered their character references, gesturing with their reassuring nods and with their hands raised as if in prayer. They had said that he couldn't possibly be the one, for they knew him to be such a gentle, compassionate, peaceful and pious man. These valedictory outpourings, respectful and effusive in their praise, were reserved not for a tender hearted priest, but for the man who lived in their block; their neighbour, a serial killer.

When I had first read The Sawman file I instinctively thought that he probably had difficulty relating to others. Psychopaths rarely revealed their true selves, often using highly manipulative behaviour to entice the unsuspecting into their trap and, like actors, their performances could be very convincing, yet I believed that Sawman had never met his victims before he murdered them. The mutilations and the decapitations were, however, clear evidence of the psychopath's common fantasies of domination and control.

The analyses of his multiple crime scenes had identified obvious recurring patterns that provided me with some insight into his personality and psychopathology, but it wasn't enough. My sixth sense told me that if I was to catch him I had to find out why he had committed his crimes and what traumatic event had made him become a remorseless psychopath. I had to go back to Muche's. The clock on my telephone showed four o'clock. So I took out my A-Z checked out my route back to Muche's place, got a car from the car pool and headed for Deansgate.

It was 4.20 when I pulled up outside Muche's flat. I nodded to the local policeman at the door, flashed my credentials and a minute later I was in the flat. Take it from me, a murder scene is an eerie place and I had visited many. The yards of yellow and black tape that forbade trespass eerily alluded to sinister goings on. And of course, there were those tell-tale stains and chalkmarks that traced the killer's handiwork which definitely contributed to the spooky aura. I would liken the atmosphere to that of a séance, weird – uncomfortable and unnatural – something's gone yet something's there. I had to be there. If I was to extract the truth, I needed to reconstruct his crime. I knew that unmasking him would be tough, the man that I was hunting was a psychopath and, by their very nature, they are not easy to identify, but that was what I had to do.

I recalled the profile I had thus far and I fixed it there. I climbed out of the back window and wandered down the fire escape. After a deep breath I walked slowly back up. I wasn't really looking for clues as such, better men than I had already exhausted that. No, I was trying to submerge myself in his mind; to reconstruct the pattern of events that he had followed and I needed to experience the specific behaviours of the killer. In the past I had found that it helped my understanding of both how and why they had done it and I had hoped it would again.

When I reached the window I stopped for a few seconds. He had slipped the latch there so I slid the window shut. It was quite a narrow ledge at an awkward height. I tried to lift my right foot onto the sill, but it was difficult and so I tried putting my knee there. It seemed to be more natural. With my right knee on the sill I pushed myself up and with a little spring from my left leg I was soon up against the window. I checked to see if I had made any mist marks on the glass with my breath. The window frame was recessed too deep and there was nothing. At this stage I had only the slightest feeling of his presence. I slid the window open, climbed in and closed it behind me, just as I had believed he would have done. I figured that he would have slowly closed the window to keep any noise to a minimum, but when it was halfway down it squeaked, so I stopped. I tried to slide it quickly, but the squeak was worse. I could feel him now. I applied some pressure against the frame and it closed without a sound. He was the careful and cautious type. I scanned the room which had the computer in it. My nose caught an unusual whiff. It came to me – basil, but it wasn't just basil it was mixed with something else, but disappointingly I couldn't put my finger on it. This was obviously what Geoff was going on about. I wondered what basil was doing in this apartment. As far as I could tell the kitchen had never been used for cooking anything other than reheating a pizza.

I looked at my sketch and went to the wall where the fibre had been found. I closed my eyes. My body chilled. I sucked in air through my teeth that was cold enough to make my gums scream with the shock of it. There it was, an outline in black, not tall about five foot eight or ten. I went up close, next to the wall. The presence was strong he had waited there. My heart picked up. I could feel each rapid pulse. I opened my eyes. I put my right hand on the door-handle and turned it until the brass latch freed itself from the jamb. I could feel my senses sharpen, my body tingled as the blood sped around. I was on his track. He hadn't touched anything in this room. I could feel his excitement, but there was calmness too.

My footsteps echoed as I walked the empty corridor. I could sense him and my leg muscles tensed. I was close. I shut my eyes. I saw his shadowy figure. He had walked the corridor, but he hadn't entered any room apart from the main bedroom. He had listened and smelled until he found who he was looking for. I opened my eyes and followed his path to the bedroom. When I got there, my heart quickened again, pulsating hard. In contrast, my breathing slowed, shallow, my throat constricted. The smell of basil filled my nose. It was though I was in his shoes. My hands were hot, clammy. I felt the latex grip my fingers. I also felt something on my neck, a chain and a pendant – it was a crucifix. My eyelids blacked out the reality and I was there with him. In my hands I saw paper; fibrous not shiny. It was newspaper, a newspaper clipping of a photograph. It was of Muche. With my eyes still closed, I opened the door and through The Sawman's eyes I saw Muche asleep on the bed. I took a few paces to the bed and stood over him, a hunting knife in my hand skimmed his body. The light was gloomy; it was difficult to clearly make things out. There were shapes and, like a slow zoom lens, I moved towards a dark heavy object. It was the chest of drawers. Latexed hands slid open the deepest one on the bottom and immediately my sense of smell was overwhelmed by camphor. One of the hands emptied the drawer of its contents and threw them on the floor. The other picked up some glossy photographs that had been hidden underneath. As I took in the full horror of them my stomach churned. The hand threw the photographs down where they slid across the floor. The hand ran along the inside of the drawer checking it was empty. The view panned to the bed. I got a close up of Muche's eyes. They flashed open and immediately filled with terror and realisation at the first prick from the knifepoint in the gloved hand. The fear and panic cut off his scream and then, like a scalpel, the knife drew its fatal line around his throat before his terror had a chance to activate his body, anaesthetising the nerves to his arms as they received their signal that sleep was over. Wakefulness for him had come too late. Suddenly, I broke free from Sawman's body. I was standing on the other side of the bed from him. For a moment his shape came into focus. I saw him or at least I glimpsed his deep brown eyes in a sea of white. He was wearing a black ski mask covering a long nose and then he was gone.

I shut my eyes and we were together again as one. I felt Sawman's pain and his hatred. That mix like oil and water, the fear and the ecstasy. Together we breathed in the smell of the dank, seedy rooms – the stench of shit and spunk swept over us. Anger squeezed my brain like a blackhole pulverises matter and in its centre a fire burned, yellow, red and white-hot, that drew me towards vengeance. His Christ commanded it. My mind wandered through a maze of corridors as I entered the world of souls, psyche and inner self. In my mind I was The Sawman and the gateway to freedom was in my hands, the hunting knife, bright and pure, and the saw, its teeth sharp and splayed, needed to taste depravity and rip it away. And I was their guide.

I saw the fat rolling body of Muche with its disgusting head brimming with hellish abomination and debauchery. It had to be removed and I was summoned to remove it. And then the pain eased, my headache stopped, his heart had slowed. He was at peace.

I was free from him, standing in the empty bedroom. It was then that I knew, The Sawman hadn't known Muche. They had never met before. I could see that the decapitation had nothing to do with torture and that the act was just a process, as second nature to him as driving. He was a profes-sional, a surgeon perhaps. There had been no thrill in the killing. I was sure he was a respectable, monochrome and mild mannered man, who blended into the background. I was equally certain that he would kill more.

I was supposed to be staying in a hotel overnight, but I had to get back to Glasgow. I had to get the portrait of The Sawman down on canvas. It would have made more sense to go straight to the airport, but that wasn't the way it was done in the bureaucratic world in which the police operate. I returned the pool car to Chester House and arrangements were made for Naylor to take me to the airport. First though there was something I needed to get closer to in his character, so I went to the airport via a ski shop.

When I arrived at the airport I was itching to open my notebook and type in my thoughts, but I couldn't, too many people, too many distractions and anyway, since dropping the photographs in front of Liz I had learned my lesson. Fortunately, I was soon sitting in the back row next to the toilets. I wasn't alone as every seat was taken. I ignored my fellow passengers and sat there, unGlaswegian like, keeping myself to myself. If anyone could have read my thoughts they would have thrown up and summoned security. I was turning over the whole crime scene. I had to. I needed to keep my thoughts framed; that look, those eyes, that mask. I tried to retain every grainy detail. We arrived in Glasgow at 8.30.

By 8.50 I had reached my flat on the 13th floor of the block. I checked the phone – there was one message. I hit the button it was my sister, Charlotte. She was only two years older, but even when we were kids she loved to point out my faults, dent my ego. Thankfully, she didn't ring much, usually it was as the go-between for her daughter Jennifer, my only niece and god-daughter, or ours, Liz and mine that is, well more Liz's – I was an atheist and generally viewed as unreliable. I called her back.

It was another lecture. Charlotte had heard about Liz from mum. The reprimand was thankfully short, even if, crammed with my shortcomings – selfishness, stubbornness and self-indulgence – "it was time to pull myself together". At the end there was at least the uplifting chat with Jennifer; just turned

13 in love with music, laughter and life and she liked and trusted me. We laughed and plotted until Charlotte enforced our goodbye.

Still smiling from my 15 minutes with Jennifer, I hitched up the laptop. I got out of my clothes while it fired up. I tended to pace around in my underwear when I painted, but I had to get into character and so I dressed for the part. I found my black roll top and my black trousers. I opened the bag from the ski shop and removed the cap. After three measured cuts with scissors on the back I slipped it over my head back to front.

I walked slowly to the mirror in the bathroom and gradually revealed my reflection. The black eclipsing the brilliant blue of the reflected bathroom wall like a thunderfilled cloud, forbidding and threateningly ominous. Even though I was squinting through the threads of fibre, my eyes drew me close to the image. They seemed to take me through the mirrored head; the sensation like being inside looking back, the reflection The Sawman's. My heart beat faster, breathing became quicker and there was a feeling of tightness across my chest.

I gazed at the grim representation of a malicious demon yet the eyes told another story, one of virtuous innocence, pure and incorruptible. I knew then that he was both. I stood there for ten minutes or so, watching, remembering and absorbing. I pulled off my mask and gasped out loud. My body shivered, my blood chilled and my spine tingled with fear. My mouth was dry and when I took a sip of water it was hard to swallow. Holding the mask in my sweaty hands I returned to the sitting room and sat on the sofa letting the rays from the standard lamp flood my body with heat and light. I rested still for awhile.

With the mask at my side I typed my security code into my computer and then rattled off my thoughts with as much detail as I could recall. I hoped that typing it out and editing what I had seen at the crime scene would help me spot the extraordinary or illogical. I considered too the behavioural characteristics that I had observed; the obsessive tidiness and the compulsive perfectionism and of course the signs of paranoia. I was certain too that he would exhibit chronic shyness. Those were the factors that tightened the profile and would narrow the selection down to an individual, characteristics that could be proved statistically – only then would my employers be convinced. Yet overwhelmingly I had a powerful image of the enigma of innocence and evil.

I started to paint it out. As soon as the eyes were formed the rest of the face moulded itself. The palette knife heaped ochre on the cheekbones and the paint swelled like grilled cheese texturing and spreading out. Burnt Sienna raised the brow and through natural lines across his forehead that bore the weight of distress. Torment and torture expressed itself in every stroke. It was complex maintaining a balance: keeping my mind open and yet I was determined to sculpt something tangible, a true likeness. I could not have attempted it if I had stopped to consider the little that I had to go on. It was my imagination that was driving the painting. I stopped around 11, tired yet exhilarated. Experience had convinced me that it was better that I broke away after a while and not look at my finished work until I had diverted my attention on to something else – it was time for The Horseshoe.

The night air chilled my body; my thin leather jacket not a match for the penetrating and freezing damp, but as I entered the door of The Horseshoe I was welcomed by a blast of hot air, noise and the smell of beer.

As a pub, The Horseshoe was a classic, built in the late 1800s in the finest Victorian tradition it wore its unique stamp from its licensee, a keen horseman, with aplomb. Its lucky motif was distributed liberally. The publican had the marks of a true Glaswegian – he was fair fond of himself; his initials JS were worked into a whip on two of the large mirrors at the back of the pub where I was soon to be ensconced. I nodded to my friend Alec the barman and my usual tipple, Lagavulin whisky and a beer (Fusty), was placed in front of me. Now that's what I called good Scottish hospitality and all just a couple of minutes' walk from Central Station and my flat. I languished at the beautiful mahogany bar, the longest in Britain it was said. I was already beginning to let the horrors of the day drift away. I smiled at Alec and number two was delivered promptly.

I drank another glass of our finest malt washed down with a pint of 'heavy'. It was late but the place was still bursting at the seams. There is something in the Glasgow psyche that, with the passing of midnight and the start of the second chapter of the day, rejects sobriety and the shackles of responsibility. While others more sober and responsible would by then have supped their final drink, eaten their curry or Thai and caught the late night bus, Glaswegians would be lovingly eyeing their reflection in a shop window and then, with a release of adrenaline, would search out a club and its dance-floor or a party to gatecrash. For once I ignored those innate impulses and headed back to the flat ready for The Sawman.

3. The Sawman waits, I worry and then get the message

Tuesday 17th September – Day two

At one o'clock he slips the lock and enters. With the door closed it is pitch black so he stops and listens. There is no sound anywhere. He switches on his torch and follows the beam along the hallway. Every room is empty. He isn't sure what to do, for until now, his God has always made certain that his subject was waiting for their punishment. He still believes that his God will guide Dean Shields, his latest sinner, to him if he waits, so he does, but not inside this house of shame. Glad to leave the strong sour smell of the apartment behind him, Sawman goes back into the common hallway and sits on the step of the stairs to the roof.

It is eight stairs from the floor to the escape door to the roof and he is sitting on the fourth in the dark where he could see anyone coming up from the stairs below, but he could never be seen. He has made sure of that by removing the bulb from the top floor and the one below. Now very little light filters up from below to his floor.

Only a fool would rent a top floor apartment, he thinks to himself.

He is right, the residents are vulnerable to an intruder, as Shields is about to find out, but he is too late to do anything about it.

He checks his watch. It is 1.30, so he relaxes and quickly sleep overpowers him.

After The Horseshoe I had gone to the hamburger wagon outside the concert hall, a wee detour, but worth it – probably the finest hamburgers and onions in the country, at one in the morning. I met a couple of my old mates there who I hadn't seen for years. That's Glasgow for you, a small place really, and intimate. We ended up going for a swift one at the Variety Bar opposite Baird Hall in Sauchiehall Street. It was a place for students, open till eight in the morning, with a DJ and loud music. I am little past all that so I only stayed for a couple of pints.

When I got back to the flat it was almost two. I was still wearing my black roll neck. I fell onto the sofa and switched on the television to settle my mind. All that I could find were the endings of B movies so I gave it a miss. I went through the motions of looking over my reports and instantly fell asleep.

The sound of footsteps wakes him with a start. His mind takes a few seconds to remember where he is. His body tenses every muscle and he sits upright. He feels the button on the side of his watch and the LED display flashes 5.30 like a neon sign. It is light outside, but without windows the morning is kept out.

He cannot be certain that it is Shields, but somehow he can tell from the dull thud of the footsteps from a long way down that it is.

Five storeys to climb and no elevator, not in these cheap apartments and no view either, even from the top, just other buildings front and back.

"Fuck." Shields swears out loud.

He listens as Shields bangs the time switch on the floor below five or six times. His feet are even noisier now; his aggression comes right through the soles of his boots as he stamps on each tread as he climbs. Despite the noise there is no sound of any of the neighbours stirring. They are probably used to this and filter it out.

Through the darkness, he sees the tiny spectre of yellow and red from the lighter in Shields' hand. Hardly enough to illuminate his thumb never mind the stairs. He watches Shields struggle with the lock. The key stubbornly refuses to engage. Shields sways to and fro and curses out loud like a drunk, but it is just the dark, just the confusion. The lighter goes out. Shields curses again and shakes the lighter wildly. He holds it close to his face. A couple of clicks and as the wheel spins the flame flares bright, tall and hot, scorching his eyelashes and eyebrows as it does so.

"Shit, Shit." The lighter is instinctively snapped shut. He slowly flicks it on again and this time carefully lowers it to the lock; his head following close behind. As the controlled flame lights up the keyhole it also illuminates his nose and then his face, just enough to confirm his identity. He inserts the key slowly and when it is fully engaged he turns it clockwise and pushes open the door.

His attacker moves swiftly and almost before Shields straightens himself to his full height the heel of the axe pounds the back of Shields' head, making a loud cracking sound. Sawman tries to catch him before he falls, but he can't restrain the dead weight and Shields' body crashes to the ground forcing the door to fly against the wall as he drops like a stone. In another neighbourhood there would have been a swarm of people to investigate the noise, but not here, noisy neighbours even at this hour are commonplace and largely ignored.

He drags the body into the room and then closes the door. He wipes the axehead on Shields' jacket to clean off the hair, skin and blood before returning the axe to its place on his belt. He grabs the feet and tows the heavy weight along the floor; slowly at first and then faster as the momentum gathers speed, leaving a crimson trail of blood as Shields' head lolls back and forth as it covers the ground to the bedroom door. The door is already open, but as he stops and turns into the bedroom it is a struggle to get the body twisted around and over to the bed, but he makes it. He rests for a minute. He spies a T-shirt on the floor and wraps it around the bleeding wound. Then he swings the body around until Shields' head faces the wall. He lifts Shields under the arms and with all his strength lifts and pulls him onto the bed where he lays him out straight. He removes the T-shirt from Shields' head and throws it to the foot of the bed. The blood from the gaping hole in Shields' head oozes out over the bedclothes.

I woke up at 5.15 on the sofa again. My head was thumping and my tongue was protruding from my mouth. I tried drinking some water, it helped, but I needed something stronger so I made myself some coffee. That revived me and the couple of paracetamol I took eased the head a great deal. I felt brave enough to review my painting so I wandered through to the bedroom. It didn't take long to see that it was a failure. The paint strokes glared back at me. They were uncomfortable and showed it. I thought I had placed them into a logical and coherent pattern, but I could see then that I hadn't. My mental discourse had missed its mark. It told me little that I didn't know. I'd wasted my time. I should have known it wasn't going to work because all the signs had been there – the rocking back and forth and those repetitive sounds;

that stupid, dull, tuneless humming. All that overlaying of theory upon theory had been obsessive. For a moment I was tempted to have another go, but I knew I wasn't ready. I returned to the sitting room.

I sat on the sofa sipping my coffee looking down at the M8 feeling a bit sorry for myself. There wasn't much activity at that time in the morning. It was still dark, but the motorway was lit and I watched the cars pass, heading for who knows where, maybe Edinburgh perhaps even London, most likely hoping to get to bed wherever that was. The thought of beds reminded me of Liz and contrasted the past and the present. The smells of the good times: dinner, laughter and her perfume were fading and I could no longer feel the warmth that once enveloped the place. Instead it was chilly and I felt the anger and frustration from the isolation and tedium of bachelor life. I checked the phone – there were no messages. It was foolish of me to think that she would have phoned. I loved her, sometimes as she had said at a distance, but always ungrudgingly. It wasn't perfect, occasionally ugly, but I had only ever loved her. I still thought that she and I were best friends, but there I was alone.

It had been four nights and I hadn't heard from her. I tried to work out where I went wrong. I dragged down our relationship from its sacred pedestal and dissected it, but I still hadn't worked out why she didn't want to be with me. It was not as if I was promiscuous, I had been monogamous. I examined what I had done to chase her away and all that I could come up with was sorry. It was pathetic. The thought of a trial separation took me very quickly to divorce and my depression closed in tight.

I padded back to the spare bedroom and stared at his face. I wondered who he was and what he was up to. The portrait had lots to tell me, but it wasn't communicating anything then. I slipped on the mask.

The Sawman studies the face closely. He mentally measures the thickness and length of Shields' eyebrows which resemble a long moustache, drooping down at either end, and in the middle only the slightest thinning, otherwise both are as one.

"Is this the mark of a child molester and paedophile? Should we have spotted it? When did they join up, after puberty not before surely? You're disgusting." Sawman says quietly.

The black and white picture of Shields flashes across Sawman's mind. It is of a wicked face and Sawman could see that it matches. Those evil eyebrows knitted together making his already narrow eyes seem even closer together.

"You thought you'd escaped. Since they let you go your only thoughts were the depraved sick lust for inflicting pain and suffering you bastard. Those poor bambinos ripped open by your bony hard fingers and their innocence assaulted by your ugly prick. Well, never again you loathsome scumbag. Mai nuovamente (never again)."

The Sawman removes his rucksack and takes out his tools: the hunting knife and his saw and sets them down on the bed. As he bends down he catches a fruity whiff. He rises up and sniffs the air. His receptors home in on the odour, drawing his head around until his eyes focus on the chest of drawers on the other side of the room. He walks over to the chest and lifts the glass tumbler sitting on top. He picks up the almost empty glass, which has a film of sticky liquid on the bottom. He takes in the sweet fruity odour. There is a hint of banana and pineapple. He recog-

nises the scent as Ethyl butyrate – rum. Satisfied that he has iden-
tified the scent he puts the glass back and pulls open the bottom
drawer of the chest. Its contents, mostly T-shirts and underwear
are laid on the floor. He places the rum glass in the corner of the
drawer and then returns to the bed.

Trying to get back to sleep was a waste of time so I decided I would catch the earlier flight. I switched on the TV, made myself another cup of coffee and swallowed a couple of paracetamols.

Slinging his rucksack over his shoulder, he takes one last look at
the message and then turns and walks quickly out of the bedroom,
down the hall and out the front door. His legs move quickly as
he ascends the stairs, through the door and on to the roof.

It takes no more than seconds to cross the roof and reach the
door to the next apartments. The door opens quietly and his feet
clip down the stairs in a rhythmic step – one, two, three, one, two,
three, one, two, three. He spins on the balls of his feet as he reaches
each landing, after a few more paced strides he returns to the
rhythm – one, two, three, one, two, three, one, two, three. When
he reaches the bottom he walks slowly to the outer door and opens
it wide. Suddenly, the bent head of a young boy facing him on
the top step startles him.

Instantly he takes in the scene. His eyes follow the boy's head
down to the bag full of newspapers. Before the boy turns to look
up, Sawman's eyes scan the street behind the boy, swivelling left
and right as far as he can see. There are no moving cars and no
people: nothing. The boy looks up at him and utters "sorry". The
word from the boy fades quickly to a breath as he stares at the
stranger. Their eyes lock for a split second, but it is the stranger's

hands that catch the boy's gaze. The boy's muscles tense so that he momentarily trembles, a shiver rippling through his body. It is the instinctive reaction to something odd, something evil.

They stand face to face. For the last 30 minutes The Sawman has been on automatic pilot, his actions directed by a programmed process, but now it is broken. His right hand slips inside his coat as he reaches for the knife. It would all have been over in a matter of seconds. The boy wouldn't even have screamed for its long serrated edge would have cut off the breath before it reached his vocal cords, before the boy knew what was happening, but it did not happen. Instead The Sawman's hand freezes over the flap on the sheath for the knife. He closes his eyes for a few seconds, just long enough for him to decide that this would be wrong. This isn't the face of someone he has to exterminate. Topped by floppy, unbrushed golden hair this is a plump face – the unblemished skin swollen by an 11 year old's puppy fat. An ashen face except for the rosy cheeks like those of a doll's and the bright cherry lips pulled apart and flashing his silver brace over two crooked front teeth – no not this face. These aren't the eyes of a rapist or lowlife, with their greyish blue hue filling the iris like a camera lens, focusing wide to take in the light; these are the eyes of hope and innocence.

"Thanks." He says as he side steps the boy and hurries on past. When he has gone about 50 yards he removes his black latex gauntlets with a snap and puts them in his pockets; he never looks back.

The boy watches the stranger's back as he races down the steps along the street until it disappears around the block. His brain registers the incident and then returns his consciousness to his imaginary game of football.

4. I get the message

I got to the office before nine armed with the disappointing output from my hours of analysis and painting. The portrait that I printed off confirmed that I still had some way to go. Whilst I was pleased with sections of the face the overall effect was disappointing and I instinctively knew that I hadn't captured him. The close up of the hand looked far more promising. I inspected it carefully and when I closed my eyes to recall the latex-gloved hand that I had seen in Conran's flat I was convinced that it was an accurate representation.

At about ten there was a knock on the door. It opened and in walked a small, middle aged woman, with brown hair and a severe looking face.

"Dr Ahearn?"

"That's me."

"I'm Joyce Carville, Assistant Chief Constable Ulis' PA. He would like to see you in his office."

"When?"

"Now."

I got up to follow her when she turned and said, "You may want to take your jacket."

She was an officious little thing.

"Please, this way." She wasn't asking. Still I didn't know where Ulis' office was so I followed her.

"The Royal called me. They said that you didn't check in yesterday," she said as we walked to the lift.

"No."

"It's where we usually put visitors up. I have never had any complaints."

I had the feeling that she wouldn't have.

I glanced at my wrist and swore to myself as I remembered it was fucked, I needed to do something about getting it fixed or get a sextant.

"Which hotel did you go to?"

"I didn't. I went home."

"To Glasgow?" That was the first sign of real animation on her face.

"Yes."

"I should have been told. We will have to pay."

I ignored her and was asked to take a seat in an anteroom while she 'checked if the Assistant Chief Constable was ready for me'. I flicked through a copy of a police magazine, but it wasn't my type of reading, anyway it didn't matter because Joyce returned straightaway. She showed me into Ulis' office and as she was leaving I handed her a file for Geoff containing copies of my painting and study of the hand.

Ulis greeted me with that ingratiating smile again. It was probably the one he used to fraternise; the one that helped him socialise and I could tell that he was good at hobnobbing; that smile could cloak shortcomings and blind you from the truth. He wasn't alone. Bert Wood was sitting looking smug as usual.

"Ah good, take a seat please." Ulis pointed to a hard chair.

"I understand that you went back to Glasgow last night."

"Yes."

"You should have told me I wanted to see you last night."

"John Naylor knew where I was."

"Yes, John told me. Dr Ahearn I believe you are used to getting the freedom to do as you wish, but I would rather you kept my office informed of your movements."

I said nothing.

"I understand from John that you went back to Muche's apartment?"

"I did."

"Did it help with your profiling?"

"It all helps."

"Have you come up with anything?"

"Not yet." My frustration with the portrait stopped me from mentioning the hand.

Ulis spread his arms in an arc over his enormous mahogany desk.

"Hmm. Well there is another matter that I wanted to speak to you about."

I said nothing and kept my gaze on his lips. He had one of those sticky white strings of rheum attached to his top and bottom lips at the corner of his mouth that stretched and recoiled when he opened his mouth. It had me transfixed and turned my stomach.

"You were with DCS Wheaton when he interviewed a Mr…" He paused and looked at an open file on his desk. "Mr Leon Melnar?"

"I was."

"I have received a complaint from Mr Melnar's solicitor concerning DCS Wheaton and wondered if you could help me." I looked briefly at Wood who had a sort of righteous smirk on his face.

"It is alleged that that he assaulted Mr Melnar. Is that correct?"

"I don't know what you mean."

"I am referring to the incident where Mr Melnar alleges DCS Wheaton smashed Mr Melnar's mobile telephone over his head."

"Look, he's a pimp and he's up to his gold teeth in the shit that was going on in that place."

"That maybe so, but did DCS Wheaton assault Melnar?"

"I am afraid that's not my area of expertise."

"Dr Ahearn you are seconded to this force and while you are here you will adhere to our codes of practice. Now did you see him strike Mr Melnar with the mobile?"

"And I repeat this is not my area of expertise."

"Look Ahearn answer the question," Bert Wood demanded.

"Why don't you answer the question? You're the detective."

"If you persist in this non co-operation I will contact the Home Office."

"You do as you see fit. I've got work to do." Ulis rolled his eyes. "My job here is to produce a profile of the killer that might assist you find him. It is not to sit in petty judgement of the behaviour of your officers."

"And when can I expect this profile?"

"If I get back to Glasgow tonight, probably tomorrow morning."

And that was that. I was dismissed. I got up and walked calmly out of his office and returned to mine. I checked my wrist again. "Fuck," I called out. I had smashed my watch on the wall in a fit of anger when Liz left. I hadn't been mad at her, just me. Liz had bought it as a present to commemorate our seventh anniversary, so I couldn't just buy another to replace it. I had to get it repaired. "Oh Liz, what the fuck are you doing, come back girl, come back," I sighed.

The office phone rang.

"Hello."

"We've got another one." It was Geoff.

"What?"

"The Sawman's got another one."

"Where?

"Stockport."

"What time is it?"

"11.10."

"Okay." I let out a hoarse rasping cough.

"Time you gave those up."

"You're right. When did you find him?"

"About ten minutes ago. I'll pick you up at the front door."

"Right."

I spun my body around collected my things and headed for the door. I felt lousy, another night on the fucking sofa and another hangover.

I jumped into Geoff's car and his driver hit the beacons and the siren.

When we reached the apartment block the place was swarming with the media.

"How do they do it?" I checked my wrist, no watch and Geoff ignored me.

The building was an old grey tenement that had seen better times. I could see the entrance through the TV vans with their satellite dishes on top and swirls of cables. As soon as I opened the door of the car they came running. They were unsure who I was until someone from Granada recognised me from a previous investigation. "It's Dr Ahearn isn't it?" I didn't reply and tried to push past. "Is this the work of The Sawman Dr Ahearn?" I ignored them as best as I could and pushed there mikes away. Geoff and I pressed on passed the sawhorses that cordoned off the building. A local beat cop spotted us coming and opened the front door.

"Get them back at least 20 yards from the entrance," Geoff shouted to him as we passed.

It was always the top floor. I shouted "Fuck". I had to exercise more. Before I tackled the stairs I scanned the hallway and landings. It looked as though it could have done with a make-over. When I got to the top I stamped hard on the butt of my cigarette and followed Geoff inside.

The evidence of his handiwork started at the front door. There was a long messy trail that looked like someone had brushed the insides of a dead animal along the corridor only this wasn't the four-legged kind. I met James Sloan half way down the corridor.

"Hi Rob, neat hairstyle." I gave him a quizzical look. "Be careful Ulis is on the warpath."

"He's here?" I couldn't believe it, I had only just left his office.

I had barely reached the bedroom when mister immaculate's head popped out to meet me and it wasn't amused.

"Oh it's you," Ulis sneered. I said nothing, but I hoped that the expression on my face conveyed my feelings. "Geoff, I need to brief the media. Once you have had a look around let me know what you've found."

I walked past Ulis and into the bedroom where Steve was busy. I looked around while I waited for Geoff to catch up. It was another disgusting pit.

"What have you got?" Geoff asked Steve.

"Well there's no mistaking it was Sawman."

"That wasn't what I asked," Geoff said firmly. "What have you found?"

"Well, it looks as he was waiting for Shields." Geoff screwed up his eyes, which Steve interpreted perfectly. "Shields' the victim. Dean Leonard Shields, aged 38, known alias's: Lenny Forest, Len Gould, Len Lane. He had a string of convictions."

"Like what?"

Steve read from his notes. "In 1978, car theft – three years juvenile; in 1982 robbery with violence – four years. And on January 6, 1986, after processing DNA found on a female minor who was raped, he was charged with a number of sexual assaults against women and children. He got 18 and was freed in February last year. In October last year he was arrested for rape and attempted murder of a juvenile male – case collapsed after the two key witnesses disappeared the day before they were due to give evidence."

"Right," Geoff said and looked over at me. I wasn't sure why because all that factual stuff was sort of irrelevant to my work and I didn't need it to know that this was another Sawman murder, it was obvious. In fact, I was beginning to wonder why I was so involved in listening to all this detection. What I needed was peace and quiet to let me connect. It was near impossible in the disturbance that is created by detectives and forensic experts at a murder scene.

"I suppose it was like the others?" I asked in response to Geoff's pressurising stare.

"Apart from the axe it was the same MO. Shields' throat was slashed open by a hunting knife, which he probably used to tattoo the message 'to the eternal fire' on his chest. The eyes were doused with acid and the head decapitated by a saw," said Steve like a record.

Geoff was unimpressed by my question and carried on: "And how did he get in?"

"Via the next-door stairs to the flat roof."

"A flat roof in Manchester," I said.

"Stockport," Geoff reminded me.

"Doesn't it rain in Stockport then?" I asked although I knew I should have left it there. Steve answered my question.

"Just like today, bouncing down. Anyway, he had unscrewed the light bulbs on this floor and the one below and waited on the stairs for Shields. When Shields came back at around 5.30, the estimated time of death, Sawman took him from behind with a hammer or similar while he was unlocking the front door. The blow probably nailed him. Then the body was dragged through here onto the bed. The head was slashed then sawn off and left in the drawer over there." Steve pointed to the chest of drawers. "He cut off Shields' left hand fingers and thumb with a hunting knife and stuck them in Shields' mouth. Then he doused the eyes with acid. After he painted the message on the wall he left by the front door up the stairs along the roof and down the next block."

"How do you know?" Geoff asked. "There are a couple of footprints on the stairs heading out. He had picked up blood on them most likely from the hallway. We think it's a size nine, which probably makes the guy five six to five ten, which fits your profile."

"Anything else?"

"No."

"Thanks. Any witnesses?" I heard Geoff ask behind me.

"None so far; he was found by," Steve referred to his notebook, " the next door neighbour, John Ferrel. It seems the door was already open. The lock on the door isn't broken, but it has been damaged and when the door closes it opens again by itself, unless you fiddle with it. Ferrel saw the blood and called us without entering the apartment."

"Any fingerprints?" Geoff asked. This was when I stepped away and started my own look around.

"Nothing so far," Steve replied.

"What do you make of that?" Ulis asked me, catching me unawares. I turned to face him and he gestured towards the bed.

In deep maroon the words 'joyi you are justice' were scrawled across the wall.

"It reads, Jesus you are justice."

"I know that, but what's the significance."

"Much like the last message. He thinks he is doing God's work. The motive is clear; all the victims had a record of serious felonies and had escaped conviction of a recent serious offence. He is an executioner and clearly determined to inflict his own punishment. He believes that he is trying to make sense of nonsense, a kind of anarchy with a purpose. He is deeply disturbed."

"Well, what am I suppose to say to the cameras?" Ulis asked.

"How about, we've narrowed it down to a religious zealot who is trying to get his own back on the many crazy fucking perverts that roam Manchester." It just came out.

"For your information, Manchester doesn't have perverts roaming its streets. But what we do have is a murderer killing people every night right under our noses who leaves us messages and thinks he could do our job better than us." There was no denying it. "And there is a huge public who agrees with him. When are you going to come up with something?"

"When I've identified the killer," I replied succinctly. Geoff came over to offer his support.

"And what do I say in the meantime?"

"At the moment his actions are articulated by the media, who advance their interpretation of his motives in ways, which perhaps persuade others to his view. From what I have seen and heard of the media coverage, nothing has been written or voiced that contradicts his views or questions the sense of his actions, may I suggest that you approach it from there." I thought 'alternatively, you could welcome his application for his employment', but I doubt that Ulis would have thanked me for that.

He pulled Geoff aside and after about five minutes Ulis left. I followed him to the apartment door, carefully avoiding the smudge of blood on the floor and the footprints on the landing, and watched him march down the stairs. He was a little uptight and a coiled spring came to mind. I had one of my moments. Ulis changed into a huge silver slinky. It jiggled then shot forward like the neck of the Loch Ness monster descending the stairs, gathering speed, tripping over step after step, whirring and chinking until it reached the bottom. I came to when the hubbub erupted as he opened the door. I couldn't see him, but I could imagine the journalists hurling questions at him. A broad smile showed I cared.

Since I was at the stairwell, I started there. The light bulb lighting the common hallway had been screwed back in place, so I closed the door to the apartment and unscrewed it again. The darkness put the space into negative. I allowed my eyes time to adjust and then walked, with the aid of a torch, to the stairs to the roof.

Those old houses were heaven sent for housebreakers. You could climb one set of stairs up on to the roof, which was pitched, but flat at the front to give the impression of being flat from street-level, go across the empty flat space and down the next flight. Sometime in the past, the doors to them would have been padlocked, but time had taken its toll; the keys lost or mislaid or the locks had simply been smashed open and never replaced. I walked back down.

The assault at the doorway didn't make sense. It would have been an incredible co-incidence for the Sawman to appear just as Shields entered his apartment so it was obvious that the Sawman had been waiting for Shields to return. This told me two things: firstly, that he would have checked over the apartment before Shields arrived and secondly, that he must have been waiting on the steps until he came back. I wondered what he thought when he first entered the apartment and Shields wasn't home. He could have been angry, yet I felt that with his attention to detail, patience and meticulous planning, he probably dealt with it fairly calmly. He would have been confident that God would not let him down. He would have most likely waited. The darkened stairs were the obvious place. I screwed the bulb back and supplemented its light on the stairs with my torch. There wasn't much sign of him, just a few bloody footprints on the first and third stairs. I put my hand on the rail and studied the treads of the stairs carefully. There was nothing untoward. I closed my eyes and bent down to sit as he might have done. As I did so my hand slid forward and I felt a sharp pain like a pinprick between my thumb and forefinger. I pulled my hand away instinctively.

I checked my fingers and saw that there was no damage done. I closed my eyes again and sat on the stairs. I could feel his presence. He had sat there and waited, for quite some time. I felt his body go limp. He had fallen into a deep sleep. I opened my eyes and said out loud "That's it, he was asleep, he was asleep." And there it was – a small black fibre on the bannister. I called to Geoff and told him what I had seen whereupon he directed someone from the forensic team to check it out.

As Forensics examined the stairs, I walked back to the landing, leaned against the banister and lit up a Marlboro. I considered what he might have done when he heard Shields approaching. He would have been calm and collected. My thought process was broken by the noise from downstairs. I turned, looked over and down. I couldn't see Ulis, but I could hear him. He was giving one of his update interviews – all teeth and that smile no doubt.

I entered the apartment again. I could see that the door had recently whacked the wall behind it. There was fresh plaster dust on the floor below the impression on the wall where the handle had banged it. The outside of the door had clues of what happened too. Shields' body had caused the heavy scrape and scratches as he had thundered to the floor, his brain almost dead, yet issuing instructions to his hand to reach out to prevent his fall. I could see that Steve had been right. The Sawman had whacked him from behind and he had crashed to the ground like a pile of bricks. I followed the blood trail to the bedroom to the indentation on the back of Shields' head – it would have made a good model for a class on panel beating. The axe had taken a thin slice of the skull out. I had another of my moments. Just then I wondered what The Sawman had done with the thin slice; a useful mezzaluna maybe. I could see his latexed hands, one at each end of the curved arc, the fingers formed in tight fists, rocking from side to side, rolling over Shields' plump fingers until they dropped off, one by one – how neat, how efficient. I wonder' did he wipe the surface clean with slippery pink tongue; the blood painting its own red hue on the tip? Pop!

After checking that Jim Sloan had the photographs I prised out Shields' index finger from his mouth. It was from Shields' left hand and sure enough, under the fingernails there were flakes of black paint there.

"It's from the front door," Steve said.

I decided then that I should leave the detective work to the professionals and come back later on my own. I would see Shields next in the morgue.

Dawn Burns gave me a lift back to the office. It was she who drew my attention to my changed hairstyle. When I checked it in her wing mirror I could see what she and Jim had meant. I didn't remember doing it, but I had slicked my hair back just as I imagined The Sawman would look without his mask. It sent a shiver down my spine and I gave it a rake with my fingers to bring it back to my usual tousled look.

When I got to my office I topped up my coffee with George and picked up the phone and phoned my Pops.

"Robbie. Where have you been? What happened to Sunday?"

"I am in Manchester and up to my eyes in it Pops. I just couldn't make it."

"A call to your mother is not too much to ask. She is mad at you for not telephoning."

"I never said I would come every Sunday."

"It's been four weeks since you came over. You shouldn't have told her that you were coming. She had everything ready for you."

"You're right. I'm sorry; I'll make it up to her. Pops, can we talk?"

"Of course, is it about Liz? Why don't you come over early on Sunday before lunch, your mum's making your favourite stew."

"Your favourite, Pops."

"Come on over anyway."

"Sure. Is there any chance of seeing you before Sunday? And it's not about Liz."

"Have you two sorted yourselves out then?"

"Pops, can we meet maybe after you've finished some night this week when we can talk in private."

"What's this about?"

"Let's leave it until we meet."

"Okay."

"Maybe we could meet for a drink and then get something to eat if that's alright with Mum." I dreaded the thought of sitting at one of my father's bars.

"Right, how about Friday in Killern's Bar?"

"Pops could we go somewhere else it would be nice to have a bit of time on our own without the rest of them joining us." It would have been impossible for the pair of us to sit on our own in Killern's Bar; most of my father's station went in there at night, mostly every night.

"What about an Italian."

"Okay."

"What about La Concertina at say eight?"

"That's fine by me."

"What are you doing in Manchester?"

"I'm on a case."

"Not that bloody Sawman."

"'fraid so."

"Robbie, isn't it time you stopped all that? The last time was bad enough. Is that what the problem with Liz is about?"

"Pops that's what I do, you know that. Let's leave it until we meet."

"Right, I'll see you then. Oh and I won't say anything to your mother; she won't understand."

"Thanks Pops. See you Friday night at eight."

I moved to close the drawer and put George away for the night when Ulis appeared around the door.

"I'd like to see you before you go tonight." He wasn't asking.

"Sure I'll be there," I replied as I watched Ulis' eyes scan my drawer.

"Got some interesting reading there?"

"Philosophy."

"I'm surprised you have time for that."

"I make time. Proust said, '*It seems that the taste for books grows with intelligence.*'"

"I prefer films myself."

"Good," I said.

"I'll buzz you when I can see you."

"Right."

He left. The people there knew nothing about me, my love of reading and classical music; that's the way I liked it. Anyway, they wouldn't have understood. They knew about my painting of course, although I doubted whether they thought much of it. They probably thought that my intuitive way of working was a bit of a joke; they wouldn't have appreciated that it was my training and experience in clinical psychology that made sense of it all.

When I started The Sawman investigation I already knew a lot about serial killers. A lack of self-esteem was usually at the heart of a serial killer's problems. They were often social misfits who got off on violence, terror and suffering. But I had also seen for myself the other type. Those that had a dual personality and who oscillated from the ordinary to the extraordinary like Stevenson's Dr Jekyll. Those tended to be terrifyingly focused and solitary, more awkward than freaky, who liked to plan every last detail. When I read the Sawman's files I suspected that he would be like them. If I were right, his personality development would have been shut down or locked out by some traumatic event in his life. I was hoping to get evidence of this in my visions and subsequent painting. I needed to get inside his head, but first I had to go to Shields' post mortem.

5. The colour red

I was in the rest room directly above the morgue. I had sensibly given lunch a miss and as I looked out the window I tried to assure myself that life wasn't all blood and guts. I watched the wind rustle the branches of a mountain ash. Each breeze momentarily flipped over its oval shaped serrated leaflets from its dark green to a frosty hue below. Soon the leaves would change from green to yellow to orange to red with autumn. A nice ordered thought, but my mind wasn't allowed to stray that far; I knew that it was just displacement activity and I had to get on with understanding the disorder that left Shield's body in the coldroom below.

The familiar faces of James Wilby, Geoff, Steve and James' assistant were in the autopsy room. There was no mistaking that I was at the right one; the shape of the two body bags – one with a body and no head, and another with a head and no body confirmed it was one of Sawman's alright. I watched James's assistant unzip the body bag and place the body on the cold aluminium autopsy table and further proof, that the corpse, was indeed he, was emblazoned on the toe tag, which spelled out '*Shields*'.

Even with no head it was obvious that Shields had liked fast food and lots of it and I wondered how Sawman had managed to move his body around, but not for long because the slight looking assistant handled his weight with consummate ease. He made Shields look light as he lifted his body from its gurney onto the autopsy table. On closer examination the assistant wasn't so frail in fact he was very muscular; I could see the muscles on his arms extend and ripple as he positioned Shields' body over a block.

The block on the table had forced the chest to protrude upwards making Shields' body look rather gruesome. The assistant measured Shields' length and weight with a simple tape measure as though it was being sized for a suit. Of course there was no embarrassing question, What side does sir dress?" for Shields' penis and testicles had been turned into mush by the acid. James scanned the body and turned to Geoff as he noted the presence of old scars into his dictaphone. According to James they were from previous knife wounds. He also commented that there were also long and deep gouges on Shields' arms and the side of his face. Again these were judged to be old, possibly scratched there by long fingernails. Good on her I thought.

The assistant made the first diagonal incision from the right shoulder to the middle of the breastbone and then another from the left shoulder. For a second it looked like he was getting ready to play tic-tac-toe, but instead he completed the letter Y when he cut deep with the scalpel from the breastbone through Shields' belly button towards his disfigured private bits.

Constant streams of water poured from open faucets on the table and as they sped towards the drain they mixed with bright crimson rivulets of blood. I had to admit to some satisfaction in watching Shields' blood wash into the gutter. I couldn't help thinking about the money that could have been saved if all the Shields in the country went straight to the autopsy table instead of prison.

The assistant picked up the scalpel responsible for the sophisticated butchering and wiped its surface clean. He picked up the heart and then dropped it into the disposal bin. He had a final look at the bared rib cage before he returned the flap of skin just like my mother smoothing out her tablecloth. Finally, Shields' abdominal organs followed the heart, all ready for disposal by incineration and the best place for them I said to myself. I wondered if Shields had ever imagined that he would end up such a grotesque figure.

The autopsy wasn't quite over. The head was unzipped from its own bag and placed on the table. Now that was revolting. It had been severed above the larynx and still had a piece of the oesophagus dangling from the skin. At that I felt my stomach going. The head too was measured before the assistant placed it in a glass jar on a platter where it sat like John the Baptist's.

"Make certain that it is sent to the forensic scientists in the lab for further analysis as soon as possible," James said to the assistant who was filling the jar with formalin. When the assistant had topped it up he motioned to another assistant nearby to collect it. It was put on a trolley and then it was off to Forensics.

"Careful with that, it's evidence," Geoff called after him rather pointlessly.

As I turned back towards the autopsy table I thought that I saw the assistant's fingers wave goodbye to Shields' remains, but I could have been mistaken.

As a final act the residue of faeces and bile from the stripped intestines were washed away, down the drain. Shields had all but gone and so had I.

6. Ulis bales out

It was half past three and I was heading back to the office summoned there by Ulis. I was on my second cigarette. I didn't normally smoke in the car; Liz thought that it was such a disgusting habit and she was right of course, but I was in a pool car and what the hell, who's to complain? I drove into the secure car park and caught the lift to the tenth floor.

I waved to Joyce and she smiled back. That tough exterior softened when she smiled, but from the lack of lines it probably didn't happen often. Ulis opened the door as I approached.

"Come in Rob." He had that smiling electioneering face on. Ulis' broadest smile was for an audience and I was right because when I got inside Geoff and Wood were there together with two men that I'd never seen before, but those guys stood out, they were Special Branch from the Met.

"Rob you know Bert Wood, I'd like you to meet Detective Chief Superintendents Baillie and Chester from the Special Branch." I wondered if either had a first name. I shook their hands and sat down as directed in a brown leather chair at the end of a long shiny table that took up some of the vast space of Ulis' office; Geoff and Wood sat on my right, facing the men from Special Branch. All the ingredients were there for the type of meeting that I hated; I didn't have the guile for conspiracy or politics.

"Special Branch believe they can help us with our serial killer," Ulis said authoritatively while looking at me.

"Oh," I murmured.

Ulis looked as though he had won the lottery and could hardly contain himself.

"This morning I forwarded a copy of your report and profile to the Special Branch and I am pleased to tell you that DCS Baillie has identified someone who might fit your profile."

Baillie, the slightly taller of the two cleared his throat.

"Thank you sir. As usual the profile was passed to our records office and compared with those on our database. A potential match was identified and as DCS Chester and I were already investigating the individual concerned we were asked to assess their findings. We both believe that he is a good fit."

"Unfortunately, the profile at this stage would fit a great many of the men here in Manchester alone," I responded.

Baillie read from a file he was holding.

"White male, aged between 30 and 40, about average height, probably obsessional, but with above average intelligence. He is likely to be a quiet inoffensive looking man, who is probably meticulously clean and neat. A church going Catholic."

"Yeah that's about it."

"It is exactly what we have been advised," Chester said. I shot a glance at Ulis who was still smiling.

Apart from the 'inoffensive' reference, our suspect Luis Beale fits the bill." Baillie said. He went on: "We have no wish to meddle in Geoff's investigation," Baillie smiled at Geoff and then returned to me with a cold stare. "All the murders have been confined to Manchester so we appreciate that the investigation is the responsibility of GMP, however, we thought that ACC Ulis should know that the murders coincide with the arrival in Manchester of Luis Beale, someone who we suspect is working for a London Syndicate and have been monitoring. We believe that Beale matches much of your profile. He is also known to carry a hunting knife." He passed me a photograph from his file. I looked at it briefly. It was of an impeccably groomed and expensively dressed dark haired male. The man in the photograph and the man in my painting only bore the slightest of resemblance, maybe a little more, the nose was the same; it couldn't be him, I thought.

"There are some similarities, but I doubt if Beale is The Sawman," I said.

"Why?" Wood poked his nose in and that was enough.

"In ways that you wouldn't understand."

"Try me?" Wood looked angry.

"You mightn' respect my methods but they produce results."

"Where are they here?" he sneered.

"These things take time. I have only been here two days."

"Yes, and while you are taking your time people are being murdered."

"I believe this case has been under investigation since May." I replied.

"Dr Ahearn, what makes you think that Beale isn't the one?" Baillie asked coolly. These guys were like ice.

"Well, I'm no detective but I don't think that the Syndicate would be wasting their time with sexual deviants and secondly, I presume that since his arrival in Manchester, Special Branch has kept him under surveillance."

"Firstly our surveillance is not yet 100% effective," Chester responded.

That was a first. I had never heard a spokesman for Special Branch suggest that their organisation wasn't perfect.

"Secondly, we understand that the victims could have been involved in the porn industry and this Syndicate is a major organiser of prostitution and is known to have aspirations to expand here. We believe that Beale has been sent to remove the competition."

"While there is case history linking the victims to prostitution only the most recent victim Ernst Muche was actively involved in the distribution of pornographic material," I said.

"You don't sound very enthusiastic. Their suspect might well be our man and I for one am keen to check him out, unless you have identified our serial killer already." Ulis delivered his words in his best politician speak, but his eyes were disapproving.

"You would be the first to know, but as yet I only have a few pointers and none of these suggest the Syndicate," I said to Ulis. "Does he live in Manchester?" I asked Baillie.

"No, in London, but as I have already said he is currently operating in Manchester."

"Beale is cool, tidy and effective. The consummate professional you might say," Chester said.

"That maybe so. Is he in Manchester on his own?"

"He is here with three other associates from London," Baillie answered.

"Is he a practising Catholic?"

"As we said, he is church going."

"Yes," said Chester.

"What about his wrists?"

"What?"

"Are they fat or thin?"

"I don't know."

"What about his fingers?" I was getting very strange looks. "Are they long like a pianist?"

"The photograph doesn't feature his hands."

"Where was he in May?" I said happy to play my table tennis. I guessed that Baillie and Chester were waiting for their chance to pass me, but that never happened because Wood butted in.

"What is this, 20 questions?"

Before I could answer, Bob Ulis stepped in, which was just as well because Wood was a moment away from the Glasgow kiss that I was itching to give him.

"Now look, we need to work together on this." Ulis looked at the Special Branch guys with those smiling eyes. "We agreed that Dr Ahearn would attend your debriefing tonight and study your surveillance reports," Ulis added through that ingratiating smile of his.

"Okay we will see you tonight," Baillie said as he stood up and a minute later he, Chester, Wood and the chill in the air were gone.

"That kind of negative attitude is unhelpful."

"My attitude is my business. I am here to provide you with a profile of the killer that might enable you to capture him. As I already mentioned in my report I believe the man you are looking for is almost certainly solitary, probably extremely shy and local. Do you think that their mobster matches that profile."

"Maybe not, but you also mentioned that he was skilled in his work and his physical characteristics are a good fit."

"I did not imply that he was a professional killer. My inference was that he had a sound understanding of anatomy and dissection."

"You do admit that he does look like the photograph of your painting?" said Geoff; his first words.

"Yes, he does have a likeness, but at this stage you shouldn't put too much store by that. I haven't got a clear picture of his physical appearance."

"I'd like you to have a look at their suspect," Ulis said.

"Look, I need to work things out in my own way and seeing pictures of suspects until I am sure who we are looking for doesn't help me."

"Nevertheless, you are seconded to my investigation and I would like you to co-operate and assist Special Branch." I felt the anger suffuse my face, but I bit my tongue.

"Geoff , Joyce has the details of the meeting, six o'clock room 24. I'd like a report in the morning."

I could feel my blood pressure soar and it was best that I left before I lost control. Two cigarettes in quick succession and a top up from George didn't chill me, so I decided it was better that I left the building. On the way out I found Naylor, in the restaurant, drinking coffee. Like the instinctive policeman that he was, he knew exactly what I wanted and where I wanted to go.

Naylor dropped me off at Shields' apartment. I walked past the entrance to the apartment next door that Sawman had used to get into Shields' unseen. I walked up the stairs to the top floor. The stairs were like a mirror image of Shields'. The hasp on the lock to the door to the roof was rusted and hanging loose. A gentle push and I was on the roof. It was flat and as I walked along I stopped to look over the edge. I feel sorry for people with vertigo; the world looks a better place when you look down on it from a height, more peaceful, ordered and purposeful. I stepped inside the door to Shields' apartment block and walked slowly down the steps to the hallway outside his front door. It was an easy journey. Sawman had the perfect escape. I broke the tape and entered his flat with the key. I shut the door it was very black. I shone my torch along the passageway. I could feel his presence and closed my eyes.

I was inside his mind. The pictures were sharp. I could feel his heart increase its speed as the adrenaline fuelled his anticipation. The sour rank smell of the old and unwashed had made him gag. I pushed open the doors, one after the other; every room unwelcoming, cold and poisoned with acrid scent. I felt his disappointment when I entered the last room and it was empty. Then I felt lifted. It was a strange feeling and at once I understood. He knew that Shields would be delivered to him. All he had to do was to wait, but not in that disgusting place.

I returned to the stairs. Shields was to be taken unawares; when The Sawman's God delivered him. I walked down the stairs and stretched up and turned the bulb until its light was cut off. I returned up the stairs and unscrewed that bulb too. It was very dark there was only a shaft of weak outside light from the door to the roof. It pointed to the stairs, inviting him to sit there and he did. He had sat down on the fourth step. I sat where he had sat, my feet like his comfortably rested on the second step. My heavy head was drawn to rest on the banister. That was where he had slept. There was a noise of someone coming into the apartment, light footsteps. I watched and listened. The sound was faint and stopped as the door of the first floor apartment closed. It was a neighbour. With Shields' weight his feet would have been louder and slower, scuffing and rubbing the stone with every tread upwards. I shut my eyes.

I was back inside his head. All was black for a few seconds then I saw him, Shields, fiddling with the lock, the light from his lighter too dull and flickering to be of much use. That was his chance. I could see the back of Sawman. In his right hand was an axe; he held it high then slammed it down hard on Shields' head. "Thank you God."

As I re-entered the flat a different scene entered my head, a bedroom in the dark. I saw a young boy and a man. My wrists felt tight as if they were being gripped by someone strong, the fingers binding me were rough and callused. My breathing was obstructed, stifled like I was being smothered, I was being pushed into a pillow. I could feel a heavy weight on my back, pushing hard, again and again and pain, a ripping pain in my anus. I let out a scream. My mind snapped free. I was soaking with sweat and shivering. I knew then that as Shields' blood, putrefied by his sins, unsalted and stinking oozed onto the floor, it erased some of the torturing memory from that part of Sawman's life.

I rushed out of the flat onto the landing. I took some deep breaths; tried to calm down. I needed to get out of the dark. I was shaking, but I managed to twist the bulb back into its socket on the landing. I wanted to stop, but I had to go on. I went back inside. I put the lights on in the apartment and walked into the bedroom. The drawer where the head was found was still open, empty, but open. I returned to the bed and closed my eyes I saw Sawman, more shape, sharper, better defined, wiry, slim and fit. A mask covered his head. He lifted the corpse's right hand and then flattened out the fingers. He picked up his knife and sniffed the handgrip. The whites of

100

his eyes in the slits disappeared as he tossed his head back and shivered. Now there was deadly calm. He opened his eyes, placed the blade across the four fingers and with some downward pressure cut them off with a single stroke. He placed the blade over the thumb and pressed down until it too was severed. I watched him gather up the fingers and thumb and carry them to the drawer. He placed them inside and then returned to the bed. The sensation I felt was similar to that described by those who have claimed to have had an out of body experience. I was hovering above him as he slid the knife across the neck and then picked up the saw. I watched it shuttle back and forth until the head bounced free. Grabbing the head by the hair he walked quickly to the drawer and placed it inside. Its grotesque face stared straight up. Then I was inside Sawman, looking through his eyes. I was taking in every detail. The matted hair thinly covering the scalp, the pitted skin with its broken veins, the popping eyes and the twisted mouth with its broken yellow teeth and its snarling expression – the face of Shields filled my vision. I saw the two latex hands stretch out before me. The fingers of one resting on the brow while the other pulled the jaw slack until the mouth opened. A black slippery hand forced the chopped fingers and thumb between the teeth. The other placed a tiny vacuum-insulated liquid dewar cylinder on top of the chest. A pair of protective goggles slipped over my eyes. With precision, fingers removed the cap from the bottle and then carefully dripped the solution onto Shields' dead eyes. There was a small white puff from each socket. The tiny clouds dispersed. The cap was replaced and disappeared from view. I opened my eyes. Shields' head was still vivid, the fingers jammed tight between his pale lips, not neatly, but scrunched up. I sat on the wooden floor. My head swooned. I felt faint. I had to push myself. I had to reason what I saw. Why the fingers? I asked myself. It came to me quickly. They were soiled hands and were placed there to let Shields taste his own baseness. I closed my eyes again. The screw tightened around my brain, pain, excruciating pain then it was gone. I saw The Sawman again. He had a sock in his hand. He climbed on the bed, his feet springing on the soft mattress. He positioned his feet just above each of the corpse's shoulders, rolled the sock up and then dipped the end of it into the cavity where the neck would have joined the head. He used the soft cotton like an artist's sponge to soak up the crimson ink and with long swinging movements he started to paint the message on the wall above the bed. He recharged his cotton 'brush' again and again until his message was complete. The blood soaked sock dropped to the floor. I watched Sawman examine the hunting knife. It had a smear of thick red blood on it. He took a corner of the duvet and wiped the knife blade clean. The knife was slipped silently into its sheath on his belt and the retaining-strap around its handle fastened. Then he took a cloth from inside his coat and cleaned the saw blade and slipped it inside his coat. He rubbed his gloved hands on the cover, buffing the front, sides and back hard and then he buttoned his coat up. I gasped, drew a deep breath and opened my eyes wide. No more, I was drained. I was sure that he believed that he was following God's will, purifying the sole of a sinner.

I had to get back to my own apartment. I had to get my new insight of him on canvas. I hurried out the door, down the stairs to the street and into the car. I told Naylor to take me straight to the airport. I had to catch the first available flight. As Naylor sped off I called Wheaton on my mobile.

"Hello Geoff, it's Rob. I've just been to Shields' place. We are looking for someone who has access to surgical tools, he may work in an undertakers something like that. He is unmarried and will have problems forming relationships, probably still lives with his mother. He is five eight, slim, but fit, with black or very dark hair and brown eyes."

"How do you know all this?"

"It will take too long to explain over the phone. He is deeply disturbed and could be having treatment for depression probably through the NHS. And another thing, he was probably abused when he was young, definitely sexually, but probably physically too. I need you to check NHS records for residents in and around Manchester."

"But there are eight and a half million people in Greater Manchester."

"Yes, but they not all black haired, brown eyed, slim, fit, work in an undertakers and have been abused."

"I'll get on to it. Oh, and the boss wants to see you."

"Tomorrow, Ron is with me he is taking me to the airport."

"He'll be mad."

"Tough shit."

"What about the meeting with Baillie?"

"Look, I just said that The Sawman is an undertaker."

"Okay, I'll let them know that you won't be there."

I hung up. I glanced at Naylor, who was staring straight ahead.

"How long to the airport?"

"You are on the right side to get there but the traffic will slow us even if I use the beacons."

"Okay as quick as you can please."

I called BA. The next plane was 17.30 but it was full. I could go on standby. I told them it was a Home Office emergency quoting my special pass ID and I was told I would still be on standby, but given first priority.

"You'll be okay, a lot of the business seats don't turn up," Naylor said.

"Good."

"How do you do it?"

"What?" I asked.

"How do you do it, where do you get that information, evidence whatever?"

"I don't know really. I just see it." Of course the forensic evidence had already told me what had happened; the details were filled in by my morbid imagination, there was something else but I didn't know what I was.

"How long have you had it?"

"A long time I suppose. I played mind games when I was a kid. Sort of observation stuff."

"What kind of games?"

"Simple things at first. I'd guess what we were having for dinner. My mother helped; she had the patience of a saint. I would sit in my room all quiet and still while she prepared lunch or dinner in the kitchen. After, I would guess what she had cooked." It was strange talking about this as we sped through the traffic.

"You mean if you were having chicken or a roast?" A car swerved out of our way while Naylor just ploughed on.

"The main ingredients were easy, but it was the more subtle smells and slight traces on her hands and clothes that I would try and identify like the herbs, spices and oil that had been used. Also, if my mother had a visitor when I was out, on my return I would use all my senses to guess who it was."

"They say you're psychic."

"I wouldn't say that."

"But you see things."

"Yes sometimes."

"Jeez, doesn't that freak you out."

"Sometimes."

Even in the marked police car it took ten minutes to get there and another 15 to reach the BA check-in. Twenty minutes later I was seated in business class in the only vacant seat available. We were soon on our way and I settled back to my BA sandwich washed down with a double helping of Glenlivet whisky and those, together with the coffee and shortbread, helped my brain drop into neutral and wander. In front of me high backcombed hair like a web of blueberry candyfloss towering high above the British Airways' antimacassar caught my attention. I watched a spider straddle the lifeless gossamer waiting patiently for its British Airways snack. I would like to have fed it a 'fly-cemetery', but instead of a piece of a garibaldi I placed a crumb of shortbread in his insensitive nest and within reach of my little confused friend. He wasn't fooled he could sense it was like his lair twice baked and dead already. The person sitting next to me gave me a look of disapproval, but said nothing.

We arrived on schedule and the Healey had me home in 15 minutes and that was without the help of any blue flashing light.

I nodded to Alec and got into the lift. A minute later, I slipped the key into the lock and pushed open the door. I started undressing before I reached the bedroom. When I got there the mess shocked me. The room looked like some kids' nursery after an emergency evacuation. Papers of every shape and colour were strewn over the sofa, coffee table and floor. The stuff on the floor looked like one of Jackson Pollock's violent paintings, but without purpose. I would like to say that the protection on Liz's polished floor was deliberate, but it wasn't entirely, for most of the papers had simply been discarded there when I had finished reading them. No matter, I had work to do. Standing in my underwear I made a beeline for the easel in the middle of the mess.

The first images that entered my mind came from somewhere deep and took me back to my college days when I used to do dope, acid and other psycho-chemical drugs while I painted. Back then some of those trips had helped me visualise things differently and the hallucinations had taken me to new places. There had been no more drugs since college, but some of the images still haunted me; that night, I knew that I had trawled some of them back from my subconscious because the images that entered my head were like those, dark and bleak, just what I wanted, that was why I restricted my palette to raw umber, yellow ochre, burnt sienna, some tantalising white oils.

I set up a new canvas and laid the oil paint on thick with a palette knife. It added texture to my thoughts and allowed me to constantly rework the imagery on the large canvas. I knew his build, weight and height. The appropriate proportions were quickly painted in. It wasn't long before I had gone from a bright white canvas to a dark theme just like the subject I was trying to create.

I worked with intensity. Colour dripped to the floor from the thick moulded head. I painted fast and furious as the memories and the ideas floated through me. At that stage no one but me could have guessed what was going on, for there was no foreground, there was no background, there was no man, there was no sun, nothing was recognisable in that painting, but I could see the shaping of something, my making of something. The scythe-like strokes, deep circles and long loops expressed the inner world of The Sawman. It was not a picture to be judged by others. It was not a question of whether it was good or bad. I wanted to get an expression of his inner forces on the canvas; his energy and anxiety. That was why I added a new colour to my palette – vermilion. It was a moving mass expressing my feelings or his feelings rather than illustrating. After an hour or so I was finished.

I took a long drink from my large tumbler of whisky and lit another cigarette. I walked around the canvas with measured paces that matched my deep measured draws. I stopped and eyed up my other canvas of The Sawman that was propped up on the bed. In that painting the high forehead and the round dark half-closed eyes stared back – they could have been mine – it could have been me. My new work was definitely not me. It had an aura of pain, sadness and hurt. I had used the red in a savage, violent and apocalyptic way. I had applied an intense interpretation of Freudian and psychological factors that I felt were influencing Sawman. I could see that my mind had built Sawman from his genes, the soft emotional seeds of his mother and the practical harshness of his father with the idea that those genes made important contributions to his personality. I had painted them all, the genetic factors that influenced his mix of fear, aggression and extrovert behaviour, as well as his physical and psychological disorders. I could see depression and schizophrenia.

The painting was drawn from my unconscious and my knowledge of The Sawman. It was a combination of nurture and nature that had created the synapses that were responsible for much of Sawman's brain's activity blending his natural inhibition and his repressed memories of traumatic experiences, a sure-fire recipe for fuelling a desire for vengeance. The eyes of the painting expressed the suffering and torment that convinced me I was right, as a child he had been abused and damaged. The selection of his victims had presented its own evidence of his rape. From my clinical training I had learned that stressful experiences could drastically alter important aspects of the brain's development and function, and my painting had clearly illustrated the effects of the disorder that fouled Sawman's reasoning. I never contrived to make him look mad and on the surface he didn't, but there was something in the eyes that said there was no denying that he was.

As a child I would discover frightening faces in the most innocent of clouds and the shapes, the painting held similar demons and in the same way I stepped back from my involuntary strokes that had created the puzzle and consciously tried to solve it. Sawman's face reminded me of the suicides I had investigated during my training, those indelible memories of the sorrow of those poor victims. The eyes had the quiet acquiescence I had seen in one of my first visions during an investigation into a suicide. It was of a 19 year old and that final glance as he went over was one of utter acceptance of his fate. His hysterical mother had told me that he had been sitting, quiet and relaxed before he got up, walked to their apartment window, slid it up to its maximum, stuck his head out as if watching the streets below and then climbed onto the windowsill. My mind had replayed his final acts. One minute he was standing there tall and straight, without panic, then he looked down, took a small step, leaned forwards until his weight pulled him out and down. I recalled that when I opened my eyes I instinctively clawed at his ethereal shadow in desperation. There was more. The Sawman's mouth in my painting had the same twist of pain of another of my investigations; hers frozen by her last breath, a 35 year old who had staggered into her bathroom and oblivion. She had carelessly thrown open the mirrored door to her drugs, smashing the glass and spilling the medicines over the floor, yet she had taken meticulous care to choose certainty and permanence by selecting the most lethal potion before untwisting, untwisting and untwisting until the gateway clicked open. Her chalk white lips bore witness to the finality of her decision to empty the contents onto the back of her tongue, throw back her head and let them tumble down her throat unfettered. Also in my painting the top teeth nipped the lower lip ever so slightly, just like my lasting impression of those of a 50 year old priest. He was anathematised by inner doubts, yet his epilogue personified clarity and conviction. He had ignored anaesthetics and reached for his razor, rolled the gnarled end until the bare blade was free and then with its thin steel held lightly between his thumb and index finger made the sign of protection on both his wrists, sluicing his crimson blood in a pulsating flow. In the aftermath of their suicides I had seen some terrible misery and in my painting of Sawman I saw it all again.

I was suddenly overwhelmed by compassion for him. I felt pity and a genuine sadness at the pain that I was sure he had suffered. And I was worried by more selfish feelings.

Sawman was most likely schizophrenic and to my horror I found that there were some uncomfortable parallels between him and myself. We both struggled with relationships, preferring to lock out others from our innermost feelings and ruthlessness, callousness and remoteness were our strong character traits. Worst of all I believed that both he and I shared a talent for self-destruction. It seemed that I too had the hallmarks of a psychopath.

I took out my digital camera and photographed the painting and downloaded it into my laptop. I held up a bottle of Lagavulin to the light, like some sommelier admiring a '54 Margaux, then squeezed a tube of black paint and drew its uncapped tip around the glass at the base of the bottle's neck. I planned to go no further. I opened the bottle and poured the first measure, looked at the level and repainted the line an inch further down. I lay back on the sofa, drank slowly and reached for the TV remote. I thought that maybe I'd catch a movie, not crime or horror, I hoped for something quiet, something homely. I have tried to watch comedies, but they didn't work for me. I hate canned laughter and I never seem to get the joke, I guess when you have been dealing with shit all day it's hard to let yourself go. Just my luck, the news was on. It was a picture of the Assistant Chief Constable Ulis. I turned up the sound:

"The police are sifting evidence as I speak and we are hopeful that our sophisticated Forensics team can assist in apprehending the perpetrator. I appreciate everyone's anxiety, but thankfully, our officers are very well trained professionals who will do their job, despite the enormous amount of pressure and publicity these killings have produced. Detective Chief Superintendent Wheaton and his team have my full support and I trust him and his team to apprehend the killer and end these murders."

Nice words; they sounded familiar. I muted the sound and then turned it off. I kind of envied Sawman, for him it was all black and white, he pleased himself and nobody got in his way, except me, maybe.

7. My day gets worse

Wednesday 18th September – Day Three

It was almost one in the morning when it hit me. She was gone. I could hear every creak and groan from the roof to the floorboards. I was gripped by its emptiness. The sounds that were once familiar had been stripped of the words, the shouts and the negotiation. The flattened tone that remained lacked the pitch, and the harmony was gone, and yet the implications were sharper. It was dark but during the day the place was always bathed in autumn glow – how could she have chosen to leave me in September.

I called Liz at her parent's 'town' flat in Edinburgh. It rang. "Hello."

"Liz?"

"Robbie."

"How are you? How you feeling?"

"Tired. How am I supposed to feel at one in the morning."

"I'm sorry. Your parents up in Perthshire?"

"Of course."

"Look I've been doing a lot of thinking. I can see that I haven't given you enough time. I'm sorry that it took this long for me to notice. I want to change things."

There was a long pause at the other end. All I could hear was her breathing and it sounded self controlled and chilly.

'It's late I mean too early for this; I was sleeping."

"I'm sorrrry," I slurred.

"Are you drunk?"

"No, I just wanted to … to speak to you."

"Look Robbie, I'm still fond of you, but not your work. It turns you into a morose melancholic. I can't stand you when you are like that."

"But I'll change."

"What? You'll give up your job?" Always the same question. She knew that I couldn't give it up, I was directionless without it.

"I didn't mean that, but I can be home more. I've bought myself a diary. I'll write things down. I won't forget things."

"You've already got a diary. I gave you one last Christmas. It's not about diaries it's about us and your preoccupation with your job and your bloody curse. You are becoming an alcoholic. I've had enough of your moods and your drinking."

"I'll stop drinking."

"Sure and I will win the lottery. Robbie, I married a bright, funny, sociable, caring man and you've become a depressed clumsy and oafish drunkard. I couldn't go through another spell of nursing you through another breakdown. I can't take that anymore."

I said nothing. I was lost for a response. All I wanted to do was say sorry again, but I had tried that already.

"Look, I want to get some sleep. I'll call you."

"When?"

"I don't know – soon – I need to collect my stuff."

"Why?"

"Look, I'll call you."

"What about a drive up to the cottage on Sunday. It'll be like old times?" I said trying to keep it going, but it didn't work.

"What?"

"Do you fancy going to the cottage on Sunday?"

"Sitting in a car for five hours – I'm going now, okay. Bye." She clicked off.

"Bye," I said, but the line was dead.

Phoning her so late was a mistake. My head was swimming with emotion and drink. Even half cut I realised that my suggestion about the cottage was a stupid idea and it was. Who in their right mind would want to drive five hours each way for a day out? What a crazy fucking suggestion. Still, the cottage was a place where we used to chill out. We bought it after I got out of hospital. Liz thought it would help me recover, get me fit like the old me; the before the smoking, the drinking and the dark moods me. By the sea, no traffic and no phones or TV, a small white cottage, no trees, just a few shrubs and no neighbours, just sheep. I was kidding myself, it hadn't worked. Things were different at first; well they would be with all the fresh air and no pub for miles, just long walks, reading and music. I wasn't as intense about everything. Maybe if we had stayed there or if I had given up work as Liz had wanted, it could have worked, but that wasn't possible. In retrospect, I accept now that she was right; I was never an easy person to live with and with my psychic experiences I could see that I was impossible. But just then when I put the phone down, I was confused and angry and had all the excuses and the pathetic justifications for my actions. I even assembled reasons for letting her go. I mused that she didn't understand me. That she was always going on about me taking up some academic post, even though she should have known that I would have hated it. I'd had enough of that highbrow reasoning at St Andrew's. And there was her nagging about my smoking, those lectures on the repugnance of the smell, the damage to my health and the surreptitious dangers of secondary smoking. And then there was her love of minimalism. Minimalism had meant that our sitting room and kitchen always had to be kept free from the clutter. And she hated my reading habits. I had liked to spread my books around me while she found the need to keep our books indexed and filed. I liked to dip into a number at a time and would leave them around the kitchen worktop or on a sofa, which again she termed passive aggression. I resented her conversion of our spare bedroom into a library. And she hated my gift. They were the maudlin ravings of a drunk. Eight years on and she's had enough and who could blame her.

I lit up another cigarette and rolled into the long night ahead.

The salty tears rolled down my cheeks and into the corners of my mouth. My bare feet gripped the ledge, slipping and sliding on its smooth painted surface. With each slither my head got more light-headed like the giddiness of vertigo. It was as if I was tottering on the end of a high diving board, yet I could see that I was standing on the sill of a window, only one floor up from a stony lawn. As I looked down, the grass shrivelled and the garden shrunk exposing grainy grey granite; a cliff overhang, the sea far below. I felt compelled to stretch out and as I did so, extending across the rocks, dripping my tears, each spilled droplet penetrating the rocks surface, staining them black, I felt something holding me back, restraining me by my T-shirt. Slowly my weight pulled on the fabric, stretching and tugging, letting me lengthen. Soon, I was past the overhang looking down on the advancing waves. My head and shoulders all the way out; my arms swept back like swallows wings anchored in the shadows behind me. I was weightless as if suspended in free fall. I didn't look up but I could feel the sky, sunless, dark and overcast, its mood – anger. The pressure was building, sitting on my back, pushing me down towards the steely grey sea. I saw the tide below advancing, its smoky waves not yet reaching the cliff, a ribbon of beach still exposed with its glistening pebbles, blackened volcanic sand and seaweed, brown speckled with black and red. Then suddenly I felt anxious; I was going to fall. The clouds above pushed me down. I heard my T-shirt rent and rip. I started to panic; my heart thumped; my body bounded in terror. My arms windmilled, slow motion at first like a fuzzy memory that gradually focuses and reveals itself then faster and faster. I was falling. I looked back and saw the black mask; the narrow slits; the whites of his eyes – it was Sawman waving goodbye, letting me go. I plunged downward, the rocks rushing towards me. I screamed and sprung up. Cold sweat oozed from every pore of my body. I was awake; my spine clenched tight, fused in fear. There was nowhere to hide and nobody to help.

I sat there for a few seconds with my head in my hands and then I rubbed my eyes. As my heart slowed its palpitations, my focus sharpened. On the coffee table in front of me sat the malt whisky bottle, two thirds empty. My panic left me.

It was only four o'clock, but I needed to wash away the nightmare and its suit of sweat. After a long pulsating shower my anxiety faded. I wrapped myself in Liz's towelling robe, made some fresh coffee, put on *Les Sylphides* and settled into the sofa willing the music to anaesthetise the memory of the nightmare. I closed my eyes and gave myself up to Chopin's romantic and melancholic ballet. Liz was right, it was just like last time, the nightmares and the cold sweats that followed, only this time, there was no Liz to hold me and help me get through them. I hated myself for putting her through those nights. She was right to leave me and get on with a normal life.

I must have fallen asleep because when I opened my eyes the clock on the DVD player showed 5.50. I decided to catch the seven o'clock flight. So I dressed quickly. As my clean shirts had run out I put my black roll neck on and instead of my suit I wore a black casual jacket and my black trousers. I made my way to the airport.

Still feeling a little rough, I caught my flight and was in the office for 8.45. I printed a copy of my painting from the previous night. It wasn't him but I could see the profile was beginning to take shape. It was a long face and it had a long nose. The detail wasn't there of course apart from the hands because of the mask. Still there was a silhouette of his whole body, which gave some indications of his proportions, but I had to get closer to his mind if I was to pick out his features. Nevertheless, my profile was almost there: he was a white male, slim but fit, aged between 30 and 40, about five foot eight, with dark hair, brown eyes, narrow wrists and long fingers. I already knew he had above average intelligence. He was probably obsessional, but likely to be quiet, inoffensive, respectable, mild mannered and meticulously clean and neat; a devoted, church going Catholic, who probably attended service daily. Someone who would have problems forming relationships; he most likely still lived alone or with his mother.

I was running off my notes on hard copy when the door opened.

"Morning. You're early," Geoff said.

"Yeah couldn't sleep."

"It's good you're here. I arranged for a case conference at nine, can you make it?"

"Sure."

"Let's go then."

When we got to his office Dawn and Steve were already there.

"What've we got?" Geoff asked.

"I passed the drawing of the hand to records, but I'm not sure what they can do with it," Steve replied.

"Any luck with the other stuff I gave you last night?" I asked.

"We're working on it. We checked through the NHS all night, nothing so far that fits. We are tackling the undertakers this morning," Steve answered.

"Good," Geoff said.

"There is something that might interest you," Dawn said.

"What?" Geoff encouraged.

"Well, I went over all the files and found something in the forensic reports that might mean something."

"What?"

"Well, I was trying to find out how he selects his victims and I was looking for things that might have been common to all the murders, part of the criteria that he used for selection."

"And?"

"Well it may be nothing."

"Christ come on," Geoff pushed.

"The eyes are brown."

"What? All the victims eyes were brown?" he asked.

Geoff looked at his list and read from it.

"Alexi Zochten, John Conran and Ernst Muche all had brown eyes."

"And Shields?" I asked,

"Dean Shields had hazel eyes," Dawn answered.

"Fuck me. You may have found something there. How common are brown eyes?" Geoff asked.

"Don't know," Steve shrugged.

"Dawn, go through the list of the remaining potential victims and identify those with brown eyes. You could be onto something. It may explain why he is destroying the eyes with acid. What do you think Rob?"

"I thought that the acid in the eyes was something to do with The Sawman's need to take control, but maybe it is far simpler than that. The trauma that I think he experienced when he was young could have been at the hands of someone with brown eyes," I said. They looked collectively unimpressed.

"Anyway it is a new lead. Great Dawn." Geoff gave her a great big smile.

"Now what else do we have? You were developing his profile last night. Any more thoughts?" Geoff anchored my eyes.

I showed him the print of my painting.

"It's not him yet, but you see the eyes are brown."

"Rob. It looks quite like the photograph of Luis Beale." Geoff passed it to Steve.

"It isn't finished. It's just an outline of The Sawman."

"I think it looks like him; the long face and the nose," Steve said.

"But Beale doesn't fit the profile at all," I responded.

"Maybe, but he bloody looks like your man. I've arranged a meeting with Baillie after lunch, so we will hear what they have to say."

"Okay," I said.

"When you were developing your profile did you uncover anything that might explain the four months gap?"

I shook my head.

"Maybe the murder in May was just a practice run," Steve offered.

"I don't buy that. I'm sure it is the key to these murders," Geoff reflected.

Silence filled the space as we turned it over in our minds.

"What did you find out about Melnar?" Geoff asked Steve.

"Nothing new, but the prostitution business looks big. Their action might interest the Syndicate."

"What colour are his eyes?" Geoff asked.

"Brown."

"Was there anything else?" Geoff asked, rubbing his hands together. Heads turned to and fro then settled back on Geoff. "Well, it's not much, but we have something new to work on. Let's hope the eyes or your profile come up with something. We could do with a breakthrough." He added.

"I'm getting close." I said. I'm not sure why I said it, maybe I just wanted to believe it.

"I hope so." Geoff said.

I got back to my office just as the telephone rang. It was my boss' PA.

"Rob, it's Audrey. Sir Anthony wants to see you today. I have booked you on the BA 4.30. It gets in at 5.25. He has also asked me to book you into the RAC Club tonight. He will probably need to meet with you again tomorrow so I have got you an open return. You can collect your e ticket in Manchester using your Executive Card."

"That's kind of him. What if something turns up here in the meantime?"

"You will have to discuss that with Sir Anthony. He wants to meet you in the Club at seven."

"Did he get my report?"

"Yes, he did."

"Right."

A few minutes later Ron looked in. He wanted to give me that tour. I wanted to see the Major Incident Room so I agreed to go.

"Let's start at the top."

We took the lift to the eleventh floor and the Chief Constable's offices. The Chief Constable was still abroad on holiday, so I was allowed to see the amazing panoramic view of the city from his room. Against the skyline, the small rows of terraced houses and sprawling estates butted against Gothic church spires and futuristic office buildings. For many people, city living is a nightmare, but living in the centre, with views across it, could be just as alluring as the open country-side. The panorama reminded me of my flat, it too had been an old office block before its conversion. My mini loft's open plan kitchen and sitting room were just about the same size as his office.

The rest of the main building was just like any other admin factory; full of people shuffling paper or staring at computers. The annexed computer and communications room was, however, very different. Linked to the back of the main building, it was on two floors, diamond shaped and totally secure, like a military establishment. I was shown the air-conditioned computer room called the Computer Hall, which was full of electronic wizardry and telecommunication equipment.

Next, I was taken to the operations room with its electronic maps and bank of motorway monitors. Then the recreation room which was basically a lot of chairs with no one smoking. The Major Incident Room was like the operations room with its computers and maps, but with sections detailing specific investigations. There, I met Dawn Burns. She and three of her colleagues were working in an area dedicated to The Sawman. The walls closest to her were covered in a collage of photographs and notes displaying details of the victims, the crime scenes, and my little profile to which had already been added – brown eyes. Dawn explained that she was investigating Melnar and the pornographic videos. I wasn't sure what more there was to pornographic videos than pornographic sex and I didn't think that Dawn's experience would add anything to the guys in Vice, but it was none of my business. I couldn't help thinking though that those videos were symptomatic of the change to our culture. Violence and sex were the mainstays of our entertainment. Kids just out of nursery were watching video nasties and the rest of us couldn't distinguish between fantasy and reality, sometimes I wonder what is to become of us all.

We finished the tour in the canteen where I had lunch served up by enthusiastic dinner ladies. The whole tour took about two hours. After lunch I went outside for a smoke. I was expected to go back to the Major Incident Room, but that kind of investigative work had little to do with what I did. When I returned to my room I was summoned to a meeting with Geoff and the two Chief Superintendents from the Met's Special Branch.

The two Met men were just as chilly as before. I listened carefully to their debriefing of their surveillance of Luis Beale and his 'associates', Tony Smedley, Johnny Carter and Alf Butcher and studied their pictures. The Beale gang looked like hoodlums. In their photographs, they looked cocky confident and arrogant. Luis, so obviously their leader, stood out from the rest. His sparkling white teeth signalled his confidence and attention to detail. Even in those pictures taken with long lenses 'without the smile please' he had presence. It was something about his bearing; the way he held himself erect set him apart from the rest. He had jet black hair smoothed over; it looked like gel and I suspected that the wisps of white that should have been there had either been plucked or coloured. His nose was strong, purposeful like a Roman Emperor's. He had brown eyes and, even more importantly, narrow wrists and long fingers. And he was a murderer, fond of large hunting knives and about the right height. There was an awful lot that matched my painting; even so, I still didn't think he was The Sawman. My only concern was that my sixth sense might have borrowed from the photograph that they showed me when we first met in Ulis' room.

Beale certainly looked the part of a big time gangster. From his silk tie to his £1,000 bespoke suit, he swaggered and bragged. Apparently, he had enough suits made, so that he never had to wear the same suit twice in the same week. On my pay, I couldn't have afforded the trousers, never mind the fancy suit. I was told that he wore an accessory, a Baretta 45 millimetre in a Venetian leather holster. If he did it was impossible to tell, but then his suit had probably been designed to hide it. Somehow, I didn't think my man would be wearing expensive suits. In most of the photographs of Beale there were also shots of Alf Butcher or at least parts of him. They evidently stuck close to each other. Butcher was a powerfully built man with a neck that any wrestler would have been proud of and ideal shoulders for knocking down doors. In contrast, his round face was childlike; silky smooth and not a crease in sight, just like his suit. He was immaculately tailored and wore the collar of his open neck shirt over the lapels of his jacket; a strangely dated look, like someone stuck in the '80s and yet he could only have been my age, early 30s.

I was certain that the gang wasn't relevant to my case, but the mug shots and history were fascinating. Tony Smedley was eating in every photo. I could see why he was called 'Fats the Fingers'. Their biography of him showed that he weighed nearly 220lbs and was only five six. Apparently, the nickname, 'Fingers' was a reference to the extra finger on his right hand. In all the photographs he looked untidy, his tie slung about an inch down from his collar, his suits ill-fitting, the jackets unfastened revealed a belly that rose in folds to meet his chin. He was more fat than cuddly. The other member of the gang, Johnny Carter, was tall and skinny. His nose, as big as Cerano de Bergerac's, dwarfed his ugly face; his mouth just a slit, with very little lip. Apparently, he had a couple irritating habits; he shrugged his shoulder pads on his suit every few seconds and flicked out his arms and pulled the cuffs of his shirt down – the insecure type.

One particularly intriguing photograph was of Luis in the arm of a beautiful dark haired woman, his girlfriend I was informed. Apparently she was 18, less than half Luis's age. She wasn't brassy, in fact the opposite, kind of understated and homely and all the more beautiful for it.

To be fair, the Met men had done their homework. Even so, I wasn't convinced that they were right about Beale. There was something about him that didn't fit. I was certain that

The Sawman would not have a girlfriend. He would be a loner I was sure about that. And I doubted whether he would have the cash or even the inclination to be such a dandy as their man Beale. I found myself yawning and looking at where my watch used to be every few minutes. After nearly an hour and a half listening to Geoff and the Met men swap theories and probabilities I'd had enough. I asked for the material to be downloaded to my private folder and reminded my Special Branch friends that I had a plane to catch. To my great surprise, they were more than a little helpful. When they realised that I could miss my flight they offered me a lift to the airport. I gladly accepted. When we got to their car, I sat in the back with Baillie while Chester sat in the front with their driver. Chester told the driver to switch on his flashing lights and sound the siren; all done in time to heavy acceleration. Meanwhile, Baillie was on to the airport security's Special Branch officers and told them to hold the flight.

We flashed through Manchester to the airport at Alderley Edge in a blur. We entered the airport through a security checkpoint at the edge of the runway and drove straight to the plane behind a Range Rover escort. No ticket to check-in and no security check. I was escorted to the plane, which had already boarded and shown to my seat at the front door. We were off.

We landed on time and I caught the Heathrow Express to Paddington station. A taxi took me to Queen Anne's Gate and I was soon swiping my pass at security on my way to the Police Scientific Development Branch. The PSDB's job was to provide technical advice to the Policing and Crime Reduction Group, as well as the police and Ministers. Its aim was to improve the operational effectiveness and efficiency of the police service and to support the Home Secretary in counter terrorism. My job was to do as I was told, though the only person that could tell me was Sir Anthony Holdsworthy. Sir Anthony was the Permanent Secretary for Crime, Policing, Counter Terrorism and Delivery. I reported to him and he reported to the Permanent Secretary of the Home Office. I was the odd-bod in the Department, but justified in support of one of its main aims 'To reduce crime and the fear of crime'.

I sat in my small office, fixed my laptop into its docking station and booted it up. Once I had typed in my security code, I checked to see if the Beale file had been sent; it had. I checked for important e-mails – none. I reviewed my latest summary report and printed off hard copies of it along with the Beale report. I was ready to see Sir Anthony. I buzzed Audrey's extension, but surprise, surprise I was told that he couldn't see me. I was to meet him at the RAC Club as arranged. I e-mailed the reports to his office, packed up and made my way to Pall Mall.

Huge fiery torches played flames above the entrance to the RAC Club, adding a dramatic touch to the sombre and impressive structure of the building. I climbed the sandstone steps and the uniformed doorman welcomed me inside. I walked through the grand foyer up the stairs to the reception desk where I was given the keys to my room. I had stayed there only once before, in a room not much bigger than a cell but with fewer luxuries, it had, however, met the frugal demands of the department's budget. The corridor to my bedroom had been given a makeover since then. I opened the door and my eyes widened in surprise. The space was cavernous and the room luxurious. I wiped my feet before I stepped onto the royal blue carpet. I felt myself sink into its soft deep pile. I placed my bag carefully on the solid beech bench that matched the huge double wardrobe and crossed to the shiny silk covering that draped the king size bed and sat on its firm and welcoming mattress. From my throne I took in the rest of this sumptuously dressed room. There was a desk, chair and a cabinet housing a large television, all in solid beech. The room had all the trappings of a five star hotel bedroom. Previously I had had to wander down the hall to a shared bathroom, by contrast my new room had an ensuite bathroom with fluffy white towels bearing the RAC crest. I opted for a pulsating shower and then killed time at my desk in my thick towelling robe sipping whisky delivered by the porter as I enjoyed my complimentary shortbread. Clearly some parts of the job had their rewards.

I met Sir Anthony in the 'long bar'. I was on my second Lagavulin when he arrived. He was tall, wore an immaculate pinstriped suit, crisp white shirt and silk tie with regulatory double Windsor knot. An old Etonian, but I didn't hold that against him. I had always found him to be astute and fair. He had stuck by me on quite a few occasions when others were trying to undermine me. He was a shrewd politician and I had his ear and that was how it would be I guessed until I fucked up. He greeted me in his usual pleasant way. His was a gin and tonic and a cigar, mine another Lagavulin and a Marlboro. We sat at a table out of earshot. After a few pleasantries, it was straight to business.

"I read your report and the Met Office's report on their suspect Beale. They appear to have quite different conclusions."

"Yes. I standby mine."

"Their man matches your profile."

"In part, but he isn't The Sawman."

"What about this chap Melnar"

"What about him?"

"This morning Beale was tailed across the bridge to an address in the Salford Quays." Sir Anthony's delivery and phrasing were perfect.

"And?"

"It was owned by one Leon Melnar."

"Maybe they are friends."

"Don't pretend to be naïve," Sir Anthony responded.

"What happened?"

"Beale never went in, he just watched. What do you make of it?"

"I am not sure. Maybe, it has something to do with the distribution of pornographic videos." His eyes hinted at impatience. "I don't know, but what I do know is that Beale isn't The Sawman. The profile doesn't fit. The Sawman is definitely a loner."

"Hmm. What about this other business?"

"You mean Ulis?"

"I mean Assistant Chief Constable Ulis, yes."

"I don't like him."

"It's not your job to like or dislike. You are there to offer support and advice. I do not expect telephone calls from Assistant Chief Constables claiming that a member of my staff is being obstructive."

"There is nothing in my job description about clipes."

"Dear boy, I am referring to the way you dealt with it."

"I understand."

"Now, the profile you have submitted should have led to an arrest by now. Why hasn't it?"

"I am getting close, but he wears a mask, that's what's holding things up."

"If he wasn't so guarded our friends in GMP wouldn't have needed you, would they? When will they get their painting?"

"Soon, I hope." I pulled deep on my second Marlboro of the conversation.

"All right I'd like you to be around tomorrow in case the Permanent Secretary wants an update. Can you keep yourself busy here?"

"Yes."

"Let's eat."

We made our way to the French restaurant and we shared a very pleasant meal and some interesting New Zealand red wine. Everything went well apart from one embarrassing moment when I was drinking my tea, my hand shook uncontrollably. Sir Anthony carried on as though it hadn't happened and I stuck to the wine. When he left about nine, I had a swim in the Club's magnificent pool and for the first time since Liz left, slept in a bed. And what a magnificent bed it was.

8. The wrong things unravel

Thursday 19th September

Despite my swim and the comfy bed I slept only fleetingly, any deep sleep was broken by more horrible nightmares and I woke up feeling worse than when I had gone to bed. Still breakfast, my first in days, was a pleasure. I enjoyed the most magnificent porridge and cream that I had ever tasted and I followed that with bacon and scrambled egg. I was no hotel inspector but if the RAC Club had been a hotel even its competitors in the AA would have awarded it five stars. The problem with my hand, shaking teacups and rattling saucers was, however, still there.

It only took a few minutes to pack my meagre belongings including the mask that I had taken to carrying around with me everywhere I went. I caught the tube to Queen Anne's Gate. During the morning I called Audrey twice to see if I was needed and both times the answer was 'not yet'. I went through all my files again then I called Geoff to check on progress, but the news wasn't good. His team hadn't found any undertaker within Greater Manchester that matched my description, also there was nothing from the enquiry into the child abuse. The lack of progress was getting to me. I could feel my chest tighten and my head ached. When I went to the lavatory for some water and air I met one of the senior managers, who promptly told me that I looked like shit. Unfortunately a glance in the mirror told me he was right. There was no denying it; I had let myself go. I hadn't remembered to take my shaving kit and the dirty looking stubble didn't help. I hadn't bought a shirt either. The black rolltop was into its second day and it looked like I had slept in it – if only. The lack of sleep had contorted my whole face, especially my eyes. They were dull and black and looked like I had packed sandbags beneath the loose folds of skin under them. I'd also lost some weight, which I supposed wasn't that surprising. The weight loss made the skin on my face look like a Sharpei's. I gave up on the assessment, took a leak, washed my hands and then headed for the front door

Outside I joined the throng of shoppers. I hated shopping in London. There was always the feeling of never-ending restlessness and aimlessness at the same time. The street where I was walking was a sea of bustling anonymity; commuters, office workers and shoppers. After only a few minutes I had had enough. I could feel my collar constricting. The tightness warned me that I was most likely to succumb to pedestrian rage so I slipped out of the crowd and into the first shop I saw selling menswear.

It was like an oasis until the salesman approached me. Right away he eyed my rollneck and tried to interest me in a ludicrously expensive designer one that cost as much as my monthly pay check and right away I disappointed him. Like most Glaswegians I am a little ashamed to say, I liked expensive designer clothes. If things had been different and Liz had been there I might have been persuaded, but his luck was out. I couldn't afford them, I was on my own and just then I had to keep up the payments on the mortgage without Liz's contribution. His phoney smile turned to a sneer when I said I wanted the cheapest shirts they had. He pointed at a shelf at the back and left me to it. I settled for three new shirts, underwear and socks that all up, were half the price of the rollneck the pushy assistant had tried to sell me.

When I left there I considered grabbing some lunch, but instead I stopped at a chemist for some headache pills. I broke open the pack, threw back three and helped them down with a free drink from their water fountain. I had to get out of the place, yet I couldn't quite face returning to my office. After a couple of turns along side streets I spotted a gloomy bar that befitted my mood.

Even though the whole city must have been doing lunch that place was nearly empty. I took a stool at the corner of the bar furthest from the door and ordered a double Scotch from the morose bartender. I knocked it back and signalled for another. While my dour bartender refilled my glass I looked at myself in the mirror below the gantry. I resembled a hobo and for what, for the wasted hours I sat there contemplating his face. My doubts came flooding in. All that effort at profiling – was he that, was he this, when all I had to do was ask Special Branch to send me over a photograph. I was bruised from the lack of proper sleep. I had to admit to myself that since Sawman, my life had been on a slippery slope. My relationships were in a mess. Liz had as good as told me I was a drunk and that I should fuck off. I felt so guilty and hopelessly inadequate. Even my mother was pissed off at me and Pops blamed me for chasing away his beautiful daughter-in-law. And Ulis thought I was a chump. Something was happening to me, I wasn't sure what, but I was seeing things differently, feeling things change and not for the better. My confidence was replaced with self doubt. The idiots and bureaucrats that I once used to spike with ease seemed to be able to keep me on the back foot. I felt that I had become as horizontal and indistinguishable from the others that I used to hold in contempt. My passion for all sorts of things was waning. I hadn't read anything challenging in two weeks and even my music had lost its ability to stir my soul. The dark clouds were gathering and dulling my sharpness and what's worse my energy to fight back was running low. I wasn't sure what I should do. I suddenly became aware of the television. It was reporting our progress with The Sawman or more accurately the lack of it, but that wasn't what I heard. The face in the picture had Ulis' unmistakable, electioneering smile, but the words didn't synchronise, and worse, the voice that spoke them was mine.

"Special Branch have tried to diffuse our efforts by inducing sleep and blabbing in light airy bubbles. I have, however, blown them out with The Sawman's tagliatelli and swept their crazy thinking into the bin. They ate the line and the hook and were left with nothing but a bobbing float. Help me sink it deep, feel free to piss on it, bash it or smash it. We have no more use for their stinking thinking and tell them from me I expect to speak directly to The Sawman soon, mighty soon."

"What the fuck," I shouted.

The bartender thought that I was a little on the deaf side and turned up the sound whereupon Bob Ulis' voice boomed, "The department has a number of leads that we are following. Once these have been fully investigated we will be close to identifying the serial killer. I'd like to take this opportunity to thank the many members of the public who are assisting us with this investigation." Ulis lifted the copy of his speech and disappeared from the lectern under a hail of media questions.

I looked at the glass of Scotch and was in two minds whether to drink it or leave it. I considered whether my mind had crossed its wires. I concluded that I must have experienced some kind of hallucination. I was confused and scared. I had somehow caught myself up in a web that I had spun. I slipped off the stool and went to the telephone booth in the corner. There I called my friend Pete Whelan.

"Dr Whelan." I was lucky his familiar voice answered immediately.

"Pete, it's Robbie Ahearn. I need your help," I half croaked.

"Robbie where are you?"

"Near Anne's Gate."

"What can I do for you?"

"Pete I need to see you."

"When?"

"Now." I didn't need to say anymore to Pete, he knew me well enough to recognise that I was stranded in confusion.

"Come to the office. Do you remember where it is?" It was two years since I had been there. It was he who diagnosed my breakdown and arranged for me to be hospitalised. It was his support and professional skill that got me through it.

"Harley Street right."

"Right."

Pete gave me the exact address. I hailed a cab.

Pete was Edinburgh born and reared. I had known him since we were freshmen at St Andrew's when we used to down drams together, we were mates, but I had only been to his office that once. I thought I was seeing things then too, and it turned out I was. He was my saviour, brought me back from the brink and he was also the person who helped me realise that what I had was a gift.

I entered his building and took the lift to the sixth floor. When the doors opened I saw the sign I was looking for straight in front of me, it said BPST. I followed the arrow below it pointing to the right. It led me to an outer glass door with another sign saying press the buzzer for BPST reception so I did. A few seconds later an attractive middle aged woman opened the door.

"Dr Ahearn?" she asked with a pleasant smile.

"Yes, I am here to see Pete, I mean Dr Whelan."

"Come in please, he is expecting you." She pulled the door wide open and beckoned me in.

I walked into the reception area, which was small and gloomy. She smiled and asked me to wait. I stood there like a lost kid as she walked over to a large mahogany door, knocked quietly and then disappeared inside. My eyes swept around the neutral coloured walls until they locked onto a plaque. It was brass or gold and gleaming. Its inscription read: Dr P Whelan Director of Psychotherapy, BPST. Underneath it there was another in black and white, which read: BPST – residential treatment for adults 18 and older for both psychiatric and chemical dependency disorders. My recollection was that Pete was the one at Uni with the dependency. I read on: Outpatient treatment including psychotherapy, medication management, group and family therapy, substance abuse treatment and marital counselling in our Centre in… I was distracted by the receptionist or nurse; anyway whatever she was she had come back.

"Dr Whelan can see you now. Please go in. Would you like a coffee?" I couldn't handle questions with instructions just then. I shook my head and walked past her through the open door into a large office come sitting room. The door closed behind me. It was not the refuge I expected. The large room was empty of any semblance of homely comfort. I could hear muted voices coming from beyond. The voices stopped and the door at the far end opened. Pete came in.

"Hello Robbie I am sorry about that – one of my patients."

"Och, that's okay." I waved my hand as though I had got all the time in the world, as if I was only there on a social call.

Pete shook my hand warmly.

"It's been ages, good to hear from you. How's Liz?"

"We've separated I think."

"Oh you sounded like you had something on your mind."

"This has nothing to do with Liz. Look, I can see you're busy."

"Hey don't worry about it. It's lunchtime so I am free for the next couple of hours. So what brings you here and why didn't you tell me you were coming? Come make yourself comfortable." Pete motioned me towards a sofa.

"It isn't a social call."

"I gathered that, sit down. Can I get you anything?"

"No, no I'm fine." I didn't want coffee, but I certainly wasn't fine. I was scared shitless. Pete sat in a large easy chair and patted the arm of the sofa next to him. I sat down at the other end and stared at my feet. My shoes were scuffed, dirty and too big. I hid them under me.

"So what can I do for you?"

"I don't know where to fucking start." I always slipped into the vernacular with him, he was a mate, a safe house.

"Wherever you are comfortable. Are you sure that I can't get you some coffee or a cold drink?" I shook my head. "Okay, please go ahead. If I don't follow anything, I'll say."

"It is the visions, the gift. I'm eh, I'm working on this case, a serial killer." Pete nodded for me to go on. "I seem to be getting entangled in it. And Liz has walked out and I'm not sleeping well, although I don't feel tired." I looked into Pete's eyes; they were sympathetic and supportive. My hands shook uncontrollably. "Anyway, I went to a bar today – that's where I called you from – and I thought I heard myself speak from the television. It was fucking weird you know, not like my visions, my voice, coming from the television." I was still uptight and the words weren't flowing. My palms were sweaty and I rubbed them together. "It wasn't me. I mean the guy on the television wasn't me. I was watching my boss. It was a news report on our investigation into our serial killer. One of our news conferences, you know. And my boss was speaking, except that it wasn't his voice or his words. It was my voice and my words." Pete didn't say anything, but nodded encouraging me to go on. "Well, I was worried, seeing things, delusions, all symptoms of schizophrenia, so I called you."

"You say this wasn't like your visions."

"No, I was just watching television in the pub."

"Have you ever had anything like this before; when you were young maybe?"

"No." I suppose that I should have mentioned my crazy moments, but I didn't.

"Okay. I doubt that I can tell you anything about schizophrenia that you don't know." It was true, I probably knew as much about schizophrenia as he did. I already knew that it was one of the most severe and debilitating psychological disorders; that it affected less than 2% of the population and that the psychological effects became apparent in the early teens to mid-20s, when most have their first psychotic break with reality. "As you have never shown any symptoms when you were younger then you should know that it is extremely unlikely that you have this disorder."

I nodded.

"Aye and I know that hallucinations and delusions are symptoms, as well as disorganised speech and paranoia – that's why I'm fucking worried. I'm sorry, I know it's stupid."

"Robbie, it is not stupid you did the right thing. Hearing things isn't normal. You said that this has never happened before so there must be some disturbance to have caused it."

I nodded my head.

"What was the voice saying to you?"

"Oh I don't remember it was sort of garbled. It was about the case, but rubbish really." I ran out of words and silence filled the gap. Then Pete spoke.

"The anxiety, lack of sleep and not eating are in themselves enough to cause you to become confused."

I nodded again.

"You mentioned that Liz had walked out, how are you coping?

"I suppose I am pretty fucking devastated... shocked."

He nodded for me to carry on.

"I feel empty kind of blunted. It is like I've lost my confidence. At times it all seems so hopeless; work, Liz everything, like nothing good is ever going to happen again. It's like I've lost my luck."

"When we play cards you always said that you make your own luck." I smiled he was shite at cards, I always beat him. "When did Liz leave?"

"Saturday."

"Ah," I could tell he was thinking that was nothing, but it was everything to me. "And you have had trouble sleeping since then?" he continued

"Before that, but now I hardly sleep at all, maybe a couple of hours if that. I have these recurring nightmares and wake up shaking, covered in sweat."

"What are the dreams about?"

Our conversation was beginning to sound like the last time, when I ended up in his clinic near Edinburgh. I wondered whether he was planning to make me go back there; paranoia another symptom.

"There are two of them. In the first I am at the cottage standing on a windowsill staring at the encroaching waves pondering my fate, awaiting my destruction. I want to keep the waves back so I shut my eyes. But that doesn't help, they keep coming. I turn my shirt collar up against the wind, but still I hear them advance one after another, their gravel sound stuck on repeat, getting closer with every churn. Each new ripple penetrates my conscience deeper than the last, stirring memories I know that I'd rather not face. Flooding my mind with things I'd rather forget, the hatred, the anger and the defeated expressions. Bringing memories from my cases. My head swims in the horrific and gruesome memories and I lean out over the cliff and it ends with me falling onto the rocks.

The other is when I am in a bath. Well there's no bath, but that noise you get when you put your head under. In my dream I am inside my mother's womb, not as a child but as

139

a man. I am floating, listening to my heartbeat and then I can't breathe. It was as though I was drowning." I stopped because I could see it all again so vividly just like one of my crazy moments.

"Was that when you woke up?"

"No, I am thrashing my arms around, pulverising the inside of the womb until it bursts open and I am flushed out on to a bed. I lay there, face down with my hands over my eyes for a while and when I uncover them my fingers and palms are smeared in blood. That's when I jolt myself awake. Of course there's no blood anywhere, but my whole body is soaked in perspiration."

"And do you go back to sleep?"

"I try, but my mind buzzes with everything that's going on and it's impossible."

"What are you thinking about?"

"Just the job and Liz, everything I suppose. My head feels like a witness box and some QC is bombarding me with pointed accusations."

"What kind of accusations?"

"Sort of barbed, sharp and cutting. Most are about my ineptitude. Like my handling of a case I'm working on now; there are lots about that."

"How do you deal with them?"

"Shit, nothing, my defence is nothing but a pathetic and uncomfortable silence."

"Are you drinking more than usual?"

"Aye. I suppose so."

"How much?"

"Nothing serious, half a bottle at night, maybe a little more."

"Still on malt?" I nodded. "I am sure you know that the drinking won't help. It won't ease your troubles and it is probably preventing you from getting a deep rest so avoid alcohol in the late evening. And you shouldn't drink anything that has caffeine in it. Do you prepare for sleep?"

"What?"

"You know, take a bath, get into your pyjamas."

"I don't wear them."

"I just mean do you have a routine to go to bed, at a particular time?"

"No my mind is too busy on this case and I paint."

"What are you painting?"

"I spend most of the night painting out a profile of the serial killer."

There was silence. I wasn't sure whether he wanted me to speak or he was going to speak. I was trying to keep my head together. It all felt so fucked up.

"You are an unusual guy Robbie, but your body is like everyone else's it needs sleep and nourishment."

I nodded again and stared at my knees. They were jutting out sharp and bony. Thin, far too thin. He went on.

"This case, I suppose it is the one that's getting all the coverage – the killer who saws off the heads of his victims?"

"Aye, that's the one." I stared at his face. It was a gentle face, serious, but generous.

"I can only imagine the horrors of it."

"It's not that. I am used to that."

"Then what's particularly bothering you about this case then."

"I don't know. He's doing terrible things, but I find myself feeling sorry for him. I can't explain it. Sometimes I feel like

I am walking in his shoes feeling what he feels. I am him. And he is lonely. I feel like I am all he's got, but I am out to get him. And when I do he will be crucified."

"Why?"

"Because they don't want to understand him. They just want him locked up for good, you know. I think he deserves a chance. I'm sure that he has been through some trauma and this is how he is dealing with it."

"That's more my area than yours."

"I suppose so but it's been difficult to remain objective." I wanted to say that I was drawn to The Sawman, his complexity and the more I understood him the more I questioned my motives. Catching him had become a quest – an obsession, yet deep down I felt that maybe what he is doing was right in a way, but it never came out.

"How do you mean?"

"All his victims have been perverted scumbags that have been abusing kids. He is achieving something the police can't but would like to, he removes them permanently. The best that they can hope for is to put them away for a while, but they know that when these perverts are released they will do it again. The police are being paid and praised for delaying the abuse and The Sawman is being hounded because he ends it. Ironic, don't you think?"

"Society makes its own rules. You are doing what you are being asked to do. We don't want to recognise his kind of vengeance. I can understand your frustration and the appeal of his freewill. It sounds like a case of transference, but it doesn't usually work that way round. According to Sigmund Freud, transference isn't unique to the psychoanalytic relationship between client and therapist. He claimed that similar patterns

142

of relationship could be formed with 'substitutes' other than psychotherapists, but I don't know how he would explain it in this context. I don't know of any eh." He was looking deep into my eyes and I could see him shift. "I'm sorry, another time maybe. I am sure you don't want to get into that now. Your split with Liz will make you sensitive to suffering in others. Do you believe that there are similarities between yourself and the killer?"

"Some."

"Like what?"

"We both struggle with relationships and are kind of remote."

"I wouldn't say that you were remote. Could the fact that he is a vigilante possibly have an appeal to you."

"No it's closer than that it is something that's happened to him."

"What do think happened to him?"

"I don't know, I can't explain it. When I paint him there is pain and sadness."

"What have you seen that makes you feel this."

"Nothing specific, I just feel it. You know how I operate," I said. He knew from the last time. He knew that I got inside their head, sort of fused, saw what they saw or imagined that I did. "It helps me paint out their profile, but when I paint him he looks like me."

"Many artists favour themselves when painting others."

"Pete, I have painted out dozens of profiles before, none of them looked like me."

"You say you are not sleeping. Is that because you are having these nightmares?"

"No, I just don't seem to want to sleep that's all."

"Apart from this case how's your job doing?"

"I can't really separate the case from the other work. It is only the fourth serial killer I've worked on. I feel as though I am getting too much interference and no one is listening."

"How can that be? Are you not in charge of the investigation?"

"Yes, but I still have a boss."

"Oh yes, the one on television."

"A guy called Ulis."

"Is that relationship going well?"

"No different to usual – me and bosses never really see eye to eye."

"Does he know how you feel?"

"No. He knows how I look that's all."

"What about Liz? Are you planning to get her back?"

"I am trying, but she doesn't return my calls."

"Why is that do you think?"

"I don't know, she probably wants some time to think it out. I don't know."

"Robbie, it sounds as though you have a lot on your mind at the moment. Being over-stressed can cause a range of health problems, such as headaches, high blood pressure and, of course, insomnia. The recurring dream is likely to be about your internal tussle with the concerns you have about your killer. You are faced with, for you, an unusual dichotomy – save him or let him go. Such bouts of conscience about the people you are hunting are unusual I suppose?"

I nodded my head.

"The womb in your dream implies safety and security, which part of you would like for yourself and for your killer, but the professional you knows that you need to stop him, catch him. And, of course, your regrets about Liz compound it. The best thing you could do is take a break from work at least until you have worked out your problem with Liz."

"I can't do that, this guy is killing people every day."

"There are others who could take over aren't there?"

"No, not this case and anyway it is important that I solve it."

"Why?"

"Because I have got to know this guy and I feel that I am not far from a breakthrough."

"Not sleeping isn't going to help you solve it nor do your health any good."

"No, I can see that. Is there anything you can do to help me sleep?"

"I can, but you need to commit yourself to taking it easier. It is likely that you are suffering depression, feeling down and perhaps overwhelmed. I could prescribe you some SRIs to help regulate your mood disorders."

"Okay."

"You should know that even though they tend to have fewer and less severe side effects than the older drugs, some of their side effects might at this stage be counterproductive as they can cause decreased appetite, nausea, nervousness and insomnia. And I don't think we want to make these problems worse do you?"

"No."

"So I think we should wait. Don't get me wrong though, over time antidepressants can improve mood, appetite, and concentration, but it can be between 6 and 12 weeks before real signs of improvement are seen. I think we should consider these later if things don't improve."

"Okay, but what do I do now. My attitude is so negative a lot of the time. I feel so useless."

"Try not to over-generalise, try and avoid the terms like 'always' or 'never'. You need to recognise the positive things in your life and if you are considering negative aspects you need to quantify them. You are a respected psychologist, an intelligent and artistic person, don't diminish those qualities. You need to try and recapture the more positive outlook on life that I've always seen in you before."

"If only."

"If you are worried that this is a recurrence of your nervous breakdown two years ago, don't be. From what you have told me, your problems with Liz are bound to be making you sad and anxious so it's no surprise that you are finding it difficult to concentrate. With the lack of sleep you are bound to feel a little lethargic throughout the day. I wouldn't worry about the television incident it sounds as though you are pretty focused on your investigation and you probably had a sort of day dream, a kind of déjà vu. You should, however, take it as a warning. You need to take your depression seriously, it's not imaginary, and it will get worse if you don't deal with it. Whilst I'm certain your anxiety and depression are linked to poor sleep and your problems with Liz you mustn't allow this investigation to be a catalyst for the return of the dangerous clinical depression that could so easily draw you back into a psychotic disorder. That could prove even more dangerous than your breakdown. Are you with me?"

"Sure, I understand."

"You need to improve your mental and emotional well-being. I suggest you start with setting yourself some realistic goals like eating at least one proper meal, getting four hours sleep each night and, even with Liz, it needs to be measured. You should set yourself a goal of meeting up with Liz, not to get her back, but just to talk about what went wrong. And you should lay off the painting and the booze for now. The painting is making you focus too hard on work and the booze is just making things worse."

"I'll try."

"Most importantly you need to deal with the not eating and not sleeping."

"I am meeting my father for dinner tomorrow."

"The food's good, but you have to avoid the drink and talking shop."

"Easier said than done."

"Robbie, this is for your own good. You need to give up work for a while, get some rest, let your body recuperate."

"Okay, look Pete I am grateful for this."

"You need to keep your work separate from the rest of your life."

"Sure, I understand."

"Take one of these before you settle tonight," he took out a small bottle of pills from a cabinet at his side, "and Robbie, try not to stay up late. Take a bath, not too hot, just warm enough for a long relaxing soak and try and get some sleep. It will make a big difference."

"Thanks Pete."

"You are with Tom Berner aren't you?" Tom was my doctor. "You should give him a call and have him give you a physical; just to be sure that everything is okay. You can tell Tom that we've spoken."

"I'll do that, I haven't been to the doctor for a long time."

"Say hi to your dad for me, when you see him. Don't be tempted to drink. I know that will be difficult, but it will help you'll see …"

"Okay."

"I'd like to see you next week, but I'll call you at the weekend and we can arrange to meet."

"Okay and thanks Pete."

When I left his office and got into a taxi I felt a lot better. I don't know why really, I suppose I was more relieved than better. Insanity had visited me once and I didn't want to meet it again. I wasn't sure whether I was in the clear, yet I was certain that I hadn't taken possession of the madness that had introduced itself in the bar. Maybe it had passed me by or maybe I had outwitted it, although I still had doubts. I doubted for the first time that my reasoning was sound. I doubted whether my role, in this particular case, was appropriate. It wasn't like me to be so introspective and this wistfulness was new. Something was happening to me and I didn't understand it. I knew that this new me was on a collision course with my other self and was a real threat to my career.

When I got back to my office, Audrey told me that Sir Anthony would be too busy to see me, so I caught the 4.15 to Manchester. It was about seven when I checked into my hotel, the Royal. I dropped my things in my room, thought about dinner, but decided that the dining room was probably going to be as boring as my 'ensuite single' so, I went downstairs and out the front door.

Being a Glaswegian came in handy on such occasions, you see we don't mind going up to perfect strangers and asking where the nearest pub is. I did just that and thankfully the response told me that The Coach House was just around the corner. That was where my good fortune ended. The pseudo-Tudor elevation on a building built around the '50s said it all. The nearest that pub got to coaches must have been buses used by football supporters; another theme pub helping to ruin our great British institution. Pubs were once places of refuge, solace and friendship: The Coach House was fake, from its beams to its ceramic stone floors, soulless, devoid of any character of its own and from the age of the clientele, a homework club. It was full of kids drinking Bacardi Breezers and expensive Hoegarrden. The only adult there apart from the bar staff was an old age pensioner who sat in the corner opposite about three feet from the telly. I was relieved to hear that I wasn't doing any voice-overs.

I got myself a pint of Boddingtons and a table as far away from the one arm bandits as I could. The atmosphere made me spare a thought for the army of sales reps who spent their evenings alone in dreary hotels and plastic theme pubs just like the one I was in.

Apart from the loud music, there was very little to distract my introspection. It had been a strange day. Pete was reassuring, yet what I experienced wasn't natural. I wondered where it would end. It certainly crossed my mind that I should give it up, all of it, work, the drink, the worry. I knew that wasn't going to happen. There I was in a pub drinking a pint of Boddingtons and there would be more to follow, it was strange how one lied when asked by a doctor how much you drink.

The Coach House could have been prescribed by Pete to get me off drinking for after only a couple of pints I returned to my hotel. Madness hadn't got hold of me but I wasn't out of my depression because as soon as I got to my room I switched on the television and watched sumo wrestling on the satellite channel.

9. A breakthrough

Friday 20th September – Day Five

It was ten o'clock and I was in Ulis' office with Wheaton and our friends from Special Branch.

"Special Branch believes Beale evaded surveillance and was abroad in Manchester between one and five on the morning Shields was murdered." Ulis took that smile around the room and nodded to the two self-righteous suits.

On cue Chester read from his notes: "At 2.10am, Alf Butcher knocked on Luis' bedroom door but got no answer, then we heard him enter Luis' room and he said, 'He must have gone out' (meaning Beale)."

"How clever of you to work that out," I said facetiously.

"At 5.25, Luis returned to the apartment." It was Baillie reading from his report.

"You saw him," I asked.

"No, but we recorded the noise of the bedroom door opening and footsteps in Luis room," Baillie answered.

"How do you know it wasn't Alf again?"

"The person entering never went out of the room again and there were other noises of clothes being put away."

"Okay, but the time of death was around 5.30, isn't that right Geoff?" I looked over and drew his eyes up from the ground.

"That was when we were advised, but we won't know for certain until the coroner has completed the post mortem."

"Superintendent Baillie has more," Ulis interjected.

"A man wearing a long dark coat and cap was seen entering the rear of the adjacent building at 5.27. He wasn't positively ID, but the weight and height matched Beale."

"He's our man I can feel it," Ulis said excitedly.

"I doubt that. The time of death doesn't tally and this guy is hardly the vigilante type, murderer yes, but vigilante no," I said looking to Geoff for support, but he kept quiet.

"He's five foot nine, owns a hunting knife, a member of the Syndicate and around the time of the killing he was out and about. And I don't think that black knitted cap was for some fancy dress do," Chester barked.

"So did we ask him if he did it?" I asked Baillie with as much sarcasm in my voice that I could muster.

"We want to get the whole gang," Chester jumped in.

"I have invited Special Branch to assist in this investigation," Ulis said authoritatively.

"We hope you will work with us," Baillie proffered with a smile.

"Happy to do that as long as you understand I do things my own way."

"And what way is that?" Chester asked.

"I use evidence to reconstruct the crime. If you read my reports you will see for yourself."

"I've read your reports. You talk of probabilities."

"High probability based on objective reasoning," Geoff said at last.

"Oh come now, objective reasoning? Don't you get your information from some spirit while you are in some sort of trance?" Chester said looking straight at me.

"No. There are no spirits and no trances. My record speaks for itself."

"Well, that may be, but on this occasion I feel that the resources and investigative skills of the Special Branch are more likely to help us identify our serial killer," Ulis said.

"Say the word and I am on my way."

"I think it is for the Home Office to decide when your participation has ended, don't you? I have sent your Director my report highlighting the evidence provided by Superintendents Baillie and Chester," Ulis said.

"Fine, but Beale is not our man. I doubt whether Special Branch could identify The Sawman if they caught him in the act."

"Now see here Ahearn I have had 20 years on the Force and Dan has 18 years," Chester said.

"Good for you, but from where I sit your combined service hasn't improved your perception. If it had, you would know that he isn't our man. The Sawman is a schizo. Do you know what that is? Before you guess let me tell you. Sufferers of schizophrenia often experience symptoms of hallucinations, delusions and disordered thoughts. They become socially withdrawn. Do you think that this fits Luis Beale?"

"Impressive Ahearn," Baillie said, the polite formality of 'Dr' dropped. "The psychology theorising may work for you, but we prefer to follow through the facts. The facts are that Beale is a very close match and we need to check out whether he is the serial killer that so far has seen you chase tails and uncover not one single lead," Baillie added.

"Your life may all be neat and tidy, but where I come from that's the kind of anal behaviour that comes back and bites you on the bum. My participation in these investigations, as Assistant Chief Constable Ulis prefers to call it, has provided the profile from which you have matched your suspect. I would add that profile is, in my professional opinion, too broad to enable the targeting of an individual. I hope this changes when I have completed my analysis, which if you don't mind I will get back to." I stood up.

"Before you go you might want to hear of some other evidence crudely identified through policework," said Ulis.

"We have some other information that connects Beale with your murders. Yesterday morning Beale was tailed across the bridge to an address in the Salford Quays," Baillie smirked.

"Doing some partying?" I thought it couldn't be.

"It must have been a one man show because he didn't get out of the car. He parked outside a converted concrete warehouse and was seen observing an apartment."

"So."

"So it was owned by one Leon Melnar," Baillie responded.

"I have made my decision, Mr Ahearn I will ask for Special Branch to take over the case if we haven't found our man by the weekend. Detective Superintendent Wheaton agrees with me," Ulis said.

"Well, let's leave the superintendents here to follow their own investigation of Beale and I will do it my way."

I turned and walked out the door. I wasn't proud of losing my temper, but those bastards had got me riled.

I had gone straight outside and around the back where I took refuge in my cigarettes. Three fags later I still wasn't calm, but I was ready to get on so I went back to my office. I ignored Pete's advice about drinking and poured George into my empty mug. Whisky rather than coffee was what I needed just then.

My desk was, as usual, full of papers. I picked them up and put them down again. I blew stale cigarette breath out the side of my mouth, spun my chair a full 360° and brought my head crashing down on the files.

There was a knock on the door.

"Come in," I shouted. "Oh, it's you Geoff. Thanks for your support in there," I said sarcastically.

"I'm sorry, but they are right – Luis Beale is a prime suspect. He could easily have been sent by the Syndicate to sort them out."

"You don't believe that any more than I do."

"Look Rob, he is a professional hitman that uses a hunting knife for the kill and like they say he fits your profile."

"No he doesn't, not his psychological profile. Our man is troubled, but he is also sensitive and deeply religious. And what hitman would bother to saw off his victims' heads."

"Italians? I don't know. One thing for sure, troubled or no, he plans the murders just like a professional. And Beale is the only lead we've got."

"The Sawman's neat and tidy but he's not a professional," I said without anything to back it up. "And what's this stuff about him and Melnar?"

"Beale was followed to Melnar's apartment building and they were convinced that he was sussing the place out."

"Yeah, my boss told me that but what was Beale doing there?"

"Probably something to do with the distribution of pornographic material. Vice says that some of it looks as though it is real footage of sadistic torture and Melnar's gold teeth are on the face of the guy inflicting it. They also found the drug Rohypnol in Muche's apartment and in Melnar's. Vice believe that the business is big and, like Baillie and Chester, that the Syndicate may be interested in Melnar's operation."

"What do you make of it?" I asked.

"I think they are right about Beale coming up to sort Melnar and his cohorts out but I don't know about The Sawman. I can't say that we have come up with anything better and I'm bloody glad for any help I can get; they have got access to resources that we don't. My guys are pissed off working all this overtime."

"I can understand that, but they are wrong about Beale. He isn't The Sawman, believe me I've seen him."

"Well, if he isn't they will eliminate him, won't they?"

This was a lost cause and I couldn't really blame Geoff, I hadn't given him much help to find our man. He went back to his office, but a few minutes later he came back.

"Have you read Alec Shunt's report on that murder in Pinks Avenue?"

"No. Why?"

"You should. Come with me."

Geoff turned and left and I followed him to his office. When I got there he looked excited like he was bursting to tell me some important news. And he was. He passed me a manila folder.

"This looks like a professional hit. Read it for yourself. I'd put money on it that Beale was responsible."

My eyes were drawn to the reference to hunting knife. 'Adam Rogerson aged 42, suspected organiser of prostitution was murdered at 3.05 in a service road in Headingly. The weapon used was a hunting knife.' I read on. 'The victim was taken from behind as he returned to his car from liquor premises. His throat was slashed from his left ear to his right in an arc. There were no signs of a struggle. Death was probably instantaneous. It is possible that an assistant from the liquor store may have disturbed the murderer.'

"Steve's on his way up," Geoff said.

When Steve came into Geoff's office we were still discussing the report.

"Why the fuck didn't I know about this," Geoff's mouth spat out the words as he threw the file across his desk towards Steve. Geoff's anger hung in the air like a barrage balloon. Steve got the message.

"Sorry, I thought you'd seen it," Steve said, obviously stunned by the ferocity of Geoff's tone. Geoff dialled Shunt's extension. No one answered. He slammed down the receiver. Without asking, Steve gave him Shunt's mobile number and Geoff dialled it on the speaker phone.

"Alec, it's Geoff."

"What can I do for you sir?" The poor soul sounded cheery. Geoff soon changed that.

"Are you on your way in?" Geoff asked, his breathing stilted.

"I should be there in about ten minutes, sir. Is there a problem?"

"Is there a problem. Of course there is a fucking problem. Do you think I am ringing you to wish you a good fucking morning? I want to talk to you about this Rogerson murder. I need you to debrief me as soon as you get in."

"Certainly sir, but everything is in the report. Do you need anymore now?"

"I wouldn't be fucking asking if I didn't need more," Geoff said, spitting anger like a river in spate. "The weapon is the same as the one used by our serial murderer, why didn't you contact me yesterday?" he shouted.

"Sir, Rogerson still had his head." It was a neat reply and to the point, unfortunately for him, Geoff wasn't in the mood for smart replies.

"How the fuck do you know that he wouldn't have lost it if the Off Licence assistant hadn't turned up?"

"The assistant didn't find him until a half hour later, sir."

"Just get yourself in here, now. Right."

Geoff didn't wait for a response if there was one. I was as stirred up as Geoff, because I knew in my bones that it could blow out Beale as a suspect in The Sawman case – and Special Branch with him.

"Steve, in future I want to hear reports like this immediately before they get to paper. Come back as soon as Shunt gets here." Steve left in quick time and I politely left for a Marlboro.

About 20 minutes later, Geoff called me back into his office. He told me that the debriefing from Alec was comprehensive. He said that Alec like Steve was a good man and had done a thorough job. Apparently, a till receipt for the smashed whisky found at the scene confirmed the time as 2.58. Alec had already contacted the customers who had paid by credit card: one had some recollection of a man in a dark coat, but no mention of a ski cap and it was average height, average weight, could have been white or black – nothing of value. There were no other reports of anyone suspicious in the area. But another customer had remembered seeing Rogerson and had said that he looked 'fine'. The guy who sold Rogerson the booze also remembered serving him. 'He looked relaxed and happy'. That witness was also the assistant who thought that he might have 'disturbed the murderer'. Alec was right, he couldn't have because he walked passed the end of the lane on his way to his car half an hour after Rogerson had left the shop. He hadn't even noticed Rogerson's body lying on the sidewalk. Alec had contacted the cab companies and got details of three fares in that area at around that time. These have all been investigated and haven't turned up anything. There was no sign in Geoff of any trace of regret for being so rough on Alec.

Geoff gave me the low-down on Rogerson. He'd been in his early 30s, born in Leeds and had a long arrest sheet. Over the last ten years he had spent a lot of time in court with defence and prosecuting attorneys, judges, juries, but no witnesses. He was suspected as being part of the same crime syndicate as Beale. Not once, since his last juvenile crime, had Rogerson been found guilty of any offence although the Crown Prosecution Service had tried lots of times. You had to hand it to the Syndicate's legal defence team – they earned their keep. More importantly, Geoff told me that his eyes were grey. Geoff wanted to take a closer look and arranged to meet Steve in the car park; I was invited to join them.

Steve drove us to the Rogerson murder scene. On the way there a taxicab pulled out in front and forced him to swerve. He immediately blasted the horn and Geoff shouted and swore at the driver.

"Take it easy," I said.

"What do you mean take it easy? That arsehole almost shunted us. The stupid bastard." Geoff's temper hadn't improved.

"What side of the bed did you get out of?" I said half jokingly.

I got a look that could kill. The rest of the drive to Headingly was in silence.

Steve pulled up a few yards from where Rogerson's murder had taken place.

"I'm sorry about back there. You are right, I am like a bear with a sore head today." It was late in coming, but at least Geoff got it out.

"Thanks for that, but you didn't need to."

Steve and Geoff looked around while I shut my eyes and got a feel for what had happened. When I opened them again I watched Steve and Geoff pace around: neither was speaking. Even though it was 10.30 in the morning the alley was in deep shadow. I certainly wouldn't have parked there if I had been Rogerson, there was no street lighting and I wouldn't have felt safe. So why had Rogerson, I asked myself? I could only conclude that he hadn't been keen to be seen in the open. If so, why wasn't he ready? I pondered.

Geoff continued to look around. I shut my eyes again. I felt nothing.

"I think he was waiting there behind that buttress," Steve said.

"That would make him about eight feet from the car," Geoff computed.

"He would have had to make about four steps to get behind Rogerson. From the reports and the photographs the bottle of Scotch was found smashed just at the curb here, so I reckon that Rogerson had the bottle in his right hand and opened the door with his left." Steve said it as though reading Geoff's thoughts. "If Rogerson had swivelled the door open he would have seen his attacker come out from the wall, so the killer would only have had a few seconds to catch Rogerson when his back was turned and before he got the door open. The murderer's timing would need to have been perfect if he was going to reach Rogerson before he was noticed. This was a professional hit," Steve said.

"I'll buy that, but what does that tell us, apart from the fact that we are dealing with a professional?" Geoff asked Steve.

"Well, it might have been a lucky break when Rogerson stopped here and parked in this dark alleyway, but the kill itself wasn't down to luck, whoever it was had done their home-work. He knew who Rogerson was and his whereabouts. He'd tailed him here and had been capable of changing his plan instantly. I'd say, it sounds like a professional within Rogerson's own organisation."

"A fair supposition, but where are the facts?" Geoff asked him.

"We need to find the murderer's car."

"Is he our Sawman?" I asked.

"N,." Geoff replied emphatically – great minds think alike, or was it fools?

Quarter to six, I was back in my flat in Glasgow. I had 15 minutes to get to the restaurant. After a shower and shave I looked almost acceptable. It was just a pity that I had left the shirts in the bar in London. I slipped on one I had worn last week. I hand smoothed the creases – Liz and I had never owned an iron. I checked in the mirror; it didn't look too bad. I was on my way.

Dinner with Pops was always more liquid than food, so as my apartment was convenient to the subway I left the Healey in the garage. I walked to Buchanan Street and took the esca-lator down to the subway. The trains come every three minutes, but as I stood there it seemed like hours. I shot my head in one direction and then another, even though my train could only come one way. I listened out for the vibrations, scanned for tell-tale headlights and checked my wrist three times. When it arrived, I almost jumped in before the doors had opened properly.

The carriage was quite full, but I got a seat near the door. As it got under way I relaxed. I thought about meeting Pops, hoping that his intense logic might help me with my case, remembering some of the many times we would sit and chat. I could see his lined face and square jaw, emphasising his trademark experience and toughness. He had been a beat policeman for 35 years and for most of that time he had worked the same neighbourhood. To local people he was their guardian and for many their mentor, big John Ahearn. My dad practised zero tolerance before it became fashionable. Young lads who stepped out of line were nipped in the bud with the back of his hand or worse if he thought that they deserved it and not once did their parents complain. They were just grateful to John for ridding them of the pushers and wasters that used to plague them and their families. To me he was Pops. I knew his other side; the patient nature and reassuring smile. He was always easy to talk to when I had problems, always very supportive and proud of me. I was looking forward to dinner with him at La Concertina.

La Concertina was unlike the usual Italian restaurants that I'd go to with Liz and her friends. The place was noisy and bustling with snippets of football news about what was happening in the West End, whereas with Liz's friends it would be confined to topics on political apathy, literary criticism or film reviews. I was sure that the cosy atmosphere and the terracotta coloured walls wouldn't have appealed to Liz or her minimalist friends, so I had never been there with her. As I turned to look out the window feeling heartened I saw my reflection and was suddenly uneasy again. I worried that I might disappoint him. I looked at my clothes and checked my shoes, quickly rubbing the toes on the backs of my trousers.

When I got off the subway at Hillhead there was the distinctive aroma of students, curries, beer, sizzling sausages and fish and chips flavouring the air: it could only be the West End of Glasgow. I hadn't felt hungry, but just then my mouth started to salivate.

Byres Road was crowded with smart couples and cleverly dressed students on their way to one of Glasgow's many welcoming venues. If you want to eat from any part of the world or drink to your heart's content then it was all there, ready and waiting. Many of the shops were still open for everything from a loaf of bread to ruby rings and body piercing. Suddenly, a board outside a newsagent distracted me. The headlines were in big letters:
'THE WHOLE OF MANCHESTER WAITS FOR VIGILANTE SAWMAN TO SLAY NUMBER FOUR'.

I was stunned that that was the big story in Glasgow. I quickened my pace turned down the side street and headed for the restaurant.

I opened the door and was greeted with the buzz of Glasgow laughter and chatter from above. I climbed the stairs and entered the passageway between the kitchens and a line of chairs occupied by people waiting for either a carryout or a table to become free – the place was thronging. I could see Pops sitting at his usual table, his dazzling white hair contrasting with the reds and greens of the walls and the plastic tablecloths. The diners were, as always, sitting cosily close together. I waved and slalomed my way past them over to his table.

"Hi Pops."

"Robbie! Good to see you lad, it's been so long. Sit down." Typical Pops, a quick barb delivered with a smile. He signalled to the headwaiter by raising his glass high in the air. I kissed Pops on the cheek, draped my jacket over a homely high-backed chair opposite him and sat down.

"Signore Robbie it's good to see you," Salvo greeted me.

"Hello Salvo," I said with a smile.

He had brought a bottle of Barolo to the table and poured a taster into Pop's glass.

"Great," Pops said.

Salvo smiled, filled our glasses and then stood awaiting my verdict. How could I stick to Pete's advice.

I wiped my mouth with the cocktail napkin and then held the glass of ruby red over the white tablecloth. I examined its colour and finally swirled the wine with an elliptical motion to create 'legs'. I lifted the glass slowly to my nose and took a deep whiff of the delicate ethereal bouquet with its distinct scent of dried roses and herbs. After I took a sip, I returned Salvo's smile with a nod of approval.

"Perfect Salvo."

"*Preggo.*" Salvo's wide mouth grinned with satisfaction.

I was about 13, when I had my first taste of wine and Salvo had taught me this routine. It had become a ritual every time since, which must have been over one hundred, he waited and watched me give my nod of approval. At 30 it was a little embarrassing and anyway I would have been just as happy with something in a carafe.

"Chin, chin," Pops said, and then clinked our glasses.

"*Salute,*" I replied, before I took a big gulp.

"I come back in a few minutes for your order," Salvo said and left us.

"This is good," Pops rolled the wine around his mouth then swallowed heavily.

"Sure is," I took a deep drink of the rich and velvety wine. "What's with the suit Pops."

"I've told your mother that I am going to a police night."

"Oh. Sorry," I said. He waved his hand to tell me to forget it. I settled down.

"You're looking tired Robbie are you sleeping okay?"

"Just work Pops." I quickly tried to widen my eyes and lifted my frown.

"Here have a look." Pops passed me the bright plastic coated menu illustrated with a concertina. He liked silence when we perused the menu, why I'll never know because we always had the same thing. The menu was typical fare for Italian pasta houses; all truly mouth-watering and plenty of choice, although not for me, I knew what was coming.

Salvo returned for our order.

"*Signoris*, are you ready to order?"

"What are you having to start?" Pops asked.

"I'll have the mozzarella and tomato," I said.

"And I'll have the prosciutto and the melon. Then, we'll have our usual Salvo."

Pops always did that. I once said that the penne was good and now he never asked me what I wanted, he would just order penne in picante sauce for us both.

"Have you heard from Liz?" Pops said, his brow deeply furrowed and his bushy eyebrows formed an arch.

"I spoke to her last week."

"Is she coming back?" He was never one to tip toe around a subject.

"No. It wasn't about that, just bills and stuff," I tried to say matter of factly.

"Oh I see," he said, not hiding the disappointment. "You need to get that sorted Robbie."

"Aye, well you know." I mumbled and then raised my voice again as I quickly changed the subject. "Thanks Pops for coming, I hope mom's alright about me seeing you alone."

"I told you, she doesn't know anything about it. She's mad at you for not coming 'round last Sunday."

"It was work. You know."

"Are you alright for this Sunday?"

"Sure, I'll be there at one."

"Make it earlier; mum's worried about you on your own."

"Okay, 12 then."

Salvo brought over our starters.

I set my wine aside and ate.

"This is good isn't it?"

"Very," I said and took another deep drink of my wine. Pops topped us both up.

"Have you seen this?" I asked waiving my folded newspaper at him.

"Is that what you wanted to talk to me about?"

"Yeah, Ulis is worried about the media. So far we've failed to discover any definite leads and he has invited Special Branch in."

"Is that so surprising?"

"No, but this is my case. I have been profiling him. I feel as though I know this guy and that they will just get in the way."

"Well get on with it." Pops gave me that look he did when I was a confused kid. He would make me focus. "Look Robbie, while you are going over all this psychological profiling your killer knocks off more people. Sometimes you have just got to act. They haven't made one arrest I hear. What's Ulis saying?"

"He's getting desperate and that isn't helping," I said pointing to the paper.

"Yeah, I've read it."

"It doesn't help."

"That's their job. Okay, so why are you worried about Special Branch?" he asked as he filled my glass and then his.

"They have a prime suspect, a professional Syndicate hitman and I just know our focus is going to be fogged by them trying to prove it is him."

"What makes you so sure it isn't him?"

"Our guy has criminal characteristics, but he is no professional. He is a psychopath. Meticulous, leaves nothing to chance. All of his killings have conformed to a predetermined order; there was nothing indiscriminate about them."

"He sounds professional to me."

"No, you don't understand his selection is very personal, he is not responding to orders and anyway where is the motive?"

"Robbie, this guy is killing arseholes that escaped prison sentences, I would have thought that his motive was obvious."

"I know who he is killing. And do you think that would be a motive for the Syndicate. Come on. They don't kill off sex offenders just because they have escaped sentencing do they? I read their surveillance reports and his records, their suspect is a smooth professional."

Salvo removed our plates and returned with our pasta. The portions were huge and steaming hot.

"*Peppe*?" I nodded and he peppered our food.

"Parmigiano?"

"Thanks."

"*Preggo*." Salvo sprinkled the cheese liberally over our dishes and then left us.

"Smells fabulous," I said.

"It tastes good too. Anyway, the people at Special Branch are no fools. Is there anything that connects the victims and the Syndicate? Were they involved in drugs or prostitution? It could be that they wanted these guys off their turf."

"That's what they said." My voice dropped for the first time I had my doubts. "Sure prostitution and drugs are involved, but those had nothing to do with it. These were sexual deviants, any use of prostitutes and drugs was personal. They were rapists, women beaters and child molesters."

"Well the Syndicate doesn't like people who mess with kids."

"Pops I've seen the pictures of the suspect, he would never saw their heads off."

"No that seems a bit gruesome for a professional."

"There are other things that don't fit with the Syndicate that aren't in here." I pointed to the paper. "He carves a message on their chest with a hunting knife."

"Yeah I heard that," Pops interrupted.

"How? No never mind. He's also taken to writing longer messages on the wall in the victim's blood." I said.

"Manson style."

"Sort of."

Pops face contorts and his expression hardens. "I see. That doesn't sound like the Syndicate. So why does Ulis think they are right"

"You mean apart from the mutual fawning of sycophants. The Special Branch's main reason is that their suspect arrived in Manchester from London at the same time as the killings."

"Was he there in May?" Pops interrupted again.

"They don't know they weren't shadowing him then." I picked up where I left off. "Their suspect is an expert with a hunting knife and he is about the same height and build as the killer. That's all they have to connect him. And we don't even know if the killer is of Italian extraction like their man."

"That seems quite a lot."

"It's purely circumstantial and proves nothing. Ulis sees the opportunity to shift the media heat to Special Branch. With a murder a day he's worried about public opinion."

"Bob Ulis don't know shit from shinola. The good folks of his parish wouldn't pee on any of the scum that this Sawman's killed if they were on fire. Joe public will have read between the lines and will be glad he has rid them of these shits, in fact they would probably pin a medal on him if they had their way and so would I." Pops strong Glasgow accent boomed out. Strangely it was getting stronger the older he got.

"What do you make of the writing on the wall?" I asked.

"Well he's a religious fanatic and Catholic I'd say."

"Yeah I had figured that."

"Hey, there aren't so many fanatical Catholics still around. So that narrows the odds."

I laughed. Meeting Pops was good for me.

"You are probably right about this. It seems unlikely that anyone from the Syndicate would waste his time with the writing on the wall and the decapitation. A shot in the head maybe, but a saw, no I don't think so. What about your own investigations?"

"I get the feeling that he is paying someone back. I can feel his pain. I think he was abused as a kid."

"Lots of kids are abused, physically, sexually and emotionally but they don't all turn out serial killers. No one's seen or heard anything? What about Forensics?"

"Nothing much so far, they have ruled out the hunting knife as the weapon used to decapitate – it's a saw, a hand saw, very sharp like an old medical tool and by all accounts he's an expert in using it."

"A doctor maybe?"

"Maybe."

"What else have they found."

"Well they identified a black synthetic fibre. They think it came from his hat or mask. It all adds up to a grain of sand. Not enough to seed a theory, never mind a solution. My profile of the killer is almost there, but there are a couple of things missing."

"Like what?"

"The motive for one."

"You said. What else is bothering you?"

"Well the gap. I can't understand why he killed in May and then nothing until September and then it's one a night."

"Maybe the first was a test."

"I thought that at first, but he doesn't strike me as the trial and error type. He is neat and plans the murders in detail."

"That sounds like a professional; keep an open mind. I would forget about Bob Ulis and if you want to keep Special Branch out you had better get on with it. There are three murders, there must be more clues. Are you sure you've checked everything?"

"I think so. If I could only work out the motive I think the rest would fall into place."

"Well I can't help you there. And how are you with all of this?"

"Och fine."

"You know what you are like with all this profiling. You get too involved. It's not healthy. You know what happened last time."

"I'm fine. It has to be done. I just need to get it over with."

"Well all this talk of headless bodies has put me off my sweet. Are you up for another drink? Salvo's commemorating a festival in his father's home town; we should at least toast the blessed San Gennaro."

"Yeah, why not Pops."

Two large grappa were ordered and delivered from the tiny bar in seconds.

"To San Gennaro."

"To San Gennaro," I said. "Who was he anyway?"

"He was the patron saint of Naples and the annual fiesta is to celebrate his martyrdom," Pops replied.

"He was beheaded for his faith near Pozzuoli, my father's old home town," Salvo added.

"What?"

"Yes. Last year I took him back home to the festival. The parade starts on the 13th and goes on to the 24th..

"A big affair then?"

"*Si.* There is another celebration in May."

"When?"

"On the first Sunday in May."

"Salvo, Pops, you're both brilliant." I slid my heavy chair back and started to put on my jacket. "I am sorry Pops, but I've got to go. I'll phone. Tell mom I'll see her on Sunday at 12." I took some notes out of my wallet and slipped them across the table to my father."

"I don't want your money. But what about the grappa?"

"You have it Pops." With that I got up and put my jacket on.

Pops waved goodbye and I was gone.

My head was swimming, hardly conscious of what was going on around me. There were so many things I had to check out. When Salvo said that San Gennaro was beheaded my mind flooded with many connected thoughts. I had to get these down quickly before the wine blurred them. I hailed a taxi and headed home.

There was no time to lose. I wanted to see those files, but first I had to get those results from old Pinder.

It was almost nine by the time the cab pulled up at the flat and I was full of mixed emotions. I had a new lead that might connect the murders to the festival. The dates were a perfect fit. My brain was sucking in possibilities like a whale sifting plankton. I had solved many cases that were more complex than that one with less to go on and I was feeling both exasperated and excited, but the gloom that had dogged me all day was lifting fast. There was still something missing in my logic, but with these new pieces I thought that I might be able to make it whole.

I pressed the light switch and my flat lit up. I went straight to the bedroom where I had left my laptop. It was still on standby, so I entered my security pin number and searched my address file – no number for Pinder. I called the morgue and got security. The guard sounded as though I'd woken him, but I gathered that Pinder had already left for home. My sleepy security man wasn't prepared to divulge his home number. I patched into the main server and finally came up with it.

I tapped the numbers into the desk phone, but all I got was his answer machine. I waited for his message to finish telling me to leave my number after the beep.

"Dr Pinder this is Robbie Ahearn, if you are listening to this please pick up." I waited a few seconds and then there was a click.

"Alan Pinder, what can I do for you Rob?"

"Doc. have you finished the post mortem on Shields yet?"

"Yes, but the report isn't written up."

"Never mind, can you recall the main points?"

"Well, let me see the time of death was between 5.30 and 6.00am."

"Are you sure?" I interrupted.

"Of course I'm certain. Shall I go on?"

"Please."

"There was a massive blow to the back of the head fracturing the temporal bone, tearing the middle meningeal artery causing haemorrhaging at angles of corpus callosum and in upper brain stem, which resulted in the victims's death. There was also a deep incision across the jugular vein and there were other bruises to the body consistent with a fall. I found evidence of the application of sulphuric acid to the eyes, abdomen and genitals. This was administered after death. Two strands of hair were identified. Neither were the victims. We are running DNA tests now and should have the results by Monday. The subject's head was decapitated by means of a surgical handsaw not unlike the one I use in the autopsy procedure. He was another of your Sawman's victims."

I waited until there was silence.

"Yeah I had guessed that Doc. The hairs, what colour are they?"

"Both were black, one coarser than the other. They were unrelated to each other or the subject."

"Can't we get DNA results quicker Doc?"

"DNA profiling is a complicated process, if I get them by Monday it will be a miracle. It will take almost that long to give the sample a computerised numeric value in the form of a 'bar code'. When we have that we can compare the DNA profile with our files and hopefully get a match."

Was this how it was to end? It would mean the rapid identification of the killer with a very high degree of certainty and absolute elimination of innocent suspects like Beale, although maybe 'innocent' was the wrong word.

"Thanks Doc. Just one thing more please. Apart from the pathologist and his assistant, who else has access to the medical instruments?"

"Well, just as in any morgue, doctors, nurses, lab attendants and auxiliaries would have access to them. If fact, most people in a morgue could get hold of them if they wanted. But if they were ours, their absence would be noticed very quickly. Many of these instruments are very old and not easy to replace. Each is stored in its own receptacle. After all, they are not the sort of thing you would take home with you are they?"

"Many thanks Doc. When are you back in your office?"

"Monday, nine o'clock."

"I'll see you there then. Bye and thanks again Doc."

I put the receiver back in its cradle. That was typical of me I always had enough going on in my head, yet I still had to take on more. DNA results were Wheaton's responsibility, mine was producing a profile. I always seemed to need to play the sleuth, but I needed to find out who had access to the saw.

I thought about making myself a coffee and then changed my mind. I threw my jacket on a chair and watched as it slid slowly to the floor. "Fuck it", I had more important things to do. I set my laptop up on the coffee table in the sitting room, ready to get down to work, but before I started I needed to take a few minutes to think, so I lit up a Marlboro and inhaled deeply. I was feeling up. Maybe, my luck was changing. I went over to the answerphone hoping that there was something from Liz. The screen showed that I had one message. I hit the play button. It was my mother wondering if I was coming on Sunday. I pressed the delete when she asked if I had heard from Liz.

I headed for the whisky. I poured myself a very large glass in last night's empty, but used glass. A quick swallow then it was back to the sofa.

I stared at the screen. It was a copy of the collage on my wall. I went straight to some of the blank sheets and started to type. When I finished I sat back and lit up another cigarette.

I added new headings: *Records of abuse; San Gennaro, Pozzuoli; surgical saw*, and the dates; *September 13th-23rd*.

I thought that solving it wouldn't prove too difficult. I put my mouse on the web icon and searched for San Gennaro and Pozzuoli. There were numerous references about pizza parlours, holidays in Italy, but at last, the festival. I noted down the main points. It was a large fiesta attracting more than a million people over 11 days in September. I typed *publicity* and *eleven* on 'post it' notes. I was sure now that the killer was Italian.

Next I looked up San Gennaro. I learned that he had been the Bishop of Benevento and was subjected to various forms of torture because of his Christian beliefs during Emperor Diocletian's persecution of the Christians. My eyes widened as I read that they had beheaded him at Pozzuoli in 304. They had tried to torture him by throwing him to lions, but the lions hadn't attacked him, instead they crouched at his feet in submission. I tried some other sites. A few sites referred to the 'miracle of San Gennaro', where his blood stored in a vial in the Cathedral of Naples, miraculously and mysteriously liquefied on September 19, 1860. I held my breath, when I read that it was said to happen twice a year, once the Church of San Gennaro at Solfatara in Pozzuoli, virtually on the spot where he was killed, on September 19th and again at the Duomo (Cathedral) of Naples on the first Sunday of May. I searched for my diary and looked up May 5th. It was the first Sunday in May.

The dates apparently had significance in that something noteworthy was to happen on those days, something which could be interpreted as a general notice of disapproval from on high. I noted *disapproval* down and underlined it. I had found one of the missing pieces – this was why he had stopped for four months. It was clearly important that he commemorated the dates in some way and his way was execution.

I eagerly looked up Pozzuoli. The city of Pozzuoli was in the province of Naples, southern Italy, on the gulf of the same name. It said that the greatest interest in Pozzuoli was the sulphur caves, which, through crevices in the earth exuded sulphured hydrogen and sulphurous acid. There were also four mineral springs, and two caverns, which exuded carbonic acid. I wrote the word *sulphur* on the 'post it' note. This explained the acid on the eyes and the groin and corroborated what I had thought, that the acid had been used to depersonalise and degrade his victims as well as eradicating memories of sexual abuse. He had been trying to exorcise some horrible childhood memories of some sick fuck feeling him up, or worse.

I stared at my matrix of information. I had all the pieces that completed my puzzle or all bar one. "I know who you are. You are a Catholic zealot, an Italian immigrant that lives or works in Manchester. You have access to chemicals and surgical tools, which you know how to use with considerable skill. You have killed three times." I looked at the date on my calendar and then corrected myself "no, probably four times already and you will kill more if I don't stop you first. I know who you are, now I need your name.

I loaded up the coffee pot and switched on the answering machine. I was close and had the feeling that things were going to turn out all right. I tried my luck with Liz. My mouth was dry and my heart pounded as I pressed Liz's number. There was no answer, just her answerphone. I left a message, poured myself a coffee, and put on some music. I had everything. My cigarettes were in front of me next to the ashtray and my trusty old Zippo; my coffee mug was charged to the brim with pitch black Arabic and the bottle of malt was standing tall and half full next to a clean glass. And to top it all Beethoven's Choral was lighting its own cathedral candle.

My laptop was propped up in front at arms length. The collage flashed its messages to me. San Gennaro headed up one note and I deleted 'Irish?' and the 'Spanish?' My man was Italian. That got rid of Beale. It had all begun to make sense. By the next day I was certain that there would be five bodies and the prospect of another eight to come before he stopped. I was sure that there would be no more after the 24th. Under *who* I typed Doc/ medic.

After I had helped myself to a whisky, I went through to the studio, to my paints and canvas. I looked at the painting; it was good. The collaboration of analysis, writing and painting had so nearly come off. The analysis had sparked a note, the note sparked an image and the brush shaped it. Sometimes it had been the other way around; a shape had sparked a thought, then a note and then more analysis. I took the palette knife and mixed large amounts of paint on the palette. The background of the portrait of Sawman's profile had been applied in flat slabs that added physical texture to the surface of a painting. The head and body had the same textured surface. The face was that of a hybrid Irishman and Spaniard, and I applied paint thinned with white spirit to remould the head. The paint was slow drying, which meant that I could rework sections, or scrape it off from a part of the painting that hadn't succeeded and start again and I did until I had the face I was looking for. Staring back at me was an Italian with a thin mouth and long nose. I had transformed the painting from a vague representation of a face to a sculpted head with weary sad eyes, a twisted mouth and a drawn look, these told their own story. They revealed psychic tension, psychological drama and a disturbance of perception.

It wasn't a sinister or macabre face even though I had given him a knitted black cap and very dark eyes. His appearance was of someone in pain, not that of a hardened, uncaring murderer. My head told me that he must have sadistically dominated the victim, but that look reminded me that it was only after their quick death that he decapitated them. Those eyes had kindness in them. I knew that there was no apparent profit from his actions other than possibly a feeling of righting a wrong. The motive was psychological, not material and this was reflected in the painting, but I also had to admit to myself that apart from the expression he looked a lot like Beale. I felt I had missed something. I took another long drink of the whisky to aid my meditative and hallucinatory faculties.

The face was coming to life; good enough to identify him I was sure. I mixed some paint for deeper tones around the eyes and cheeks. I was just about to apply the dark mauve when the telephone rang. My heart raced at the thought of Liz, but my head was anxious to see the finished work, so I let it go onto the answer machine. It was Geoff Wheaton so I picked up,

"Geoff."

"Ah, Rob I thought you were out. I'm sorry to bother you at this time of night, but I had a call from Alan Pinder. Have you anything for me? Did our visit of Rogerson's crime scene trigger something?"

"No, nothing about Rogerson, but I had dinner with my father in an Italian restaurant and the waiter said something that I think has given us the breakthrough we need. I have a lot of new information, but I haven't finished it. I'd rather feel sure before I hand it over, if that's all right."

"If you have found something I need to know. We need to get him before he gets another one."

"There have been no others since Shields then?"

"None that we've found. Beale's movements have been monitored closely; apparently he stayed in a bar until one, then went home where he remained all night. Special Branch had their people posted outside the homes of those named on our list of potential victims and there were no reported sightings of men in black ski caps."

I should at least have been pleased that The Sawman had a night off, but right then, news of another murder might have been useful. Despite my painting I was still sure that Beale was not my man and I convinced myself that no murder and Beale's night-in was just coincidence.

"Look Geoff, I need a couple of days to get my head around this, I'll fly down first thing Monday with my latest picture and a deeper profile, okay?"

"Speak to you Monday."

10. Friends, relatives and acquaintances

Saturday 21st September – Day six and Sunday 22nd – Day seven

My nightmares were getting worse just as they had done before my breakdown. I slid my hands through my hair, like an obsessed phrenologist feeling my skull and looking for the holes and bumps. It felt like my brain was trying to escape, my hypochondria looking for its release or another preoccupation. I tried to reassure myself that it was totally irrational that I was being drawn into psychosis in my search for indicators, yet that in itself confirmed my fears. I had the feeling that the sentinels that Pete had helped me install to guard my fragile stability had been overpowered by the visions of The Sawman and his acts. I decided to try and keep clear of the painting and anyone connected with him for what was left of my weekend.

I had to get my life into some kind of order. I got dressed, put on some music, made myself a fresh cup of coffee, and despite my hangover, set about tidying the apartment. My previous efforts at smartening the place up had been pathetic. In my rueful melancholy I had gone about picking up the rubbish and the remains like a claw in some amusement arcade. I focused on an individual item and picked it up before pathetically dropping the detritus as soon as I could. The room looked different, but it was still a mess. I was determined to sort myself out. I thought about what I was going to do and got on with it. I busied myself around the place methodically, clearing the rubbish, vacuuming and generally tidying up. I even managed to put away the many books that were scattered over the sofa or laying on the floor. In deference to Liz, I placed them all in their alphabetical slots on the shelves in the library. I tied up the newspapers ready for recycling. When I finished it wasn't as neat as Liz maintained it; her commitment to minimalism had always been greater than mine, but there was at least order where before there had been chaos.

About one o'clock I had a call from Al, a friend who ran his own business setting companies up on the internet. He was at The Horseshoe (where else) so my afternoon was taken care of. I wasn't a great fan of all male drinking, in truth I preferred the company of women to the detached, yet intense, chaff about football and work that dominated most collective male conversations. Still, that afternoon it was just the embrocation I needed for a swollen brain.

Al is a big lad for a Glaswegian, I was six foot and stood tall among locals; Al towered above me, which was good because he was easy to spot and on a Saturday The Horseshoe was thick with bodies all the way around the bar. I waved to him and as I squeezed close I heard him order me a 'Fustie' and a Lagavulin; that was another thing about big Al, he could always be relied upon to catch the barman's eye.

Al was with 'the Snip,' so called because it was said that after he had his vasectomy when he was 20 he never finished a sentence.

"How you doin' Robbie?" Al asked.

"Not so bad."

Al passed on my offer of a cigarette.

"Too strong for me those," he said.

"We're off tae…" said the inimitable Snip, as he took one of my proffered Marlboro.

I lit my Marlboro and took a deep draw as I tried to guess where. Al saved me the trouble. "We're off to see the Gers, but there's still time for a few bevies," he said as he passed me my drinks.

"Cheers," I said sipping the pint. "Not my scene as you know."

"Ya heathen, no interested in." Snip started, but never finished a reference to my indifference towards our national game.

"Aye, I hear you've been down tae Manchester," Al said.

"Did yea?"

"Pardon," I said to Snip.

"Fly an' that."

"Afraid so." I had to be careful his affliction was catching.

"Couldnae dae it," Snip uttered.

"That Sawman guy was it?" asked Al.

"Yeah," I answered succinctly.

"Ave ye?" Snip asked.

"Caught him?" I enquired and then answered on his nod that confirmed I had got his drift. "No."

"They say he pours acid on their balls." Al opened it up with his usual subtlety.

"Look Al I'm up to here with that case, could we leave it?"

"Sure."

"His balls an'?" Snip asked Al.

"So I read, but Robbie wants us to drop it Snip. To change the subject, any word from Liz yet?"

"No," I screwed my face up and he got the message.

"Sorry, another difficult subject."

Our party was swelled by Barry Neardon, an accountant and Ben Wiseman who had his own car dealership.

"Can I get you a drink?" I asked.

"The usual," responded Barry.

"I'll just have a half pint," said Ben. Everyone stared at him. "I've got the car."

I nodded to Al and he shouted the order to the barman as I passed him the money.

"Two pints of Fustenberg a pint and half of 80 Shilling and," a quick look at my whisky glass and on cue I knocked it back, "another Lagavulin," Al shouted.

"Any word from Liz?" Barry asked." I shook my head.

"You're better off on your own if you ask me," Bill said. The others darted him. "I only mean – just think of the money you'll save." He shuffled.

Al's long arms delivered the drinks over the heads of the first two rows at the bar and gave me my change.

"Are you going to the game?" I asked Barry.

"Of course, season ticket holder am I not? Wouldn't miss it for the world."

"Aye only cause you've already spent the money," chipped in Al.

"Money well ..." Snip quipped.

"...spent." Al finished Snip's poignant statement.

"I trust you have other plans?" Barry asked me.

"Not really. I'll probably spend it here."

"Aye spends right. Two quid a pint," Al spat out.

"Well Slainte," I toasted my friends and knocked back the malt.

"I hope you don't mind me saying, but you look a bit rough," Barry said in a loud whisper over the raucous chatter.

"I think I'm catching something." I offered my cigarettes around – no takers.

"You need to watch yourself. What are you doing tonight?"

"Nothing probably."

"Why don't you come over to ours for dinner. Shona will be pleased to see you."

"I don't think so. Thanks for the offer though."

"Well, you're welcome anytime. You know that."

"Thanks."

"We're going to Mother India for a curry tonight, aren't we?"

"I'm not sure that I am up to it Al," I said.

"Don't be daft, we'll pick you up after the match if you are still here."

"You should ease up on that stuff," Barry said, gesticulating at my 'Fustie' with his pint of 80 Shilling. I smiled and drunk it over.

"Not yet. Whose round is it Snip?" Snip was the best plumber in Glasgow, but as tight as his microbore.

The conversation moved on to our favourite topics, politics which ranged from anything anti-tory, anti-government and the Scottish Parliament, to religious segregation in schools and then their beloved football. Fortunately, the football surfaced just as they had to leave to watch their opposing football teams. My friends joined an exodus of The Horseshoe's customers; some headed for Ibrox, others went east to Parkhead and probably a few towards Maryhill, the home of Partick Thistle. I sat at one of the empty tables had a few more drinks until I nodded off. And that was the way of my afternoon; The Sawman was kept at bay and I got plastered.

She was sleeping; she was always sleeping. His mamma used to make the pasta sauce then he made it for her, now he makes it for himself. He didn't need to go to the deli every night for he already has everything he needs at home, but this was what his mamma had done for years and if it was good enough for mamma then... Anyway the things that he bought from the deli tasted better when they hung around awhile so he never used anything he bought that day in the recipe that he cooked that night.

He picks up a tomato, holds it in the palm of his hand and smells it; he always selected vine-ripened tomatoes. He is reassured by its heavy weight. He checks it for soft spots, admiring its vibrant colour in the process. He caresses its tight skin and checks its temperature, "Perfecto".When he was a kid his mother had told him never to put them in the refrigerator and he never forgot her saying that cold temperatures made the flesh pulpy and killed the flavour. He puts them in boiling water for 30 seconds then takes them out, peels their skins and chops them precisely.

It takes one long slow hour to get it right so he won't be eating till ten, like always, in front of the TV.

The memory of the blood takes his eyes to the tall bottle of deep red wine. He lifts the bottle, pauses for a moment; it feels just right. He pours himself a glass of vino, not just any old wine the very best that he can afford, barbaresco. The dark ruby red fills the bottom of the glass and he holds it up to the light, then sniffs its delicate ethereal bouquet.

The barbaresco is perfect; ripe fruit with distinct scents of dried roses and herbs. It slips over his tongue easily and washes the back of his throat.

He returns to his cooking. He puts two glugs of the best virgin oil in a pan and then a large chopped onion that he sweats with two cloves of garlic.

Slicing the onions had brought no tears; he never cried now; his tears had all run out many years ago. His father and his work had seen to that. His life had been full of blood and guts and he had learned to shut off pain.

After four more glugs of oil, he adds the pomodoro, chopped in big chunks, which he stirs into the onion and garlic. He grabs the mill and fills it with just enough black peppercorns for this one pot. He cracks the pepper, catches the scent and then adds the 'secco sale'. The basil won't be needed until the last 15 minutes, but still he rubs some between his fingers and then holds them up to his nose. He loves the smell; for him making pasta was as much about the smell as the taste. In an hour and it will be ready. It should be good for it was always perfect. Time for a little more vino. He pours another glass.

You'd think that after all these years he should be able to put it on and leave it, but he can't. In between slurps, he stirs, not fast, a slow hand; he'd be good at foreplay if he ever got the chance.

He likes this time. He listens to the regurgitated news, the same sordid stories night after night; the names and the places change, but the tales are the same. It gives him the chance to turn over the day in his mind. His day is like every other. His behaviour borders on the obsessively compulsive. It starts at six with the making of 'mama's lunch', which he leaves by her bed. Then early morning mass, which prepares him for the horrors that await him in the 'shop', allows him to work on those arms, legs and bellies, lying out, ice white, marble cold, drained of life and well and truly dead. He takes only 30 minutes break for a pastrami sandwich at lunch. He never has coffee breaks. He can't understand the attraction of 'that sludge, that evil harmful filth', he thinks, never voicing his opinion. Then it's more bodies until time to leave for the shops for the ingredients for dinner. He omits his visit to Miss Delores, even though, she is the real reason for him attending mass – to purify his lusting voyeurism.

He recalls his last assignment. The head removed neatly and branded uniquely with the words 'In God we trust'. Not tattooed, but carved with a knife. It was the same as the one last May and the one the day before. Three now. He knows that there will be a lot more before it stops. He has a great deal of work to do in September. No he won't stop until they catch him, if they do it will be God's will, he thinks to himself.

He gets up and gives it another stir. It is ready. He drains the pasta and gently lowers it on to the plate and then adds the steaming sauce. He carries it to the table by the window, which is lifted high. The cold night air and the street noise fill the room. He likes it that way; he likes the city to shroud him like a favourite sweatshirt.

He tries to enjoy the pasta, but the memories flood his mind, the pleasure from the food and wine is overwhelmed with the pictures of his stepfather waking him from sleep. Once more he revisits the dark, the pain and the guilt. He puts the plate in the sink and returns to the table with his special tin. He takes out a rolley and lights the end. The 'wet' marijuana cigarette, laced with embalming fluid, administers the hit he is looking for in the first deep draw.

The substance fuels his psychoses.

I woke up about nine on my sofa. I don't remember how I got home from The Horseshoe. On the coffee table was a packet of filter coffee and a bottle of Lagavulin with a note stuck to it. On it was scribbled:

'Found you in The Horseshoe and thought that you would want to give the curry a miss so brought you home. Here's a hair of the dog, but the coffee will be better. 4-0: we cuffed them.' The mystery was solved. I picked up the bag of Italian coffee and smiled.

I ignored my gift and lit up a Marlboro. After a long choking cough I wobbled to the shower. I managed to get all my clothes off and survived the initial cold spray. I stayed there a very long time, until the forgotten cigarette fell sodden to the tray and then cruised to the drain where it lay trapped.

Surprisingly, when I eventually got out I felt okay – no headache. There was something in Glasgow's water that kept hangovers at bay. I reckoned that they had brought me back about six, so I must have had four hours sleep plus the kip in the pub. No nightmares. I dried off and made myself some strong black coffee. Thereafter, I watched television until about three in the morning – mostly second rate American films and that was the last thing I remember until I woke up at ten. So much sleep I was almost perky as I got ready for my visit.

The drive only took about ten minutes. Even before I opened the door I could sniff that smell. The Ahearn scent, a mixture of wax furniture polish and bleach. My mother liked to clean. I used to call it my place. It was the flat where I grew up until I went to university. Nothing much had changed since my earliest memories of it. It must have been painted many times since then, yet the colour of the walls had remained exactly the same. I still had my key, but no washing with me – that was in a past life.

As soon as I opened the door my mother was there to greet me.

"Oh look dad, it's Rob." It was though I had just come back from the Gulf. "And look at these beautiful flowers, white lilies. Are they for me?"

"No, they're for Pops." She laughed and carried them away.

"How are yea boy?"

"Good Pops."

At three, we sat around the same dining table where every meal in the house had been eaten. I didn't have to see the menu; it was Sunday: vegetable soup, followed by home made stew, mash, peas and carrots, and then apple pie and custard, not gourmet food, just tasty. From the first piece of bread until the last cup of coffee, my mother relayed all the family gossip about my prosperous brother-in-law, my pregnant again sister Charlotte, and her two kids, Jennifer and Josh. This included the latest batch of Charlotte's photographs of the kids to the accompanying eulogising about her granddaughter's piano playing, horse riding and latest school successes. There was no mention of Jennifer's real loves: boy bands and Robbie Williams. I also got a couple of lectures on how badly I had treated Liz and a warning that I was getting too thin, everything was as it always was.

About six, when Charlotte called mother on cue, I escaped to my old room. My window looked out over Great Western Road and I leaned out. A bottle of Guinness in my hand, it was like old times when the hours unfolded in time frames, each heralded by different noises. I didn't need a watch then, from six till eight our neighbour's televisions from below would pace the evening. Then there would be the clicking castanets of high heels on the pavement and men's deep laughter growling through their smoke-ridden lungs. Later, there would be restaurant din and faint music from the bars and clubs. After midnight the noise would get louder and change ominously: ambulances would howl followed by sirens squealing above the shouts, the football chants and the screams. Sometimes there would be the fights and once a murder right on the street below, in front of our flat, a policeman's home. As it turned out, looking down on a dead body was to become a regular part of my daily life.

Pops never mentioned La Concertina, Salvo or The Sawman. That was our secret, his and mine. I left about seven to a list of dos and don'ts from my mother ringing in my ears.

When I got back to the flat I relaxed for a while put on some music and even tried to read, but that wasn't possible so at about ten o'clock I started to review my file for Geoff, that was when the telephone rang:

"Hello."

"Robbie darling, it's Sarah Bosanne."

"Sorry."

"You know, Sarah from Omega." I was none the wiser. "I am a friend of Liz's. We met at the Contemporary Art Show."

"I'm sorry Liz isn't here."

"It was you I wanted to speak to. Did Liz mention that she showed me your work a few months ago?"

"Oh yes, I recall something about it."

"Well I took the photographs of your paintings and I showed them to a few people and we wondered if you would like to exhibit your work."

"What?"

"My associates would fund the show and make all the arrangements. All we would need are about 20 pieces of your work and if I'm right you have at least that many in the apartment."

"Look, I don't know, I'm not an artist."

"Darling your work is psychoanalytic and there is a great interest in that kind of work. Have you heard of Lexicon?"

"No, and I'm not sure that I want to."

"Your paintings are powerful and intimate, an encounter with an impossibility, a mixture of reality and the psychic that brings together the spiritual and the physical."

"I suppose I should thank you, but I'm not sure what you are saying. These are paintings of murderers, people that I tracked and chased. Who would want to see them?"

"You would be surprised darling. I believe that if you were prepared to sell them they would attract significant interest."

"I could do with a few quid, but no I don't think I'm interested."

"Robbie darling, I believe that your paintings would sell for thousands of pounds."

"I doubt whether I have enough of them to make a thousand pounds in total."

"Oh silly, each painting should make much more than that."

"You're crazy."

"Darling eccentric maybe, but crazy no. I have been in this business for ten years I know what sells, believe me."

"I'll have to think about it."

"What's to consider? Why don't we meet to discuss it?"

"Look, I'm busy with a case. Can I get back to you?"

"Of course darling, but don't leave it too long. My associates would like to have the show next month. You can catch me at my Gallery, the Omega. Just ask for me darling."

"Okay and thanks for the call it was Sarah wasn't it."

"Sarah Bosanne. Can I have your mobile number?"

I gave it to her. "I'll be in touch Sarah thanks, bye."

"Bye."

I remembered her as soon as I put the phone down. She was a tall leggy blonde in her early 30s, quite good looking, but in an over made up way, not really my type.

11. Undone by DNA

Monday 22and September – Day eight

I had another long sleep, well about six hours worth, so when I awoke at five I decided to drive to Manchester. The Healey was in great form and I was in Chester House by eight.

The place looked strangely empty except for Geoff who was already in his office.

"You're early, thanks for coming in sharp. Have a good weekend?" he said. I never…" His phone rang. He nodded and answered it. I gathered it was Alan Pinder with good news.

"That's great Doc." Geoff signalled the thumbs up.

His face was beaming when he put the phone down. "We have him!"

"Who?" I said rather naively.

"Beale – The Sawman, who else?"

As I got ready to deflate his spirits and refute the evidence with my painting and theories he beat me to it.

"That was Doc Pinder, he has a DNA match with Beale."

"It can't be, what about Rogerson? You said yourself that it couldn't be Beale. And Beale never lived in Manchester; our man is of Italian descent and what about the medical skill?"

"Look Rob there is nothing I can say about that, if Pinder has connected Beale to these crimes through DNA then that's it. Anyway, your profile wasn't so different from his and the last picture that you gave us could have been Beale couldn't it?"

"Yes, he looks like him, but I am certain he isn't Beale."

"Let me see your latest painting."

As I handed over my updated profile and supporting picture I knew what was coming. The print of my painting that I had in my file was an even better likeness of Beale. I hadn't any substance to undermine his arrest I was going to look like an idiot. I handed over the print.

"Shit. This is Beale." Geoff said.

"They're wrong." It was a pathetic statement, but it was all that I could muster.

"Rob, DNA matches are rarely wrong."

I explained my theory about San Gennaro, Pozzuoli and the medic, but Geoff wouldn't listen, Doc Pinder had matched the DNA and that was enough. He was right, of course, it placed Beale squarely at the murder scene and yet, I remained unconvinced. As far as I was concerned Ulis was wrong about Beale and Doc Pinder must have made a mistake. I couldn't accept that the test had been carried out properly because a match of DNA was one in over 9,000,000,000 – about twice the earth's population and if it was right I was fucked.

I had to see for myself. I was sitting on the back porch waiting for Doc Pinder, not that I expected to see him there, but it was the only place where you were allowed to smoke. It was only 12.30 and I could have allowed myself to be happy that I had worked it out and that Special Branch had fingered Beale. If they were right, we had our serial killer or at least we would soon, but I knew they weren't right. Yet I was in a no win situation; if I supported Beale's arrest for murder in the first degree, my professional pride and reputation would be in ashes and the killings would stop and for the moment I didn't want that. If I was right, the killings would continue.

I had to come up with some evidence that proved that it couldn't have been Beale, which meant proving the DNA evidence was wrong. I took a final draw then stamped out the butt. I went inside and along the bare plastered corridors to Pinder's office. He still hadn't arrived. I sat on the wooden bench facing his door and waited.

While I waited I reminded myself that Pete had said to keep a positive perspective, so I decided that I'd discuss my medic theory with Doc Pinder when he arrived.

"Afternoon Rob, what brings you here?" Doc Pinder said benignly.

"Afternoon Doc. I'm here about your DNA report."

He unlocked the door and I followed him inside.

"I sent the DNA report to Geoff Wheaton."

"I know, I've seen it. I'm troubled by your findings."

"What specifically bothers you?"

"Is there a chance that a mistake has been made, the wrong fibre was tested or something like that?"

"I hope you are not questioning the integrity of our analysis." There was an accusing look in his eyes.

"No, but mistakes can be made."

"Well it's possible, but it has never happened before. I'll get the report up. Now let's see." He switched on his PC and after a long minute it opened at the menu.

"Don't you use a protective password to get in?"

"No. I never remembered the darn thing so I don't bother now." He looked tired. His thin eyelashes dropped slowly every few seconds, like dead leaves falling to the undergrowth.

"Can't you access our criminal files from this server?"

"I don't know. I never look at anything other than my own files and the e-mails," he sighed.

"Isn't that's a bit risky Doc, anyone could use your system to access confidential information without you knowing about it."

"Who would want to?" He was just a few years from retirement and I suspected that they couldn't come quick enough for him. "Ah, here is the report from Don."

"Was the sample taken from Shields or his flat?"

"Just a minute. There were two samples, one from the flat and another from the body. He says that they extracted DNA from both. The one from the flat has not yet been matched against police records. The other was a perfect match for no. 2784099, a Luis Beale," he said matter of factly. "I am sorry if it is not what you wanted to hear, but I can assure you the analysis was correct."

"I accept that, but is there any way, that the sample analysed could have been taken from another investigation and become misfiled?"

"No, that could only happen if the evidence purportedly gathered at the crime scene hadn't been. You are not suggesting that one of our forensic people were involved in planting evidence?"

"No."

"Well, that only leaves our police colleagues open to suspicion. I don't think so, do you?"

"No." I watched his eye lashes flutter like a camera shutter on slow.

"Thanks Doc I just had to be sure." I turned and left.

I was almost at my office before I remembered that I wanted to ask him about the medical saw, that was the problem with dealing with guys who had all the time in the world, you lost yours while they waited theirs out. I remembered that I should try and eat something so I went off for a sandwich and a coffee.

When I was waiting for my sandwich at the deli I saw my reflection in the chrome splashback. I looked like a tramp.

I was mindful of Pete's and my mother's advice so when I got to the office I ate half the tuna sandwich straightaway. The supporting coffee and cigarette were great accompaniments and the polystyrene beaker was a bonus. I was fed up with those thin leaking plastic efforts that the office machine served up. I ate the rest of my sandwich as I worked through a pile of paperwork, some of which didn't concern The Sawman, even so, he was never far away from my thoughts.

The cuffs of my shirt were a constant reminder of how grubby I looked and after a couple of hours of trying to ignore them, I put my jacket on. It was no good, I had to buy some more and I had to get my watch fixed. I found out from one of the guys in the outer office where the nearest jeweller was, grabbed an A-Z and took the Healey out of the car park.

Harry's Place was in a downmarket row of shops sandwiched between a barber and a chemist. The shop had a heavy wire security blind across the window that diffused a rather pathetic display of cheap rings and watches. I had second thoughts about leaving my watch there. I had been told that Harry, the owner, was a great fixer. His rates were reasonable and the police and their friends were given a discount. I was told that I was to mention GMP. Apparently, he had been caught fencing some stolen goods and had since felt duty bound to make amends. I stepped inside.

It was a gloomy place, the lighting was pathetic and smoke hung around like fog in a horror film. It wasn't an antique shop yet everything looked old. There was a film of dust over even the brightest of metals that dulled their sparkle. I was reminded of Dickens' *Old Curiosity Shop*. There was no rusty armour or little Nell, but there were old relics from churches and strange looking clocks all at different times. I took a deep breath and waited at the grill which protected the counter.

There was no sign of Harry, but I could hear someone in the back office rattling glasses. I waited and eventually there was the shuffling of feet, then a crumpled face, that I assumed belonged to Harry, appeared at the service hatch. I showed him the watch and with some embarrassment mentioned that colleagues in Chester House had recommended him to me. There was a definite reaction and a promise that it would be ready within a couple of days so I left it with him.

Next, I bought some shirts from a menswear shop. Nothing expensive, but any one of them was bound to make a huge improvement on how I looked, I then headed back to the office.

I swapped my shirt and had just started on more paper-work when I checked my messages. There was one from Steve. I called him as I laced my coffee with some more of George.

He told me that he had worked out the list of possible Sawman victims as promised. His theory was based on geography, the seriousness of their misdemeanours, but primarily the colour of their eyes. He wondered whether there was any point in me looking through it as Beale was to be arrested within a few hours. I tried to convince him that it might not be Beale. It was a waste of time.

I was about to sink further into my depression when Jim Sloan popped into my office. And he soon cheered me up. Jim may have been big, but he was agile, graceful even and together with his ear for accents and his witty mind he had the ability to mimic anyone. That day he chose to do Bob Ulis at a press conference, so I suppose I was bound to find it funny. When he asked me to join him for a drink I found myself saying yes.

Jim had suggested a place a few blocks away from the office, but I didn't fancy a police watering hole so I persuaded him to stop off at a run-of-the-mill Irish bar that I had heard about near my hotel, well I had to find an alternative to The Coach House.

I had never liked bars favoured by policemen: they were all pool tables, darts. You invariably found yourself jostling for space with sports fans peering at TV screens (guys yelling at whatever team is losing) waving their glasses filled with brews I'd never heard of. Unfortunately, when we got there, the pub I had chosen was just like those. Jim said that he had been there a couple of times before and that they made the best Bloody Marys that he'd ever had – freshly mixed, no horse-radish and nicely spiced with lots of Worcester.

"What's it to be?"

The Bloody Mary flashed across my mind and right out again.

"Guinness would be good."

"Right then, Guinness it is," he said in a thick Irish Brogue. "And how about a little chaser?" I shook my head.

Jim grabbed a handful of peanuts from a bowl on the counter.

"You obviously haven't heard about the analysis of nuts lying open in a bar Jim."

"Life's too short. Anyway, I think all food should be eaten with your fingers. Except soup, of course."

I laughed.

"That's the problem for scientist types like you, you always want to know what's in it, not what it tastes like. Well, I can tell you that these taste great, spunk an' all."

"I'll take your word for it."

"You're a strange one. I've been here 20 years nearly and I've never known anyone like you. How did you get into this? Surely it wasn't because your old man was a cop."

"No, it wasn't much to do with him, it was more my whole family."

"How'd you mean?"

"Well, I suppose it was my extended family with all its aunts, uncles and cousins that started it off when I was a kid. At first I was overwhelmed by them but once I understood them I was fascinated by their behaviour. I suppose it was the eclectic mix of humour, eccentricity and banality that did it. Later in my middle teens that interest in human behaviour turned into an obsession. That was when I read about Charles Manson and his charismatic power. I was hooked."

"He was a crazy bastard."

"Well he was a bit more than that. He had a sort of Machiavellian guile and I just had to find out more about it. So, when the time came I chose criminal psychology at college."

"And how did that bring you here?"

"You brought me here remember." We laughed some more.

"At college I was really fascinated by psychopaths and I discovered that when I studied their crimes I could visualise them taking place."

"Gees that sounds weird."

"It was, freaky even. When I qualified as a profiler I decided to use my 'freaky' skill to explore my obsessive interest in them.

Forensics was an obvious career to consider and when I looked into it I was directed to the Home Office and the rest is history."

"Why didn't you just go into psychiatry?"

"Well I sort of did in a way. I practised as a clinical psychologist when I first left uni, but murder investigations were a great opportunity to study psychopaths close up so I joined the Home Office."

"Christ, with your brains you could have done anything you wanted. Me, I always wanted to be a barman in a lap dancing club." I didn't find it particularly funny but I laughed anyway.

"So why didn't you?" I asked.

"Their owners thought my face would scare the punters. No, I suppose in a way I was like you. I don't mean I was interested in behaviour, I was kind of fascinated by people or their faces at least. Well just look at this." He pointed to his face. "All the Sloans have this weird shaped face. You know as ugly as we are, we all kind of look interesting, even fascinating in photographs. So I took lots of photographs. The police was just a safe way of making money and having a job for life. Well weddings are not so popular today are they?"

"Not as popular as divorce anyway," I said.

"Don't I know it."

"I thought you were happily married."

"Yeah, three times."

"What happened to the first two."

"They just walked out and never came back."

"That must have been tough."

"You know like a kick in the teeth, it leaves a few bits missing but you get over it. I didn't blame them." I gave him a blank look. "Well it's not easy being married to a cop is it?"

"No."

"A lot of people just see the label. You're married to a cop, a plod, a dick, a flatfoot – I'm used to being called the fuzz or worse, but my first, Katie, found it difficult to ignore. She also resented its impact on our social life. Being a cop affects old friendships. All of a sudden friends have something to hide, become careful about what they say. That hits the wives hard."

I could relate to all that even though I wasn't a policeman.

"And with no kids, forming new friends was also more difficult, unless they were in the job themselves," Jim added.

I thought about Liz for a brief second. She hadn't wanted to make friends with the police people I came across in my job even though her father had been a judge, but then again I wasn't keen on making police friends either. I saw and heard enough police work during the day not to want more when I was off work and the cops I knew always talked about work when you were in their company.

"Helen, my wife is different; she knows what it's all about. She was in the force when I joined her. Myrtle my second wife always hated my hours, the late nights, Saturdays, Sundays, and most without paid overtime. So it didn't work out. She's married now to some accountant guy. They've three kids and she is as happy as Larry."

"Never mind, you are happy now."

"You are dead right."

The next hour was spent listening to Jim's repertoire of jokes and impersonations. I don't mind admitting some of them were funny and that I enjoyed his company; he never discussed anything that demanded brain cells nor talked about work; I suppose he learned his lessons in that regard. However with me work was never far away and a chance remark he made gave my mind a tweak. He had been talking about when he was a kid and used to deliver newspapers at six o'clock in the morning and the time suddenly clicked with Shields' murder. I wondered whether we had made enquiries about newspaper deliveries. Something told me it was important. I excused myself, headed for the toilets but stopped on the way to call Geoff, but he had switched off his cell phone. I convinced myself that if he had checked it out, it would be in the reports. I needed to get into my PC. I had to get back to the hotel. When I came back from the loo, I bought Jim a drink and headed back there.

When I got back to the Royal, I quickly read through the various reports on the interviews with Shields' neighbours in the next block. A quick scan confirmed that they had little of interest to add and there was no mention of the newspaper delivery. I knew it was a long shot, but somehow I felt it would be important to speak to the delivery person. I found the name of the neighbour that found Shields. He was called John Ferrel. I looked up his number and called him.

"Hello?"

"Mr John Ferrel."

"That's me."

"Mr Ferrel this is Rob Ahearn of the Home Office. I am working with Detective Superintendent Wheaton. I'd like to ask you a few more questions relating to the murder of your neighbour, Mr Shields."

"I told you lot everything I know."

"Yes thanks that was helpful, but all I wanted to know was what time your newspapers are delivered in the morning."

"I don't get a paper you can't be sure that kid will deliver them. Frank in the flat below said he didn't come again today. He needs a good kick up the arse if you ask me."

"What time are they normally delivered?"

"Well they are always there before I go to work about seven, think he probably comes around five or six."

"Do you know the kid's name by any chance?"

"No I don't think I do, but he works for old man Woodery."

"Woodery?"

"He's got the newsagents on the corner of Whitticomb Street."

"Many thanks Mr Ferrel. You've been a great help."

"Well, if you are speaking to Woodery you tell him from me that he should give that boy of his a kick up the arse."

I looked up Geoff's home number in my PC. I rang him.

"461."

"Geoff?"

"Who's that?"

"It's Rob Ahearn. Sorry to bother you, but I was out with Jim Sloan and to cut a long story short, he gave me an idea."

"Jim Sloan; that must be a first."

"He was talking about delivering papers when he was a boy and I suddenly thought that maybe some newspaper boy or girl might have seen our man."

"Who? Beale?"

"No, Sawman."

"What? I don't follow."

"Sawman left Shields' place around 5.30 and 6.00, that's when the papers are delivered."

"How do you know?"

"I talked to one the neighbours who was interviewed."

"When?"

"Tonight, a Mr Ferrel."

"That's not your job."

"No, but I couldn't get hold of you and…"

"I have been home all evening."

"I didn't have your home number and tried your mobile. Anyway, he told me that he thinks the delivery is between five and six. The newsagent is a Mr Woodery. The shop is in Whitticomb Street."

"Okay, so what, we have Beale and the DNA, why bother with this now?"

"Because Geoff, I told you I don't think that Beale is The Sawman and anyway, I hear that Beale has a solid alibi."

"Of course he has an alibi, but we've got his DNA. Which of those would you believe?"

"Humour me. You had some doubts in the office."

"No, Rob not doubts. I just agreed that parts of your profile didn't fit Beale that's all. I never said you were right."

"But what if I am?"

"What about the DNA?"

"Okay, I can't explain the DNA, but I have got a feeling about this. I think the kid saw him."

"What the newspaper delivery boy?"

"Yes."

"Rob I am at home with my feet up, do you know how rare that is?"

"Sure I do, I'm here and my home is in Glasgow remember."

"I'll tell you what I'll do. I'll call the office and see if we have his home number and I'll call him."

"Will you get back to me?"

"I'll call you as soon as I have spoken to him. I'll call your mobile."

"Okay."

He hung up and I waited on my bed. I scrolled through the reports again. It was an age before my mobile rang.

"I've spoken to him. He told me that the boy who delivers the papers was off today. Apparently, he had some kind of an accident and the last he heard was that he had been taken to the hospital. I've got the boy's name and address. I thought it was better to go and see them rather than call. Are you up for it?"

"Now?" I was taken aback that he was prepared to go that far.

"Sure. The Royal Hotel is on the way. I'll meet you outside reception in about 15 minutes."

12. Charlie sticks his nose in page two

We parked at the end of a row of neat terrace houses in the only space available on the street. My long shot just got longer. This was the sort of place where if the boy had seen anything he would have told his parents and they would have told us. We got out the car and walked back along the street because the number we were looking for was somewhere in the middle. As we neared the house a football rolled in front of me. It belonged to a couple of kids probably about Charlie's age and I wondered if he was one of them. I resisted the temptation to ask and instead resolved to let Geoff do the policeman thing of speaking to the parents first. I kicked the ball towards them but sliced it badly; it banged off a new looking Mondeo and shot off down the street with the kids running after it sort of groaning; as I previously said, I wasn't really into football. Geoff unsnecked the gate and I followed him up the narrow path lined with small white pebbles between two neat lawns with rose bushes set into little squares dug out of their centre. Not really my taste, but I was no gardener. I peered into the room overlooking the garden and could see that the television was on so they were at home. From what I could see through the curtains the place was small, but cosy.

As Geoff rang the doorbell I put out the cigarette that I had lit when I got out of the car

"Mrs Willis?" he asked apologetically.

"Yes. What do you want?" I took in the hallway, which was clean but pokey.

"I am sorry to bother you so late. I am Detective Chief Superintendent Wheaton and this is my colleague Dr Ahearn from the Home Office." He flashed his identification.

"What's this about?"

"I wonder if we can come in for a minute?"

"Of course, come on in." she replied. Her face flushed with suspicion and fear.

I could hear voices, muted, but loud enough so that I was able to make them out and the one that was speaking loudest was the boy I guessed.

"Dad, why doesn't he blast it."

"Power isn't any good without accuracy. He needs to place the ball. They are shooting too far out, they'll never score like that. They've got the skill to beat that defence, but they need to keep control and pass it around." My eyes followed my ears. Mrs Willis noted my distraction.

"Sorry. They are watching a football video. Is this about Charlie?"

"Yes it is, but there is nothing to be alarmed about mam, I am investigating a murder on Broome Street and I think he might be able to…"

She interrupted. "It's such a dreadful business we go to the Most Holy Crucifix next door to where it happened. It was that Sawman wasn't it? But what would Charlie know about it?"

"I understand that your boy delivers papers around there and I was wondering if he saw anything unusual, that's all."

"I don't think so, but come through to the lounge."

We followed her.

"I thought that you were calling about his injuries," she said as she walked on ahead.

"I heard he had an accident. Is he okay?" Geoff said to the back of her head.

"Oh, he's better now, but it was a worry," she replied.

"Sure dad, but these guys are professionals they should be able to blast curved shots past the keeper."

"They should, but you've seen how many shots they've wasted."

Frank was passing his son a napkin when we came into the room and our entrance behind Mrs Willis stopped their conversation dead

"Frank, this is eh, I am sorry officer I didn't catch your name."

"Evening Mr Willis I am Chief Superintendent Geoff Wheaton and this is Rob Ahearn from the Home Office." I proffered my hand and shook Mr Willis'.

Charlie had a huge burger in one hand and was wiping tomato sauce from the corners of his mouth with the other. The boy was a typical skinny kid with a round podgy face that hadn't yet suffered a single attack of acne, but his lips were swollen.

"You must be Charlie," I said holding out my hand while scanning the bruises and contusions that covered his arms and lower legs. And there was a strange black and blue band across his forehead.

"Please to meet you sir," he said revealing a brace over crooked front teeth.

He was a polite boy, just as I expected in that neighbour-hood.

"He has been in the wars. Came off his bike yesterday and hit a street lamp, cracked three ribs, banged his mouth and was concussed. We only got him home from the hospital this afternoon."

"You feeling okay?" I asked rather stupidly.

"It still hurts when I cough or breathe hard."

"Charlie has a bruised liver as well as his cracked ribs, so he will feel sore for awhile. He has some painkillers, but basically he has to rest as much as he can...about six weeks before he's back to normal. Anyway, what's this about Chief Super was it?" Mr Willis asked.

"Geoff."

"I'm Frank."

"We are investigating a serious crime that happened in Broome Street."

"The Sawman." It was Mrs Willis again.

"Take the weight off your feet won't you. Why don't you sit down." Frank said and pointed to a padded and heavily patterned sofa facing the boy.

"Thanks Frank," Geoff said and we sat down.

"How can we help?"

"Your son delivers papers around there and I wondered if he might have seen anything."

"Charlie didn't see anything or he would have told us."

"You're probably right but do you mind if I ask him a few questions for the record?"

"What do think Charlie, are you up to it?"

"Sure Dad."

"That lot looks painful Charlie?"

"A little."

"How did it happen?" I asked before Geoff had the chance to ask him about The Sawman. He wasn't pleased with my interruption.

"I was on my paper round, on my bike, when I came off."

"I suppose those papers are heavy," I said.

"Yeah."

"Yes Charlie," his mother said with a rather embarrassed look.

"I mean yes sir, they are. I deliver over 150 packed with advertising flyers."

"He's fit, can run or ride his bike for miles and never gets out of breath," his father said.

I could see that he was fit; the smooth supply of red blood from his pulmonary artery to his cheeks was a testament to his dancing heart. Though his respiratory cycle didn't sound so good just then it wasn't difficult to imagine that before the accident it was performing like a French horn.

"What age are you Charlie?" I asked.

"I am 11, nearly."

"Isn't that young to be working?" Geoff said.

Mrs Willis jumped to her son's defence.

"Lots of children deliver papers."

"Charlie saw the advertisement in Woodery's shop. He had to start at 5.30, so I thought that it would be good for him and checked it out," Charlie's father explained. "It was a chance to make some extra pocket money and apart from getting up early he could do it easily." Geoff was nodding patiently and allowed Frank to continue unimpeded. "He is a bit young, but Woodery was happy to get someone, anyone to take over the deliveries from him because no one wanted the job apart from Charlie."

"Don't get me wrong, I think it is a good idea for kids to have a job. I had one myself delivering papers; teaches you to get up in the morning," Geoff backtracked.

"That's for sure," Charlie agreed philosophically.

It was easy to see that his pre-puberty development would pack him with energy, but he didn't look to have the body weight and muscle needed to cope with the burden of the papers.

"How do you manage to carry all those papers?" I asked.

"Dad's bogie carries them real easy," Charlie answered.

"I built a bogie that trails behind Charlie's bike," Frank said with pride.

"With the bogie it's easy peasy. I could do it with my eyes shut," Charlie said cockily.

"So how did your accident happen?" I asked.

"I'm a United fan," Charlie said. His face was bright, alert and animated. This was definitely a favourite subject.

"So am I," Geoff volunteered. This was news to me then again we never had spoken of anything outside of our gruesome work.

"You should see his bedroom, it's covered in pennants and pictures of the team," his mum said.

"We're struggling a bit," Geoff said with a look of deep sincerity.

"They're great, the best in the Premiere," Charlie said proudly.

"We seem to have forgotten how to score. The match last week was a horrible result."

"We should've beaten them," Charlie defended. Geoff was nodding completely oblivious to why we were here.

"Charlie's dream is to see every match in a season, home and away," his dad chipped in. I still couldn't see the connection between United and his injuries.

"One of the best things about delivering the papers is that Mr Woodery lets me read every morning paper's sport section for free, so during my round I see everything there is about United."

"That's how he had his accident," Frank said. I still hadn't got the connection.

"I was reading about the match." I still didn't follow. "I was replaying it. We had lots of chances but we didn't take them. That's when I came off my bike." Frank read the confusion in my face and came to the rescue.

"A passer-by saw him come off. Charlie was pretending to be 'Nisty' replaying every shot from the newspaper reports. He said Charlie was leaping up and down."

"I was heading it."

"And he is pedalling, hands-free, just balance and momentum, ramping along with the newspaper spread out over the handlebars," Frank said. I got the connection at last.

"That's easy. I always read the sports pages when I am pedalling. I hit a stone or something, clipped my front wheel and it threw me. A little wobble doesn't bother me, I usually grab the handlebars and it's okay. I was too slow because of the paper."

"The man said he saw him grab for the handlebars and a second later he saw him fly up into the air," Frank said.

"I don't remember much about it, but I think I hit a lamp post."

"Thank God he was wearing his helmet," Mrs Willis said with a face that revealed what might have been.

I had one of my moments and saw it all. The front wheel turned sharp right acting like a brake while the bike and bogie wanted to carry on. Charlie's flight was brief; a lamp post terminated his airborne body's departure from his saddle. His chest was first to strike the immovable upright and even though his flesh and bones were malleable and tried hard to absorb the impact, the force of his propelled body drove his body on. His ribs bent, then cracked from the thwack. The helmet cushioned the thump as he reached the end of his flight to the pavement. The crash was enough to knock him out cold, hence the bruised ring around his forehead. I could see his soft young body lying spread-eagled, battered, grazed and bruised on the pavement.

"Ben Phail, that's the chap who picked him up and took him to the emergency hospital, said that the newspapers were scattered all around him in fact a part the front page covered his face."

Yes I saw it – the page fluttering down and landing on Charlie's blank expression; it was page two that rested there I was certain and page one pointed skywards with the headline: '**SAWMAN KILLS AGAIN**'. My opening I hoped.

"Well, it is good to see that you are on the mend," I said.

"Yeah he will be fine soon," Frank affirmed.

"You normally deliver papers to apartments on Broome Street, don't you," I asked. Geoff was back with me.

"Yes."

"The day before your accident did you see anything unusual when you did your delivery to Broome Street?" Geoff asked.

"Like what?"

214

"Oh I don't know. Did you see anyone you didn't usually see?"

"No. No sir." He glanced at his mum.

"Are you sure? Think now, this could be important." Geoff was wearing his policeman face, all stern and demanding.

"No." His little brow furrowed and I saw his eyes slip northward. "Well, there was a man who nearly bumped into me when I was going into one of the flats." He turned to his dad. "Where Mr Tister gets his three papers." He returned to Geoff. "I've never seen him before."

"He was coming out?"

"Yes, in a hurry."

"What time was this?"

"I don't know, Broome Street is at the start of my round."

"So it was probably around 5.30," I prompted.

"Yeah maybe."

"What did he look like?" Geoff asked.

"Not sure. He was wearing black and he had weird hands. Yeah, I remember, he had black hands."

"He was dark skinned?" Geoff struggled to find the politically correct phrase.

"No."

"Was he wearing gloves?"

"Sort of. Like mom's washing up gloves, but black and see through."

"Did you see his face?"

"Yes."

"What did he look like Charlie?" his mom said. Geoff shot her one of his grisly looks that said please let me ask the questions and she mouthed back "Sorry".

"Eh, I don't know, sort of ordinary."

"What colour hair did he have?"

"He was wearing a ski-cap. I think."

"Was his hair dark or fair?" Geoff was in full interview mode, his questions were coming straight and fast.

"Dark, yes black, the same as his hat."

"What about his eyes, what colour were they?"

"I don't know."

"What height was he?"

"Smaller than dad."

"You are what six, six two, Frank?"

"Just over six."

"What about his weight Charlie?"

"I'm not sure; he was wearing a coat, but he wasn't gross."

"Thin?"

"Not very. I suppose he was thinner than dad, but I can't remember."

"You are doin' great Charlie. What colour was his coat?" Geoff asked, at last remembering that he was speaking to a young boy.

"Black. That's all that I can remember." The kid looked a bit spooked.

"Charlie that's fantastic. Thanks a lot," I said enthusiastically.

"I'm going to have a chat with your parents okay?" Geoff said to him while looking at his parents.

Charlie nodded.

"Let's go through to the kitchen," Charlie's mum directed.

We went into the hall and then to the kitchen, another tiny room.

"Do you think he saw him?" Frank asked me.

"The Sawman. Oh God. I said he shouldn't be doing a paper round," Mrs Willis squawked.

"I am not sure who he saw, but the description fits," I said.

"I'd like to bring some photographs around for him to have a look at and maybe one of our identikit specialists. Would that be okay?" Geoff asked Frank.

"When?"

"Well there's no time to lose, can I do it now?"

"It's late, he should be in bed soon," Mrs Willis said.

"There's no school, it won't hurt to keep him up a while will it?" Frank said hesitantly. Geoff took it as a yes.

"If you are sure then, I'd like to make a phone call."

Geoff called Chester Street and arranged for a support team to come over straightaway.

I was worried that Charlie might be overwhelmed when the guys came over so I decided to have a chat with him.

"Hey Charlie how's about showing me your room and your posters of the team."

"Sure, this way."

I followed Charlie and Frank through to his bedroom.

One look impressed upon you that he was a real fan. His walls and ceiling were covered with pennants and pictures of every player on United's books.

"This is amazing, where did you collect these?"

"From magazines and at the games."

"When he was nine he used to come with me to every home game. We had season tickets," Frank said.

"Yeah, we had seats in the West stand," Charlie said proudly.

"Last year I lost my job and my new one doesn't pay as well so I couldn't renew them. Now we only go to every other home match. That's why Charlie wanted the newspaper delivery job and the extra money."

"I would like to save up so that some day I can go to every home and away game, well every home game at least." Charlie's face looked serious and determined and I was sure that he would. "He's my favourite." He pointed to a glossy picture.

"Yeah, he looks fit."

"He's terrific," he shouted and then winced.

"Is it sore son?" Frank asked. Charlie nodded. His dad gave him a look that told him that he thought that he was brave.

"I remember I cracked three of my ribs playing football," I said.

"Yeah?"

"They strapped me up so that I could hardly move."

"They don't do that now," Charlie said confidently.

"Yeah, he gets some kind of magnetic field therapy," Frank chipped in.

"Ultrasound treatment it's called dad," Charlie corrected him.

"Gees that sounds like something out of Star Wars." I said.

"The doctor told me that the ribs protect vital organs in your body like the heart and lungs." Charlie was a smart boy and I had a good feeling about his evidence.

We talked about football for a while; Charlie told me that he was the star of his team in the scouts. He was a nice kid. They were a nice family. Charlie was a lucky boy, particularly if he had met The Sawman – a few broken ribs could have been the least of the family's worries.

Steve Cale arrived with Al Cobert, the photofit artist, and about ten minutes later the kid had guided Al's photo collage into a good likeness of Luis Beale.

"That's him."

It was so much for my profile and hats off to the Special Branch. I felt sick.

"But he looks different."

"In what way Charlie?" I asked.

"I don't know, sort of older."

Al made a few minor adjustments and showed Charlie the finished identikit.

"Yeah, that's more like him. I think." Charlie said.

It still looked like Beale.

"Okay, you've been a great help son." Geoff nodded to Steve who left the room to phone the office. "When you are better you and your parents can be my guest in our box and maybe I can fix it so you meet up with the players. How does that sound?"

"Great, did you hear that dad?"

"Sure son, but now it's time for bed. Say goodnight."

"Goodnight sir," he said to Geoff. "Mr Ahearn." He shook our hands.

"Goodnight Charlie," I said.

13. The profile finds a lead

Tuesday 23rd September – Day nine

The office phone rang: it was Dawn Burns. "Rob I'm in the refectory with Steve. You better come here right away."

I wasn't into cryptic clues and that one was too short for me too make anything of it. I walked down the two flights and through the doors into the canteen. Dawn, Steve and Dan were in the corner drinking coffee. I crossed straight to them and sat down between Steve and Dawn facing a uniformed sergeant.

"Rob, this is Dan Coomber."

"Hello." I shook hands with the heavy built sergeant who was probably around 40; he looked like he had been a policeman since he had left school.

"What's all this about then?" I asked.

"Dan tell him what you told me," Steve said.

"Well Dawn was telling me about the profile you drew up for The Sawman and she was saying that there were a few things that didn't match the suspect Beale. The way she described the profile made me think of a pervert I arrested yesterday. When I told Dawn about him she showed me a copy of your painting and it was this guy's double."

"What do you mean? Luis Beale."

"No, your painting looked like my man Cerboni, Alfredo Cerboni."

"Okay."

"We arrested Cerboni yesterday morning after a peeping tom complaint. He was a strange one. A decent enough guy, lived with his mother and a churchgoer, but it turned out that every morning for years this guy had been staring in her window, watching her get dressed."

"You say he looked like the painting," I said.

"A ringer."

"And you hadn't seen pictures of Beale before?"

"No I have been on leave. Majorca, I just got back yesterday.

"Where is Cerboni now?"

Steve spoke up. "We had to let him go with a warning after the complainant changed her mind and said she didn't want to file a charge."

"And you're sure he looked like the painting?" I asked Dan.

"I thought it was Cerboni."

"I thought that the painting hadn't been circulated?" I asked.

"Steve gave me a copy and I showed it to Dan," Dawn said looking apologetic.

"Okay," I said to Dawn and turned to look at Dan. "What about this?" I took the photo of Beale out of my wallet and passed it over to Dan.

"They look very alike. Beale looks flashier in the photo, but the nose chin eyes are similar," Dan said after he studied the picture.

"Where does he live, this Cerboni?"

"Grand Street. He is an attendant at the morgue."

"At the morgue. Have you seen him?" I asked Dawn and Steve.

"Never without his mask. He is the little guy who helps in the autopsies," Steve replied.

"Helps? He's the one who does them," Dawn said.

"I suppose Geoff knows about this?" I asked.

"Not yet. I just missed him. His mobile was off, probably boarding his plane to London. He's meeting people at Special Branch. I've left a message for him to call me."

"What about Ulis?"

"He's with him," Steve grunted.

"So what are you going to do?" I asked.

"I'm trying to get a photograph of him from his morgue ID."

"I'll try Jim Wilby," I said.

"Okay I'll get the car organised. I'll meet you out front in five," Steve left us sitting there.

I grabbed my mobile and dialled the morgue.

"Can I speak to Jim Wilby? Tell him it's Rob Ahearn and it's urgent."

"Have you got any more on this guy?" I asked Dan while I was waiting.

"Have I. He gave us his life story."

Dan started to give me a few more details, but the guy at the morgue came back on the line. I put my hand up to quieten Dan.

"I'm sorry Dr Wilby is off duty."

"Is Alan Pinder around?"

"Yes I'll try him for you."

"Dr Pinder."

"Doc it's Rob Ahearn, I need your help."

"Rob I'm busy."

"It's important."

222

"It's always important. Oh how can I help?" he sighed.

"You have an attendant working there called …" I looked at Dan.

"Alfredo Cerboni," Dan said.

"Alfredo Cerboni," I repeated.

"Yes. He assists with post mortems."

"What can you tell me about him?"

"There's not much to tell. As his name suggests he is Italian, but brought up here. He's dark haired, good at his job. What else do you want to know?"

"Everything."

"He's worked here for as long as I can remember. He doesn't say much. He's really not a socialiser, a bit of a loner, who keeps himself to himself. I don't know much about his personal life, still lives with his bedridden mother I think and is devoted to the church. I know that because he raised over a thousand pounds for the church earlier this year, money for needy kids, but really, Jim would be able to tell you more I'm sure. Why the interest?"

"He fits the profile of our killer."

"Rob you must be mistaken. Alfredo wouldn't say boo to a goose."

"You may be right. Is he on duty today?"

"Just a minute and I'll find out." I waited.

"Rob he should be, but he telephoned in sick yesterday."

"Doc if he comes in or calls let me know, but don't mention this to anyone."

"Certainly."

I ended the call. Dawn was still there and I looked at her and said,

"He's our man. I know it." I turned back to Dan. "You were saying…"

Dan told me that Cerboni had worked in an undertakers before he got the job at the morgue; the rest just repeated what I already knew and a little more detail about the peeping tom incident.

I was excited again. A morgue attendant, so he had the skills and access to the equipment, no wonder there weren't any clues on the body. There was still the boy's identikit of Beale, but he could easily have mistaken him for Cerboni. Of course there was the DNA. That was still a problem.

Dan had lobbed a Jumping Jack into the case that made my mind spin like a Catherine Wheel. I wasn't sure whether I was feeling happy because at last I had a lead to prove my profile or because I had been right all along – Beale wasn't our man.

I went to the office to pick up a few things and have a quick glug of neat George then headed downstairs. Dawn was waiting for me at the door of a Volvo. She was telling Steve about my call.

"He called in sick yesterday. Doc Pinder told Rob."

"It was probably because we nabbed him for the peeping tom thing. Get in, I've got his home address."

Dawn got in the front and sat in the back. I pressed the button and the window slid down.

"Jeez Rob, it's a bit cold for that."

"You don't want secondary cancer do you?" I lit up my Marlboro.

"What do you make of this?" Dawn shouted over the burbling engine as he handed me a photograph of Cerboni.

"Well they look like each other. He and Beale could be twins. Cerboni is our man. It fits: he has access to the tools, he has the know how and he's a bit strange ."

"What about Beale?" Dawn asked.

"I said before, if he was our man I'd give Baillie my year's pay checks. Tell me what you know about this Cerboni."

"Well, he has dark hair going grey at the sides, five foot nine and has lived in Grand Street all his life; in that row of three storey tenements between Baxter and Mulberry. Maria and Tomaso Cerboni, devout Catholics, adopted him; his step-father, Tomaso died of a heart attack when Alfredo was ten and his stepmother Maria brought him up on her own. She's a bedridden invalid. By all accounts Alfredo is devoted to her and spends all of his time attending to her when he is not at work or working for the church's charity for kids," Dawn said without reference to any notes.

"Or not spying on naked women," Steve added.

"He has worked at the morgue for 20 years and before that was an undertaker's apprentice. I've seen him lots of times but not without his mask. He is the solitary kind, keeps himself to himself."

"Yeah Alan Pinder said he was a loner," I proffered my single contribution to her background report on Cerboni even though I probably knew more about him than most. "God, if it was him he was right under our noses."

It wasn't far to Grand Street, but time seemed to stand still and it gave me a little time for reflection. It was a good day and getting better by the minute. I started to enjoy the drive, even if it wasn't in the Healey. The light through the windscreen was the colour of those Italian Masters, gold, yellow with a hint of pink. Even though it had turned colder over the previous couple of days and the dryness of the air suggested that snow was just around the corner. I thought about those autumn drives up to the cottage with Liz in the Healey with the hood down but it didn't go far. Steve piped up.

"Debs and I had once thought about renting there, Grand Street, but we couldn't afford it at the time," he said.

"I hear that they are real nice," Dawn commented.

"Built in the early 1900s for wealthy merchants: big rooms with fancy cornicing and plasterwork."

To state the obvious the journey was important, crucial even; an opportunity for me to restore my reputation, pride and self-esteem, which I had to admit, had, with a little under-mining by Special Branch, been on the slide. If it was Cerboni, my reputation would be restored and I would be able to spare the time for Liz and rekindle what we had. And, of course, we would lock up a serial killer. It's funny, but that last outcome didn't hold much appeal. The more I found out about those depraved bastards that he had killed, the more I wanted him to carry on, succeed. And maybe even help him, yet there I was probably going to stop him and enable some scumbag to inflict more pain and spread his poison among other bastards.

We pulled up outside the apartment on Grand Street.

I had to remember that it was still just an enquiry. We only had adventitious suspicion that linked Cerboni with the murders, not even circumstantial evidence, at that time.

We walked up the stairs to the third floor and stood outside the solid wooden door. Steve gave it a hard knock and waited. Nothing happened. I tried again harder and louder – still nothing. Why wasn't he there? I asked myself. The answer was obvious, why should he be? Steve banged the door hard. The neighbour across the hall came out to see what all the banging was about.

"Are you looking for Alfredo?" He asked

"Yes."

"He's at work and won't get home for another couple of hours."

"Oh thanks." I stood there not certain what I should do. I already knew he wasn't working.

"What are you doing here?" The voice came from behind. When I looked round I saw that it was a cold, serious and forbidding face framed by a nun's habit.

"Is there a problem with Mrs Cerboni?" she asked. She was up close and fiddling with door keys.

"No, we are looking for Mr Cerboni," Steve said clearing his throat and putting on his most authoritative voice.

"Alfredo? He is never home at this time," she rasped back.

"Yeah that's what I said," the neighbour volunteered.

"Is Mrs Cerboni at home?" Steve asked – a stupid question since she was bedridden, but we wanted to get a look inside.

"Of course Mrs Cerboni is an invalid, who are you?" she said as she put the key in the lock.

"I am Detective Inspector Cale, this is Detective Constable Burns and Dr Ahearn from the Home Office." I watched the neighbour's face brighten up, but there wasn't any change to the nun's.

"I trust Alfredo hasn't been in any kind of trouble."

"We just think he might be able to help us," Dawn said.

"Is it possible to see Mrs Cerboni?"

"That's out of the question she is too ill to see anyone unannounced." I stared back at her grave looking face. "Do you wish me to give him a message?"

"Oh no sister we'll call back later. Can I help you with that?" I pointed to the key.

"No thank you. It is very stiff, but I will have the better of it." I was sure she would. "Alfredo said he would sort it weeks ago, but still, I am sure he has had more important things to do."

She opened the door. I was tempted to follow her in, but I knew that I better not unless I got invited. And that wasn't going to happen.

"Thank you Inspector, good day to you."

We looked at each other and the neighbour, who turned around and went back inside. We headed for the stairs. My mind was buzzing. I had to get a search warrant.

"Help! Inspector! Help!"

I turned and ran the few steps back with Steve and Dawn at my side. The door was still closed, but a few seconds later it swung open and the nun appeared, clearly in distress.

"Oh help, please." I followed her into the apartment with Steve and Dawn. Before we had time to say anything the Sister blurted out: "It's Mrs Cerboni. She's dead." She pointed to an open door and I crossed the hall and looked inside. I wasn't sure what I expected to find, Mrs Cerboni with throat cut or headless maybe, but all there was was an old woman. She looked to be asleep, but a closer look confirmed that she was dead. Mrs Cerboni I presumed. At first glance, it looked like natural causes. A closer look suggested that the old lady had passed away some time ago – probably sometime the previous day.

"Dawn call an ambulance and her doctor. And you'd better check with the morgue just in case Cerboni has turned up. Oh, and contact the coroner's office and see if they can send someone over here," Steve commanded.

"I am sorry she is dead," I said.

"Oh the poor woman."

"Can I get you something, a cup of coffee?" I asked.

"Oh no, I am sorry."

"Please sit down. Let me get you a drink of water." I stepped into the kitchen and the pungent smell of basil filled my senses. When I returned to the sitting room the nun was lost in a fat armchair. The place had a kind of dated look; it could have been back in the 50s, good solid furniture but utilitarian; heavy and too dark for today's tastes. I passed her the glass of water. She sipped it like a gnat.

"Sister – I... sorry, I don't know your name."

"My name is Sister Scolastica from the Sisters of Florence. I apologise for making such a row, Maria's death took me by surprise." She looked pale, but dutiful as she sat there. The pious sneer had vanished, replaced with respectful solemnity; her trembling hands cradled her glass of water as though she was praying.

"Oh it wasn't expected then?" Steve asked.

"Well yes and no; she has been ill for a very long time, many years in fact, but she looked her usual self when I was here yesterday."

"You were here yesterday?" I asked.

"Yes. I come in every day normally about eight and stay until about three. Usually on Tuesdays I come about now and stay until Alfredo comes home at about five."

Steve had an unofficial look round as I chatted to Sister Scolastica whose shoulders were visibly shaking.

"Are you sure I can't get you a coffee?"

"No thank you."

"Have you known the family long?"

"Forty years. Maria and Tomaso adopted Alfredo when he was a baby. Maria was a wonderful woman and loved him as if he was her own child. And it was hard for her."

"Oh. Not money surely, this is an expensive property."

"It's rented. No, Tomaso died of a heart attack on Alfredo's tenth birthday and she had to go out to work to support her son."

"What had happened to Alfredo's real parents?"

"It is a tragic story. They had emigrated from Italy in 1962 while his mother was pregnant with him. And tragically Alfredo's father caught an infection just after they arrived here and died shortly after. She was left pennyless and couldn't work because of the pregnancy. She was placed in our charity hospital where she gave birth to Alfredo. I am afraid the trauma proved too much for her frail body and she died leaving poor Alfredo an orphan."

"He was adopted then?" I asked.

"Yes. With the help of the Fathers he was found a good Catholic family. So I have known Alfredo since he was six days old. I carried him as the sweetest innocent baby in my arms up these very stairs where I presented him to Maria and Tomaso."

"What were they like?"

"They were devout Catholic people, but unfortunately childless. They too had emigrated from Italy, 15 years before, so they understood the problems."

"And was it a happy home?"

"In certain respects, but there were some problems too. Mr Cerboni was a physical man and liked to drink too much."

"Did he ever beat Alfredo?" Her posture straightened and stiffened. She was a nun, but I waited for the lie.

"We are talking about over 30 years ago. Parents smacked their children then."

"Sister I don't mean smacking. Was there anything more serious than that?"

"Maria was a wonderful woman, may God rest her soul." The arrival of a priest and the paramedics ended our conversation.

"Poor Alfredo will be in need of comfort. I am sorry there is much to be done, I have to assist Father Mckenny."

Steve took them through to the bedroom and left them there to look after Mrs Cerboni whatever that meant. I pulled Dawn aside.

"What about her doctor?"

"I couldn't reach him."

"Have you called the coroner?" Steve asked Dawn.

"Yes, Jane Warren should be here any minute."

Sister Scolastica hadn't told me the whole story, but the situation demanded that I didn't press her for more.

I waited for Jane and the local police to arrive and then I left.

I was back in my office at three o'clock, swinging in my chair, rolling George around my mouth, waiting for the pieces to fall into place. Another corpse, but I felt elated again. Cerboni fitted my profile perfectly. When at last Geoff called in, I shared my good news. Steve had already told him what had happened, but I still felt like there were two moons in the sky.

The phone rang. Great, I thought, they'd found him. My stomach clamped tight.

"Ahearn," I answered.

"Rob, it's Jane."

"Jane. All through with Mrs Cerboni?" Maybe it was thinking about Liz, but Jane's soft voice puffed up my groin.

"Rob, I've just finished the post mortem?"

"And?"

"Well she didn't die of natural causes although she had plenty of reason to. She was suffocated."

"What?"

"Suffocated. It looks as though someone used her pillow to steal what little breath she could muster."

"Jees. Can you get the report straight to me Jane?"

"On its way."

"I'm not totally surprised. There was enough history to suspect natural causes, but she looked a bit odd. Jane, thanks a lot for calling me. I owe you."

"You could pay me back with lunch tomorrow."

"Would love to, but can't make tomorrow."

"Okay, maybe another time."

"Sure, I promise."

"Bye."

"Bye."

I was crazy, she was probably being sociable, but my stirring loins had rejected that thought.

I pressed Steve's extension.

"D. I. Cale."

"Steve, it's me."

"Rob, what can I do for you?"

"I've just had Jane Warren on the blower. She tells me that old Mrs Cerboni was murdered. Suffocated by her pillow."

"I heard."

"Have you found Cerboni yet?"

"Not yet. Don't worry I'll let you know when we have him."

"Thanks."

My heart was racing. I was sure that Cerboni was our man. I gripped the edge of my desk, swung back and just managed to save myself from clattering to the floor. "Fuck these chairs," I swore under my breath. I looked up and scanned the office and was reassured that no one saw me. It struck me like a bolt. It was obvious; if Beale's DNA matched he had to be Cerboni's twin. It was the only explanation. I'd never dealt with a case with identical twins, but I knew that their DNA was the same. I dialled Doc Pinder.

"Pinder," a gruff voice said.

"Doc, it's Rob."

"Yes." I heard him sigh.

"Sorry Doc it won't take more than a minute of your time honest."

"What is it?"

"The reason I'm calling is that I wanted to ask you about the match with Beale's DNA."

"Rob, I'm sorry to disappoint you, there was no mistake, the match was perfect."

"Okay, but that wasn't what I wanted to know."

"Oh."

"Have you run any tests on Alfredo Cerboni's DNA?"

"I don't think so. Why, should we have?"

"There was a warrant to search his house this morning. Your forensic boys were there and I just thought that they might have uncovered a sample."

"Well they might have, but even if they have it won't have been done yet. We're busy you know."

"Sure Doc I know. Can you do me a favour and make some enquiries?"

"Okay Rob I'll look into it."

"You see I have this theory."

"Do I want to hear this?" he sighed.

"What if Beale was a twin."

"What do you mean?"

"His twin's DNA would be the same wouldn't it?"

"Only if his twin was identical, then both siblings would share the same DNA."

"I think that Cerboni and Beale are identical twins."

"That's an imaginative leap, are you sure that you aren't fitting the evidence to the case?"

"No Doc. Cerboni was an orphan. I don't know about Beale, but I bet he was too."

"Rob what do identical twins share."

"I know, the same parents and the same birthday."

"And was Beale born on the same day?"

"I don't know, but I'm sure as hell going to find out. If he was, would the identical twins be the answer?"

"Well it's more likely than my department making a mistake."

"Thanks Doc. Look I'm sorry to have bothered you, but you can see why it was important."

"Yes. I'll call you tomorrow with the results of Cerboni's DNA."

I called Geoff about my twin theory and five minutes later he called me back saying that Pinder had given the analysis priority.

At ten to five the telephone rang.

"Rob it's Alan Pinder."

"What can I do for you?"

"It seems that we have already carried out an analysis of Alfredo Cerboni's DNA." I waited glued to the receiver and all that I heard was paper shuffling back and forth. "Rob can I phone you back? I've mislaid the report." Surprise, surprise I thought. Before I replied the phone went dead and just then I had one of my moments. Doc was emptying a huge bag of mail; he was picking up each letter and then steaming it open with an old kettle. Inside the kettle was a salmon poached pink. Doc stripped then squirmed into a rubber suit. He put on a scuba mask and reached into the kettle; deep inside his whole arm disappeared and then as he fished out his arm, his fingers turned into hooks, fish dangling on the end. He bit one of the fish and the hook stuck in his throat. As he pulled it out, his tongue, gullet, stomach, the small and large intestine, and then his anus spilled out onto the desk. The extractions writhed about over the letters like the tendrils of a slimy octopus, wriggling and sliding over the neat papers until the gooey secretions shrivelled and melted the print as though each was an eraser made of acid. After a few seconds all that was left were ruptured cell membranes oozing Cytoplasm and short strands of DNA. The phone interrupted my mind pictures.

"Rob?"

"Doc."

"I've found it. You could have something; they are the same."

"Cerboni and Beale identical?"

"Yes."

"Great!" I shouted.

"Oh there was one thing, the other sample we took from Shields we now have a match with Record number M84523, a Mr Leon Millar."

"E-mail the report Doc, now please."

"I will. I've e-mailed the report on Millar to you."

I reached for the computer and opened up records M84523. Up it came – Leon Miller. Of course that snake Melnar, Leon fucking Melnar. I picked up the phone.

"Drug Squad."

"John, it's Rob Ahearn."

"Hi Rob, how's things?"

"Just great John. I was wondering where you were with Leon Melnar."

"I am sorry Rob I thought we got word to you that we've booked Melnar for distributing pornographic videos."

"Yeah I heard that. His DNA has just turned up at another murder scene."

"Not one of your Sawman jobs?"

"Yeah, the victim was called Shields, murdered a couple of days ago. Are you still holding?"

"Afraid not, he's on bail awaiting a date for trial."

"You got an up to date address for him?"

"Sure, just a minute Rob."

I drummed my fingers as I waited.

"Found it, Welland Heights. It's on the e-mail to you now. Is this something I need to be involved in Rob?"

"Not sure yet, I'll keep you posted."

"Oh, there is one thing you might want to know. He's on file as Leon Millar, M84523. Got five for pimping some time back. "

"Yes I heard." I hung up and headed for the coffee room.

I filled up my mug with lukewarm and tasteless decaffeinated and went back to my office via Steve's desk. He was on the phone. I indicated with a nod that I wanted him to come to my office when he was free.

"Dr Ahearn can you keep your office door closed. We don't want to breathe in your disgusting smoke." It was Angela, a civil servant, cigarette buster and ballbreaker. I ignored her and walked on.

"She's right you know Rob. Your office has a permanent haze of smog."

"Lay off Steve."

"You'll have heard that Forensics have sampled Cerboni's DNA and that it matched Beale's. Your theory about them being identical twins looks to be correct. We're still trying to get a copy of his ID, apparently Cerboni started before the pictures were computerised and there's nothing on file. Geoff has asked me to check with the registrar for details of the births."

"Have you found Cerboni yet?"

"Not yet."

"Look, I had Doc Pinder on with the results of the DNA analysis of one of the hairs we found at Shields'. You'll not believe what he found."

"One of them is Melnar's."

"How did you know?"

"Forensics passed the report half an hour ago and then Tony at Vice called me after John spoke to you. The local guys are looking out for him. As soon as they find him they will bring him in for questioning."

"Good. What time is it?"

"It's ten past five."

The rest was frustrating. I just hung around waiting, getting nowhere fast at least it looked as though my theory about San Gennaro and a medic was back in play. At seven o'clock I gave up and drove to my hotel. Reception told me that they had a message for me. It was from Sarah Bosanne. She was in Manchester and wanted to meet me for a drink. I called her number.

"Rob darling, you got my message. I'm in the Piccadilly Hotel. I'm just about to go down to the cocktail bar; can you join me later?"

"Sure, I'm not far from there, give me 15 minutes."

"No rush darling I'm meeting some gallery people half an hour should see me rid of them."

"Okay, half an hour it is."

I was like a little kid all excited. The last time she called got me thinking. She was right I had over 20 canvasses. Most of them were unfinished, but not far off. I wondered whether she could do something with them. I headed for the bathroom. Half an hour later I was in the Piccadilly Hotel.

The cocktail lounge was on the top floor. It was an elegant place with a clubby atmosphere. The panelled bar was busy with city types and businesswomen. I spied Sarah at one of the checkerboard tables in the corner. She was on her own.

"Sarah."

"Rob darling, lovely to see you."

"I didn't expect you to be alone."

"My business here is over, I have been waiting for you. I'm glad you could make it."

"Can I freshen your drink."

"A Metropolitan please." I must have looked confused because she added. "Martini with 'Absolut Kourant', cranberry and lime juice."

"Won't be a minute." I wasn't sure what I had got myself into, but I was there, so I got on with it.

I went over to the bar and ordered a Metropolitan and a Lagavulin. The barman nodded and said he would take them to the table, but I waited.

I gave her the Martini and made myself comfortable in one of the plush red chairs.

"Chin, Chin." She said and we chinked glasses.

"I was flattered by your offer of an exhibition, but I'm still not sure that it's something I want to do."

"But you must darling. Your work will fire their imagination."

"I don't know about that. I was never trained, apart from school."

"I have seen your work it is gripping. It will sell-out."

"That's another thing, I wouldn't know what to ask."

"Darling you don't worry yourself about that. You have no need to get involved. I can look after that for you."

"How does it work?"

"You simply hand over the paintings and I will do the rest."

"That sounds easy."

"It is darling, all you have to do is turn up at the preview."

"Oh."

"Don't worry, you won't have to do much, just mingle and smile. In fact it is probably best that you don't smile, just look tough."

"What do you need?"

"About 15 pictures."

"I have those."

"What about this serial killer, The Sawman."

"What do you mean."

"How many of those do you have?"

"Four. They are all at different stages."

"That's good. They will be the major attraction."

"We can't use those, we haven't caught him yet."

"No darling, but you will. If you do it before the show then even better."

I had never been with anyone like her. She didn't look real. Everything about her face seemed designed. Her contemporary clothes, which were obviously very expensive, had been made to look old.

"Have you eaten darling?"

"No."

"We can eat here if you like."

"No, I'm fine I am not hungry and anyway I don't want to be late." I didn't know what to make of her. It was awkward. It was the way she looked at me. It felt like she was hitting on me.

"You've finished your drink Rob. Would you like another?"

"Yeah." She flashed her eyes at a waiter and he came over immediately. "The same again please."

"That will be a Metropolitan and a?"

"Lagavulin thanks."

We chatted about art and the market in London and I have to admit I warmed to her. I hadn't planned to go back to her room, but that's where I found myself. We were both the worse for alcohol and a coffee seemed a good idea. I hadn't expected the suite overlooking the park. It was all a million miles from where I operated. We never had the coffee. Instead, she put on some music, showed me her cuttings of the various shows she had arranged and we shared some champagne. She was amusing and interesting, effusive and colourful, kind of sexy. Even so, I never thought that anything would happen between us and when it did, it took me by surprise. One minute she was laughing and drinking the next she pushed open a door and pulled me inside her bedroom. I haven't any excuses it wasn't even lust for her, long thin delicate bodies don't turn me on, I just accepted her invitation. Even so, I couldn't go through with it. I apologised and put my shirt back on. Sarah never said a word. As I picked up my tie I noticed a bag of white powder. The cocaine explained some of her mystery, but not all of it. I let myself out, caught a cab back to my apartment and crashed out.

14. The worst news of all

Wednesday, 24th September – Day ten

I got into the office at ten nursing a sore head from the previous night. I don't know what I had been thinking about mixing whisky and champagne. I never did that. I had come close to a one-night stand and it disgusted me.

Hungover or not, I needed to find Cerboni. I had to speak to him. Manchester was a big place, yet I was sure he couldn't hide out for long. I checked my phone for messages, one was from Sister Scolastica from the previous night saying that she had something to tell me about the Cerbonis and the other was from Steve timed at eight that morning. Steve's message said that Melnar still hadn't been found.

I tried Sister Scolastica number, but it was engaged. I started to write up my report. Two cigarettes later, I tried her again.

"Oh Dr Ahearn thank you for calling. I am afraid I was a little circumspect when I told you that the Cerbonis had problems."

"What do you mean?"

"I would prefer not to discuss it on the telephone can we meet?"

"Sure. Let's see it's almost 11.30 now, can I come around one?"

"Of course, that would be good."

"Okay. It was the Sisters of Florence wasn't it."

"Yes."

"I'll see you there then?"

"Goodbye."

"Bye."

I was intrigued, but I had to get this report off before it went cold. I poured some of George into my coffee as a hair of the dog and got down to it. There was a lot to write up and the time seemed to fly by. It was well after one when I had finished so I called her again and told her I would get there about two.

At ten to two I arrived at the Sisters of Florence. I rung the doorbell and was answered by Sister Scolastica. She showed me into a small room off the hall.

"I'm sorry about earlier, I just didn't notice the time." Liz had heard me play that record a hundred times.

"It was good of you to let me know that you would be late. I expect you are a very busy man."

I followed her through to a sitting room with old-fashioned sofas and chairs.

"Please sit down Dr Ahearn, can I offer you some tea?"

"No thanks Sister. I am keen to get on."

"Have you heard from Alfredo?"

"No, I was hoping that he had contacted you."

"No, I am afraid not."

"You said you had been a little circumspect." I was tired and my patience was running thin.

"As I said on the telephone I didn't tell you all that I should have yesterday."

"Oh?"

"When I said the Cerbonis had problems I realise now that I should have told you what I know of them."

"That would have been helpful Sister."

"I mentioned that Mr Cerboni was a physical man and liked alcohol too much."

"Yes."

"It was more serious than that."

"Go on."

"Tomaso was an alcoholic and used to beat Maria and Alfredo."

"How serious?"

"Mostly bruising, but once he broke Alfredo's arm."

"Were social services involved?"

"No, I don't think so."

"The police?"

"No, Maria wouldn't allow me to contact them. She said it was the alcohol."

"Probably, but it's no excuse."

"No. Maria was very difficult. She was very opinionated and there was a lot of friction between her and Tomaso, but when they argued he always held the upper hand and she always came off worse. Alfredo would try and defend her, but Tomaso was a big man and he never stood a chance." She stopped and composed herself. There were no tears, but she was hurting. "There is more." I suspected as much. "One day, when I visited Maria, Alfredo looked very distressed. I tried to talk to him, but he wouldn't tell me much. From what I could gather I suspected that he had been abused, sexually. I approached Maria about it, but I am afraid she denied that anything was going on and for the next couple of years I wasn't made welcome. It was Tomaso's death that allowed us back into the home. Things were better then, but probably because of the problems with Tomaso, Maria had become terribly over protective towards Alfredo. She smothered him, he wasn't allowed any friends or to go out on his own except to attend chapel or run errands. If ever he had the slightest sniffle she took him for medical attention. When he was about 17 Maria became ill and Alfredo spent most of his time attending to her. We tried to help, but he insisted that he looked after her. He was a bright intelligent boy who could have gone to college, but he wouldn't hear of leaving Maria. He must have been in his late 20s when she became bedridden and it got even more difficult for him. When eventually he allowed me to help, Maria confided that Tomaso had been sexually abusing Alfredo, although she swore she didn't know anything about it until after Tomaso's death."

"Why didn't you go to the police with your suspicions?"

"Mr Ahearn we are talking about a long time ago, people sorted out their own problems."

"He was a child. He needed protection. How could you leave him there?"

"I have thought about that often and prayed for forgiveness."

"What about Alfredo?"

"I prayed for him too."

I rose to my feet, all this goodness was getting to me. I said: "It is not enough sister, children have to be protected. You should have gone to the police with your fears, but thank you for the information. We need to track him down."

"Track him down?"

"I am afraid Mrs Cerboni was murdered."

"No, that is not possible."

"I am afraid it is."

"You can't possibly suspect Alfredo. He loved his mother and he is such a gentle and compassionate man."

"Still rivers run deep Sister. I have to go now." I got up to leave and Sister Scolastica rose with me instinctively, but I could see that her mind was somewhere else, the burden of the shock horror of it all weighing heavily on her.

"Oh there is one thing more Sister what was the name of Alfredo's real parents."

"I am afraid I don't know and we wouldn't have recorded it. You see I just collected the baby from the hospital and took him to the Cerbonis."

"Okay thanks. Oh, you wouldn't happen to have a photograph of him?"

"Sorry, no."

I found it difficult to stay there any longer. I was mad at Sister Scolastica, mad at Tomaso Cerboni, mad at Maria Cerboni, mad at Special Branch and mad at myself. About the only person I wasn't mad at was Alfredo. I knew then for certain that Alfredo was The Sawman. Alfredo had stuck by his mother despite his father's abuse and his mother's denial and smothering; a difficult combination for anyone and for a young boy, debilitating. An orphan and abused child who had seen little compassion in his life, one could see why he would find it difficult to feel sympathy for others and to build successful relationships. He needed compassion and help, and I was offering neither. I thought about his life and the contrast with my own. Liz was positive proof that I was selfish and at best inconsiderate more likely I lacked compassion. I mulled it over and wanted to prove to her that I had changed. I went back to my hotel.

When I got back, the receptionist gave me a bouquet of white lilies that had been left for me with a card that said simply thank you. It was from Sarah.

"It's his bloody mobile phone," I could hear my Pops say. "He must be there." I heard my mother chime in the background.

"Pops?"

"Oh Robbie thank God. Where are you?" his voice was quavering on the mobile.

"I'm in Manchester what is it, what's wrong?"

"It's wee Jenny."

"Jennifer?"

"She's been attacked."

"Where? Who by?"

"She was coming back from some friend's place and some bastard assaulted her."

"Is she alright?"

"She's in hospital, in shock; they think he raped her."

"Oh God no."

"Bill has just called. He's at the hospital with Charlotte. She was unconscious when they found her but she has come around. Mum and I are going down there now."

"Oh Jeez dad. How are you getting there?"

"We are on our way to the airport now. I think there's a plane at seven. We can get the Express and then a taxi straight to the hospital from Paddington."

"Which hospital is she in?"

"Eh, I'm not sure. Your mother's got it written down somewhere?"

"Have you got Bill's mobile number?"

"Aye jist a minute."

He gave me the number; I could hardly write it down, my whole body fused by a sense of dread. There were more questions: what time did it happen? Who found her? What were the police doing? I may have asked them but if I did I never registered the answers. I called Bill. The news was all bad. The doctors were still examining her; there were knife wounds, broken bones and bruising. The police were calling it attempted murder. Bill never mentioned rape and I couldn't bring myself to ask.

I was stunned. Here it was for real, not some case I was working on, and close, my sister's daughter, my niece. I grabbed the bouquet of flowers that Sarah had sent and threw them in the bin. Two minutes later I was packed, out the door and on my way to London.

I met my mother and father at Heathrow. There was a mutual comfort when we embraced even though few words were spoken. We shared the grief from opposite ends of the spectrum. The reality of it all too horrible to contemplate for each of us, but their resistance was one of regret and sorrow while I felt loathing and hatred. Hatred was a new emotion for me, I had always accepted that there were people that I disliked, but that was a passive thing. The hatred that I felt then was active and strangely aspiring.

As we neared the hospital Pops got more information from Bill. It had apparently happened just after five. Her friend's mother had asked her to stay for tea and then offered her a lift home. Jennifer had said that she needed to get back – it would just take a few minutes if she cut across the common. After all, it was still daylight; it was busy, yet no one saw her being attacked. He had grabbed her from behind, pulled her into the bushes with a knife at her throat. She had struggled and he had punched her face and body. They had been heavy blows, her jaw broken in two places. He had also cut her under the chin and slashed her leg, the doctor had told Bill that the outward scarring wouldn't be permanent.

At the hospital's main reception I stuttered and blurted like a fresher enrolling on the first day. "My niece was attacked in Basildon – Jennifer Brown."

Bill met us outside the children's intensive care ward where Jenny was being treated. His usual bold upright stature drooped and hunched, his face red and puffy. His chin wobbled as he said "Mum" and then he burst into tears. He sobbed the only good news of the night – she hadn't been raped. Mum was allowed in to see Charlotte and Jennifer while Pops and I waited outside with Bill in the hallway to infuse our grief.

Mother told me that she had contacted Liz. Apparently Liz had been getting off a plane from Leeds when they spoke and Liz had got straight on another to London. She was at Charlotte's looking after our nephew Josh. I selfishly wished that she was with me at the hospital, I needed her comforting even though I knew that I didn't deserve it.

I had never had any children so I can only guess that my nerves were like those of an expectant father. I paced, sat down, stood up, ran my hands through my hair – I was crumpling under the weight of my imagination. The lack of cigarettes didn't help, if ever there was a time to smoke a packet of 20 it was then.

At last mum came out, her face white but no tears. Pops went in with Bill. I waited with mum, fetching scalding tea from the machine as my displacement activity. When Pops came out, his eyes wet with sadness I dared to go in.

I was nervous and wary; always when we met there were jokes and jesting, I wanted so much to cry out, take on her pain, but I had made up my mind that I had to be strong. I mentally prepared myself to be calm and 'normal'. In the end, all my meditation was wasted. She had been heavily sedated and was asleep. Because of the bandages I couldn't see much of her. What features I could see, were almost obliterated by swelling. Her face, black, blue and red except for her lips, the rose taken from them replaced by porcelain white and yellow cracked with crimson cuts. The pretty smile would be gone for a long time, the openness that was her character and endearing quality banished forever. I wanted so much to get hold of the bastard that had done it. If I had, I would have ripped him apart limb from limb starting with his vile prick. Poor Charlotte five months pregnant and so much worry and heartache, she looked done in. We had never thought of us being close, but I felt the bond when we hugged each other.

Charlotte wouldn't leave the hospital without Jennifer, so mum stayed with her while Pops went with Bill to see Josh. I waited in the corridor outside the ward. Mostly my time was spent fetching tea or coffee, but I did get the opportunity to speak to the police. The local police couldn't tell me much, but when I rang the head of the CID I learned a lot more. It was the first time that he could remember any sexual attacks in that area; it was normally a safe place. A safe place, broad daylight, plenty of people passing by, but my little niece was violated under their noses. He was confident that they would find her attacker; a local man of that they were certain. They had taken samples from Jenny's clothing, but not from her underwear – her pants had been taken.

15. Pushed over the edge I find a way

Thursday 25th of September – Day eleven

Bill had left Josh with my dad and was waiting with Charlotte to see the doctor. At about half past eight the consultant was able to see them and I joined them. The doctor was young, softly spoken with a strong Asian accent. He delivered the news with great sensitivity. In his gentle phrasing, there was always hope and encouragement. Her spirit and determination had saved her and would help her heal. His report was factual and clear, but with the clarity came the knowledge that things were bad, but could have been worse. She had not been raped. There was internal damage, probably from the handle of the knife that had been used to slash her legs and neck. Jennifer had also suffered a broken jaw, cracked ribs and a broken nose. She had just turned 13.

It was around ten o'clock when I got to see her again. I tried to be strong for her, but she saw it all in my eyes. All I could do was hold her hands and try to force a smile. Tears squeezed out from her swollen eyes and rolled down her cheeks until mopped by her bandages. There were no sounds, no sobbing just a steady stream of brutal acceptance. He hadn't killed her, but when he had laid that first clawing hand that had clasped her mouth and shut it tight, he had smothered her joy and destroyed her childish naivety. The damage to my sister, I was certain, was going to be just as difficult to repair, the extent of which was made clear to me over a few minutes in private conversation.

"It's my fault," Charlotte said, her face torn apart by guilt.

"Don't think that. You are an exemplary parent."

"Some example, look at her Robbie, she's covered in bandages."

"You can't keep them swaddled all their life."

"Yes and look what happens when you let go. Perverts pray on them. Even in nice neighbourhoods kids aren't safe. I shouldn't have let her come home herself," Charlotte said angrily through rolling tears. Her belief in the security of her middle class fortress breached. "I hate myself as much as I am disgusted by the man who did this to her."

"This had nothing to do with you Charlotte. It was some crazy person who couldn't control himself. It wasn't you or Jennifer that motivated that."

"I'd castrate him." There was anger in her eyes; those that had often scorned the women's liberation movement, which offended her liberal tolerance. "That man you are after, The Sawman, should get a medal for killing those perverts.'

On the drive back to my hotel, I thought hard about Jennifer and what my sister had said about The Sawman. Jennifer would come through her ordeal; her injuries would heal. There would be more emotional trauma, but her self esteem would carry her through. Charlotte was another matter. Her emotional scars were deep. Her loathing of men was understandable and her irrational praise of Sawman's murders was partly due to her frustration, yet there was something in what she said that stirred me. Ever since I started The Sawman investigation, I found myself wrestling with reason and once again, Jennifer's assault demanded that I examine my own liberal sensibilities. When I laid out the facts, they flipped reason and logic on their heads. His acts of apparent evil seemed to remove its actual presence. Society, as we wished it, was more secure and safe as a result of his actions and I knew that if I led the police to him that more innocent people would suffer. I had never believed that all serial killers were totally evil people and despite the depravity of his killings I came to the conclusion that for once Charlotte was right – The Sawman was to be praised for what he had done.

I found it easier to comfort Jennifer than Charlotte. Warm words, a squeeze of her hand and a stroke of her hair or face were all that I could offer Jennifer, but they seemed to be enough. It would have been some relief if I had been able to console Charlotte in some way, but it didn't happen, I couldn't find the words to say to help her overcome her nightmare. I was totally inept, fortunately my mother and father were more useful, their love marshalled to wrap her in hope. There was no hand wringing or helplessness, just reassurance in their all embracing love. My inadequate sensibilities were obvious even to me so I left around lunchtime feeling neutered with only one thing on my mind, that was to catch the bastard. I never spoke to Liz.

I drove to the spot where Jennifer was snatched. It was about 12 when I got there, a few minutes early for my rendezvous with a detective from the local police investigating the case. I used the time to look around. It could have been any recently built middle class suburb in England. The street was bordered by symmetrical, sanitised modern semi-detached homes, each with their own block patterned driveways, tidy gardens and venetian blinds. From where I was parked I could see the neatly paved path where Jennifer was assaulted. I closed my eyes. Immediately, a vision took hold. I saw her enter the path. The square shoulders of her oversized school blazer disappeared behind the bushes. I opened my eyes. It was rare for my vision to be so clear so quickly. I followed her imprint and walked along the path. On either side of the path bushes slightly overgrown, but still conforming to the air of neatness. Street lamps marked out the path. Even if it had been dark, the path would have been well lit: a safe suburban pathway. This was not the sinister thick wood that I had imagined when Pops had first phoned.

I had only gone a few yards when I heard a car pull up just behind me. I turned and saw a blue Vauxhall parked where the path joined the street. Two men got out. Although I had never met either before, I knew one of them was the detective who I had arranged to meet. He also seemed to recognise me.

"Dr Ahearn," said the taller of the two, as he held out has hand. I shook it.

"Yes."

"Detective Sergeant Trainer. This is DC Burns." I nodded, then turned and walked on without saying anything.

I didn't need either of them to show me the place where Jennifer had been snatched. I already knew. I followed the scuff marks on the decorative paving. A heavy score rasped across its surface. Instinctively, I knew it had been made by the buckle on Jennifer's school shoe. I crossed to where the bushes were broken and squashed.

I closed my eyes, my throat constricted and the picture of the sky filled my eyes. I saw a face, white, scrawny, unshaven, a hooked nose and cropped hair shaped in a widow's peak.

I saw her legs pumping and kicking his arms, shiny and black wrapped in some sort of satin, a puffed sleeve tightening around her neck, pulling her back. I saw the knife – short, cheap, with a black plastic handle and a pointed tip digging into her jaw. I was drawn to a gnarly hand and its thin wrist; a cheap diver's watch. And the smell of old rancid sweat filled my nose.

Screams, cries "Stop or I'll kill you". I wanted to reach out and save her. Her mouth twisted and distorted as he punched again and again. Still she shouted, scratched; her nails clogged with her attacker's skin, blood and DNA. Her pleats in her skirt twisted and flattened as his rough fingers pulled and tugged. Her thighs pinned by his weight, his foul breath and spit smothering her screams. I could sense the sharp lift and chill as she felt her clothing being ripped away and then, the fear and panic as she is gripped by the pain from the foreign object inside her. With the realisation she harnesses all her strength into one last effort. There is a piercing scream, the shaking ceases, the bearing down stops, the force slackens and then the lightness – air. He's gone.

I have his face, the eyes, his nose, those pointy ears, he would be mine and I would have him. My words to the detective were succinct "You have his DNA and I have his face". I ignored his bewildered look and walked back to my car.

I drove all the way to Glasgow stopping only for petrol. With each mile travelled, my emotions were driven further into a seething fiery aggression, ready to burn the bastard. I wanted to bugger him with a flagpole, inflict pain, rip his flesh apart and watch him bleed to death – all the time I held the picture of his face fixed in my head.

Throughout the journey, the traffic was a nightmare and progress was painfully slow, but by seven, I was back in the flat. I dropped my bags and walked through to the studio. I looked at the painting on the easel. The face was undeniably that of Beale, but now it could also be his identical twin Cerboni. I threw the painting aside and replaced it with a fresh canvas. I painted and painted, not stopping until that face was as sharp as a photograph. I took a couple snaps with my camera and downloaded them onto my laptop. A minute later they were on the police desk, a simple note attached. It read, 'This is the rapist, early 20s, unemployed, drug user who lives close by.'Those huge dilated corneas, stared back at me – the unmistakable evidence of heavy drug taking.

That was that, but it wasn't enough. I craved revenge, even though I knew it to be the very essence of neurosis, nevertheless it was that very motive that I longed to satisfy. The thirst for it pulsated through every fibre of my body; fluxed every neurone connection and tainted my saliva, anointing my tongue with the desire to quench it.

There was a message on my mobile. It was from Liz "I'm so sorry" was all it said and then, "She'll be alright, be strong." I called Charlotte – there was no change in Jennifer; I never mentioned the painting, but said they would get him soon. It seemed to be enough I could sense an easing in the hopelessness she felt and for those few minutes we spoke with a sibling closeness I had never experienced before. When I talked to my mother and father later, their sense of pessimism hung heavy – voices hushed, sentences shortened as though there was a death in the family – a grip on their emotions. I understood. Their foreboding, held their pain in check, bound them in solitude, fearful that that they might open the sluice and cause a mass drowning in the grief they collectively shared. I thought about going to The Horseshoe to find the courage to fight the despair, but I reasoned that quiet contemplation would be my best salvation. I decided to let the desire for revenge blow itself out. I poured myself a large malt and took it with me to my CD collection. I selected Gustav Mahler's fifth symphony – the *Adagietto*, the fourth of its five movements. It seemed a fitting accompaniment. It was time to get drunk, but first I removed the face of the paedophile. I returned The Sawman to the easel and as I looked into his eyes, saw the hurt and the pain, I felt empathy. I knew then that no matter the likeness it wasn't Beale. I sat back and stared. The sense of his despair added to my own. I let the music take-over, flood my head. It consumed my thinking, creating its own links, switching neurones on and off. With every chord of the music my misery unfolded just like the human drama within the music itself. For the moment it seemed to mirror my life – once so full of vitality and love, simple and serene, but then tragedy. It was drawing me back into depression.

By the time the music had ended I had already drunk half the bottle and it was only midnight. The heating time control had turned off the boiler automatically, but I was oblivious to the cold, the warm feeling from the whisky within and the terrors of the previous day blanked my senses. I made a move for the kitchen and with much effort I filled up the coffee machine. A peer into the fridge revealed nothing, nothing without mould that was. With Liz, the fridge had been like a theatre full of bright colours, textures and shapes, now the bulb out and the space within void, just cell bars pathetically protecting an old yoghurt carton and a half used jar of ginger. I shut the door and drank my coffee black determined to keep sleep at bay.

16. Black clouds gather

Friday, 26th September – Day twelve

The bright sunshine forced my eyes open. My head was bursting, my neck creaked and my mouth was as dry as cotton wool. I stirred slowly from the sofa and hobbled towards the bathroom undressing as I went. 10.00am. I stood under the shower and flinched as the freezing cold water met my body followed swiftly by the scalding hot when I over compensated. As I braced myself against the stinging spray, I leaned my head against my outstretched arm looking along its flattened hairs. I settled on the white moon shape where my watch face used to be. It reminded me that just then nothing seemed to be working.

I dressed, drank mugs of coffee and spent the next few hours thinking. The phone buzzed.

"Hello."

"Rob, it's Pete, how are you?"

I wasn't sure how to answer.

"Pete I'm okay," I said eventually.

"I heard about Jennifer. I'm sorry."

"Who told you?"

"Liz."

Liz I hadn't even spoken to her. The guilt pummelled my inside.

"How are you coping?"

"I am chilling out, listening to music."

"What are you listening to?"

I held out the phone into the airwaves.

"Chopin's Tarantelle. It is the end. I used to love that piano-bashing end piece, like fireworks whizzing and flashing." I usually held my breath as the music climaxed with its fierce run up the scale and would exhale loudly with the two final chords, but just then I did none of that. I simply held the phone up to the sounds that filled the air again.

"Did you go and see Tom Berner?"

"Not yet, it's on my must do list." It was down there somewhere among my priorities, between making sandcastles in Alaska and planning my old age.

"When can I see you?"

I had no plans to go to the funny farm just then, I said nothing.

"Can we meet up tomorrow?"

"That's no good."

"How about Monday?" I had to end that conversation.

"Okay."

"How does 11 sound?" he asked.

"Okay."

"That's great. At my office?"

"Sure."

Pete's call drained away what little energy I had. I went out to a local café and plumped for an all day breakfast. I had never eaten there before, the misted windows and oily curtains having put me off, but last night's drinking demanded that I get to the place nearest my front door. I could have chosen better because I soon gathered that the plate of Scottish fare given to me had been waiting under arc lights from eight in the morning and it was by then midday. The greasy black pudding, solid potato scones and chewy bacon shocked my empty stomach lining. The fried egg that sat on top of the lot, glad at last to be free from its shell so long after it was due to be released. I never complained I swallowed the lot aided by a disgusting mug of instant coffee.

When I got back to the flat I deleted my messages without listening to them, my journey to the sofa was diverted to the bathroom where my gobbled repast reconstituted itself in my toilet pan. And so my day rolled on much as it started, only my thumping hangover was joined by stomach pains and raging diarrhoea.

By around five my stomach had settled and the diarrhoea had stopped so I made a few calls. The news from Pops was the same. I called Bill at the hospital, Jennifer was asleep most of the time, but he had been told by the police that they had some leads and were looking for a young man they were convinced was responsible. They anticipated an arrest later that day.

I had just put the phone down when it rang.

"Hello?"

"Rob, it's Geoff, I heard about your niece and wanted you to know that they've caught the bastard."

"Bastard is too good for that shite."

"He's a young local, 22 no previous convictions for sexual assault but he is well known for thieving; pays for his drugs. He was out of his head when he was taken."

"They're sure it was him?"

"They found an item of Jennifer's clothing in his pocket. They believe once he has come round he will confess."

"Let's hope so, we don't want a trial; that would be too horrible to contemplate."

"How is she?"

"Not good; under heavy sedation. She was badly beaten up. Her face and legs were slashed."

"I'm sorry. They have DNA that will nail him, but it was your painting that identified him. I suppose you know that it looks just like his mug shot."

"That was one that I never wanted to paint."

"I understand. Are you taking some time off?"

"No, I'll be there tomorrow. Will you be around?"

"Saturday, of course," Geoff sighed.

"Have you found Cerboni yet?"

"No nothing so far."

"Right."

"I just wanted to say how sorry I am about Jennifer. I'll see you tomorrow morning."

"Yeah thanks."

Cerboni – branded evil, but I couldn't see him as an amoral person. His crimes were premeditated; he had cut their heads off. They were heinous in the eyes of our laws, yet, for me, he was doing society a service. He had been abused and degraded, but I knew that wouldn't save him. They would want to lock him up and throw away the key, but I wasn't prepared to help them. He was a crusader, not a villain, his victims were, if anything, worse than him. He was bringing them to justice and right there and then I shared his view that the only sentence befitting their crimes was death.

I had to find Cerboni, not to catch him, but to help him. He was out there and waiting for me. I was beginning to think that I was on the wrong side. If I was going to stop other children suffering at the hands of perverts I had to enable Cerboni to carry on with his work. Forensic psychology catching Cerboni wasn't going to prevent more kids being abused. I had to change. I needed to be like the rowans on the streets below. They knew how to adapt and change. I stared at their grey-green upper leaf colour. These were already changing to greenish yellow and vibrant scarlet, despite being shrouded in exhaust fumes they looked proud and contented in the middle of town not bothered by the pollution. They just sucked it in and blew it back out as clean air. I drew from their strength and then it happened. My cells split into two. The rational cells were no longer dominant. The others had made a pact to use my own inventiveness to find Sawman.

Slizzz, crack, shehaw, shehaw, shehaw, clunk. The saw blade slue to a halt, its teeth biting against the skin at the back of the neck. A long draw of the blade sets the head free and it rolls gently to the side.

17. Contact

Saturday 27th September – Day thirteen

They were surprised to see me, not because it was a Saturday, but because everyone knew about Jennifer. Dawn was the first, the others followed; even Bob Ulis offered his sympathy. They mirrored my abhorrence, yet I knew their intentions self-impotent. In their hearts they wanted to volunteer for the posse, build the gallows, affix the rope and string up Jennifer's assailant, but I knew that they wouldn't. That was the one difference between them and me I was going to do it; I was going to help Sawman get a few more of those bastards, I just had to work out how.

The first thing I had to do was to communicate with him. There had to be a way, after all, he seemed to be able to get very close to the people he wanted to meet. My mind focused, blinkered by seething revenge, shutting out distraction, it concentrated on the task in hand – how to meet with The Sawman. I realised that if I could find out how he selected his victims it would lead me to him.

When I opened up my laptop there were a lot of messages, most of them from Audrey, Sir Anthony's PA. I read the first of his, a simple message – as Sawman had been identified my assignment was over and I should return to London. The others were messages of sympathy including one from Big Al. It said: If I can help, in anyway, just ask. That was all it said. I came out of my e-mails and got on with my investigation, but not long after my mobile rang.

"Robbie, I'm sorry I missed you when you called."

I stubbed my cigarette out.

"Liz."

"I tried earlier, but there was no answer. I didn't leave a message… so anyway how are you?" She sounded confused, but bright enough.

"I'm sorry, I'm in Manchester. Are you still at Charlotte's?"

"No, your mum is looking after Josh I caught a flight this morning; I'm back in Edinburgh." I should have known that from the 0131 read out on my phone, some detective I'd make.

"It was good of you."

"She's my God-daughter too, you're the atheist remember." Her voice tingled with castigation and reproach.

"Yes, I'm sorry. How were things when you left?"

"Much the same; Jenny's still in hospital, sedated most of the time; Charlotte seems to be coping; Bill's shattered. Your mum and dad have been great, keeping things going, you know."

"Aye."

"I heard that you helped catch him."

"Who told you?"

"Your dad. He'd been speaking to the CID. Apparently, you are the talk of the place."

"A bit of luck, my download was received by a sergeant that had arrested him before. He thought it was a picture from the police files," I said.

"They don't know what to make of you."

"They had his DNA; they would have found him anyway. I would love to get my hands on the bastard. Has he come down yet?"

264

"The drugs? I don't know. How are you coping?" she asked. I knew exactly what she meant: was I losing it?

"Dealing with it. A bit hapless, you know?" She knew exactly how it was.

"Well at least they've caught him. I still can't believe it. It is the most terrible nightmare, so awful. I can't believe it. Poor Jenny, she's so young. I don't know how she will get over it. And Charlotte and Bill, it is just horrible."

"Yeah he's fucked up their lives. I'm planning to go back down in a few days. What about you?"

"Oh, I don't know yet."

"How's Edinburgh?"

"Okay. Look I eh… are you going to be in Manchester all this weekend?" She asked.

"Probably," I said excitedly as a wild thought that just maybe she was reconsidering, entered my head.

"It's just that I plan to go over to the flat to get the rest of my things."

My anticipation blown away, I desperately tried to recapture it.

"Can't we talk about this?"

"What is there to talk about?"

"I'll change." That old pathetic line again.

"We've already gone through this."

"Well I think we should try and…" Steve appeared at my window. I waved him away and he disappeared.

Liz took the gap to shut it down. "I've got to go now. I'm sorry. Be careful. Bye." There was feeling in her voice, love, hidden, but still there.

"Be careful," she knew me so well. She could see inside my skull as though it was made of glass. We had been there before and I couldn't blame her for not wanting to do it again. She had dutifully supported me through my six months in hospital the last time I got fucked up. And she was right Sawman had brought back the depression, but Jennifer's attack had galvanised me. I replayed her voice in my head only this time she was saying "That would be great let's meet for lunch and we can sort it out." I put the phone down. I had work to do.

We pulled up at the apartment or as close as we could because the place was swarming with police and the media. As Naylor and I walked to the front gate, cameras and interviewers surrounded us. Naylor brushed passed the poking microphones and shouted to the beat policemen to get them back behind the tape. I clocked the black Jaguar. Ulis was there already.

"Ahearn, they found you." When the first calls had come in I had been at my hotel. I had left my mobile in Chester House and hadn't told anyone where I was going – I had my reasons. "That's Colson." Ulis pointed to the crumpled headless body on the floor.

I acknowledged Geoff and Steve with a nod and walked over to where the body lay. I took in the spilled blood and the butchered neck where the head should have been; it was a few feet away, lying in profile, with stringy skin and slimy, gooey bits trailing out from the base. I moved closer to it and could see that the eyes had been gouged out. The craftsmanship wasn't really up to his standard, even so, this was no copycat; it had the unmistakable handiwork of The Sawman.

"Sawman was a little untidy," I said.

"Yes. He didn't use acid and there was just the one message; the one on his chest," Ulis said, nodding towards the body.

" 'In the name of the father.' Doesn't sound too original," I commented as I read the message.

"He might have run out of acid after Elizabeth Street," Steve volunteered to Geoff.

"What do you mean?" I asked.

"The eyes and abdomen of the other body in Elizabeth Street were drenched in acid. Maybe he used it all up."

"Elizabeth Street was the *first* murder?" I asked.

Steve nodded. "A neighbour found Reglen, the other victim, at 12 o'clock and Reglen directed us to Colson," Geoff said.

"How?" I asked.

"There was a note stuck in Reglen's hand. It said twinned with Colson 41."

"How did you work out it was here?"

"I looked up Colson in the phone book and there was one listed and underlined at 41 Mulberry so we checked it out."

"So, he wanted us to find him?" I asked.

"It looks that way," Geoff replied. "The message was written with a piece of a TV aerial dipped in Reglen's blood on a page of the TV guide."

"No sign of Cerboni I suppose," I said and Steve shook his head.

"Colson here was killed about one o'clock according to Jane Warren," Steve said.

"Jane's here?"

"No, she's just left, gone back to Elizabeth Street," Geoff answered.

"I wanted her over there to complete her assessment. She was needed here to confirm the time of death," Ulis said.

"It looks as if our man was in a bit of a hurry; then again, he was a busy man wasn't he?" I said, stating the obvious.

"We know now for sure it wasn't Beale because Special Branch had a surveillance team on him all night, so it looks as though it's your Cerboni," Ulis said looking at the ground and awkwardly shifting on the spot.

"I thought that you were arresting Beale?" I enjoyed the moment.

"We couldn't find him and then with the news about Cerboni we decided to hold back." Ulis looked almost embarrassed and I revelled in it.

"What about Melnar?" I asked.

"There's no sign of him; looks as though he's done a runner too," Geoff answered.

"We got some interesting stuff from Vice," Steve piped up.

"What?" Ulis demanded.

"Muche's computer had a pornographic sex site. There was a lot of code, but once you got through that it offered access to kinky masochistic sex, paedophile stuff and a contact network. It made a direct appeal to perverts." I volunteered.

"How did you know?" Steve said.

"That's where I was when you were looking for me," Geoff looked at me suspiciously.

"And Melnar's mixed up in it?" Ulis asked.

"We think so, sir. Some of the videos feature him in action," Geoff replied.

Ulis moved away and Geoff pulled me aside.

"What were you doing at Vice?"

"Oh Dawn mentioned something about them checking computers taken from Muche and Shields. I thought it was worth a look."

"What were you looking for?"

"I don't know, I thought it might kick something off."

"And did it?"

"No."

"Next time you want to look into some new angle in one of my cases come and talk to me first."

"Okay." I never mentioned that a DCI in Vice had given me a download to work through.

I had a good look around. There had been a computer in one of the back bedrooms, but Steve had already arranged for it to be taken to Vice.

I left Ulis and Geoff and checked out the place. It was another seedy apartment, in need of cleaning and redecoration. There was a similar smell to the others: piss, shit and death. The place didn't look as though anyone lived there. There were no clothes or personal items. I returned to Steve. We poked around a little more. The murder looked messy; so unlike his previous neat jobs. I wondered whether Sawman was losing his cool.

"Steve, what do we know about the victims?" I asked. I was moving from my world into theirs.

"Quite a lot." He opened his notebook and read from it.

"Charles Reglen, 38 on bail awaiting trial for rape of a juvenile. He claims she looked 18 and that she consented. Has a history of sexual abuse, child molesting, that kind of thing. Elliot Colson aged 50, served 18 years for sodomising an eight year old boy and raping his older sister. She was 12. He was released in 1998; on the register, but nothing since."

Steve's eyes left his book and caught mine. "I'm sorry, are you sure you want to stay with this?" Steve's young face twisted awkwardly as it forced an expression of sympathy.

"It's alright. They caught the bastard that attacked Jennifer." I tensed momentarily. "It sounds like Cerboni didn't stray too far," I said.

"No, he probably did us a favour," Steve said.

"Don't let Ulis hear you say that," I responded.

Geoff rejoined us. "Steve did you ask Vice to check if their names were on Muche's computer?"

"No. Won't these guys be using an alias?" Steve asked.

"Probably, but check it out."

"Did Vice find anything at Melnar's place?" I asked.

"Loads of pornographic material," Steve answered.

"Didn't they mention that when you were there?" Geoff asked me with a suspicious look.

"I never asked."

When Naylor found me and first told me about the murders I had just got back to my hotel via Vice, where I had been given printouts of Muche and Shields' system software. I was hoping that these might help me find Cerboni and I was itching to get back to them.

"If we could find Melnar we'd know more. He is an important cog in this shitty wheel," Geoff said.

"What have Forensics come up with here?" I asked Steve.

"Quite a lot. There are a lot of fibres where they scuffled and Forensics are pretty confident they can extract DNA from some sweat and facial oil on the carpet. Maybe, Cerboni wants us to know it's him."

"Maybe he does, maybe he just doesn't care." The case was gathering a pace and I felt that they would soon have

Cerboni in custody. I needed to find him first. "So back to Colson here, how did Sawman get him?"

"At about 12.45, Sawman forced the front door lock and entered. We think Colson surprised him at his bedroom door. There was a scuffle and both men rolled around the floor. A neighbour thinks he heard it; he noted the time, but as it didn't last long he didn't bother to investigate or call anyone. It looks as though Cerboni stabbed Colson on the leg during the fight and he probably took advantage of that to cut Colson's throat. That was the cause of death. We think that he then used the knife to gouge out Colson's eyes and to make two large wounds in his abdominal area. The head was then sawn off and left where you saw it. The carving on the chest was probably the last thing he did and then he left by the front door. As you can see he made no attempt to straighten the place out. In fact we don't think he was in any of the other rooms."

"Are you sure?" I asked.

"Pretty sure," Steve answered.

"Have you been to Reglen's place?"

"Of course. Two hours ago. Dawn is still there with the team. I am planning to go back when I'm finished here. Are you going there?"

Ulis interrupted us. "Right Geoff, I have a media conference at six, what can I tell them?" Before Geoff responded, I stepped into the question.

"How about? In the early hours of this morning, two white males Charles Reglen 38, and Elliot Colson 50, were murdered. We are following up a number of leads and we would like to interview a man aged between 35-40, between five feet seven and five feet nine, black or dark hair, weighing around 130lbs. We would also like to interview a white male Alfredo

Cerboni, to assist us with our enquiries. Mr Cerboni is aged 38, height five foot eight and weighs around 130lbs. He has black hair growing grey at the sides."

"Don't get smart. Geoff, I want a case conference before I meet the press."

"Sir, it's two o'clock now," Geoff said.

"You should be through here and Reglen by say five, so let's say five thirty."

"Right."

"I want Vice and Special Branch there."

"I'll organise it," Geoff responded dutifully.

I left with Ulis, but in separate cars; he in his Jaguar to Chester House and me in Naylor's to Reglen's place.

With police Forensics and the media it was like a zoo there, so I asked that he drop me off at my hotel instead. I had other more rewarding work to do.

Tommy Lees, a technical support assistant in Vice had already done most of the work – he had found references in the memory of Cerboni's machine to a site called 'Sweet Dreams'. The site had been set up by a known alias 'Shiva', an associate of Melnar. Lees' analysis of the 'Sweet Dreams' site identified that it was part of a paedophile network. Tommy had told me that there were hundreds of hits to this site. Most users had used aliases, but he had positively identified that there were messages from machines owned by Muche and Shields on there. He had also given me printouts of the conversations from the site's chat room facility.

I e-mailed Big Al. I tapped out my problem and pressed send. His reply was swift: 'The chat room records will tell you who and when. Download records and I will sift or do it your-self – look for a single code word – 'doctor' or other link to

Sawman – don't waste time reading the chat – will only confuse.'

The computer sheets were spread out on my bed. I kneeled on the floor beside them and leafed through page after page – I expected a long night ahead and I wasn't to be disappointed. At first I spent time trying to get a feel for the main users, but after an hour it hadn't taken me very far. I then started again and went through each one referencing them against the deleted items on The Sawman's victims' machines restored by Tommy and copied on to a CD for me. It was a long and slow process and I didn't want any interruptions so I switched off my mobile and ignored the occasional call to my room phone.

It was like building an intricate jigsaw combined with a cryptic crossword and just like those I needed to get that all important start. After two hours of sifting it came. I noticed that there were a number of messages by an *Alexei*. The name stood out because of Alexi Zochten. One of the people that this *Alexei* was chatting to was called Sega. I could hardly believe it. Sega means Saw in Italian. My throat dried and my stomach twisted in nervous knots. I searched Cerboni's machine for any files related to these and there it was, a copy of a note, which I cross-referenced to a message listed on a page of the print outs. It read: MUSEGA4522.

I could hardly contain myself. Once I had identified Sega it was relatively easy to decipher the message – MU Sega. Meet You Sega – 4522 – the date for the meeting – May 4– the day before Zochten was murdered, at 2200hrs – only two hours before he was murdered.

My mind started to spin. I poured myself another minia-ture of whisky from the mini bar, I was entitled to celebrate;

I had found what I was looking for. I turned my findings over and sorted them in my head. Cerboni had tapped into a paedophile ring. That was how he made contact with his victims. It all made sense. Those networks were like a toxin and the poison emanating would fuel those with depraved minds as well as coercing prurient debased and obscene fantasies. All I had to do was link a message to this network and wait for his reply. It was a long shot of course; he didn't have his machine, but the site was still operational. Tommy told me that Vice hadn't closed down the site, they were still monitoring the activity and he could still be accessing it remotely. All I had to do was pass this to Geoff and they could trace the location. That wasn't what I wanted. I wanted to speak to him, help him with his cause. I used a spare e-mail account and left a message in the chat-room. It was simple. It said 'SEGAIWTHELP'. I hoped he would find it; I hoped he would decipher my offer of help and I hoped for an early reply. All I could do was wait and see.

I wanted to shake my mind free of Cerboni and 'Sweet Dreams' so I cleared the printouts from the bed, lay back against the headboard and pressed the TV remote control. Getting away from Cerboni wasn't as easy as that because the first programme that came into view was the late news. Ulis filled the screen; I turned up the sound: "We are seeking additional evidence in connection with several homicides and a conspiracy to commit murder investigation. We are appealing for anyone that may have seen the suspect or who may have any other information about the crimes to contact us." The studio presenter ended the programme. "So a breakthrough at last in the hunt for the serial killer, who until tonight, was known simply as The Sawman. That was Assistant Chief

Constable Ulis of Greater Manchester Police appealing for anyone who knows the whereabouts of Alfredo Cerboni, an assistant at the city's morgue, to come forward. GMP who only yesterday issued a warrant for Alfredo Cerboni's arrest in connection with the suspicious death of his mother Mrs Maria Cerboni of Stockport is now seeking Cerboni with regard to The Sawman serial killings that rose to five following the discovery of the bodies of two white males in the south of the city."

So it was out at last, Alfredo Cerboni was suspected of being The Sawman. I switched off the television, turned on my mobile and put out the room light. I didn't bother to undress; I just relaxed in the pale green gloomy light emitted by my laptop. A minute or so later, the cellphone went onto standby mode and my eyes closed.

At two in the morning, I was woken from my sleep by the ringtone of my mobile. I scrambled sweaty and disoriented from my bed and picked it up, the number withheld. I pressed the receive button.

"Dr Ahearn?" I didn't recognise the voice, but I knew it was Cerboni.

"This is Dr Ahearn." I was formal, but not cold.

"I am Alfredo Cerboni." He paused, but I let the empty space widen. "I received your message."

"How did you know it was from me?"

"I have been watching you for some time Dr Ahearn. I know a great deal about you. I know about your god-daughter Jennifer. You helped catch her attacker. I also hear that you are alone now. I am sorry about that. We are alike in many ways you and me. I know you want to catch the perverts who mess around with the children doctor. Me too."

"How did you get my mobile number?"

"Dr Pinder's address book. You said you wanted to help."

"Yes."

"You know that I have done something terrible."

"What do you mean?"

"She was ill and suffering pain, such awful pain."

Again, I let silence fill the space.

"I couldn't bear to see her suffer anymore." His voice was like a child's, innocent, emotional and desperate. "She was sleeping; she was always sleeping when I came home, but her body was twisted with the pain. I woke her up and gave her more of her medicine. It didn't help and she was crying, wanting me to help. She would have screamed out if she had the strength, but she hadn't. She just hated me for not making it stop. I called the doctor, but he said there was nothing he could do; give her more sedatives he said. I didn't know what to do. I went out and walked around the streets, but when I came back she was worse. Her eyes were shut, but she knew it was me. She cursed me for not helping her Dr Ahearn. I tried, I gave her more sedatives and she eventually stopped being mad at me. I made her stop Dr Ahearn." I could hear him sobbing. Long deep gulps and then wet blurts of air. Then there was a long pause and I was drawn in.

"What happened?" I asked.

"I tried to contact Sister Scolastica. She was out. They said she would phone, but she didn't."

"What did you do?"

"I knew that if mamma woke up she would hate me again. So I stopped her."

"How?"

"I made her sleep," more sobbing. "I made her stop."

"How?"

"I, I took her pillow and placed it over her face, gently at first, then hard very hard." He was sobbing. "I held on and on, until she stopped pushing, until she stopped breathing, until she stopped hating and then it was over."

"What did you do then?"

"I made my pasta." It was an amazing transition. The snivelling had stopped and his voice was steady.

"And then?"

"Then, I went out."

"Where?"

"I think that you know where."

"Where are you now?"

"I am not at home."

"Where are you?"

"Safe."

"Why haven't you gone to the police?"

"I don't need the police."

"What about the others."

"What others?"

"The others that you visited."

"The pigs. I made them stop."

"How?"

"You know how?"

"You killed them."

"I made them stop."

"You should give yourself up." As soon as I said those words I knew I had made a mistake it was the forensic psychologist talking not me.

"I have work to do. I must go now. I make a mistake calling you"

"Wait I want to help you."

He was silent.

"Where are you? Let's meet." I proffered.

Silence.

"Alfredo, why don't you give me a number where I can contact you?"

"No, I can't do that." His voice sounded anxious and forlorn.

"Alfredo, I want to help," I tried to reassure him. He was silent now.

"We should meet to discuss it," I said.

"Soon, doctor soon, Sunday at ten I'll call you."

"Sunday I... I..."

"Ah your god-daughter Jennifer, I understand. I will call on Monday evening at six."

"Yes, Monday would be good." The response was mechanical, my brain fused with processing options of maybes and what ifs.

"Oh and doctor, have you had your watch fixed yet? You'll need it now, you have so much to do."

Before I replied the line went dead.

18. A time to reflect

Sunday, 24th September – Day fourteen

I skipped breakfast, got into the Healy and left for London. I settled into my bucket seat and switched on the CD player and Mahler's symphony filled the cabin, competing for my attention with the deep burble from the heavy metal under the bonnet. Neither was successful because, even before I got out of the car park, my conversation with Alfredo was all I could hear. My hands felt clammy. The waves of serious doubts about my capabilities and aptitude for the role of vigilante threatened to drag me under as my brow moistened with beads of sweat. My mind was swimming against the logic that had taken me to my new role as Sawman's accomplice. I realised that I had jumped, feet first, into dangerous, and for me, unchartered waters. I wriggled in my seat uncomfortably as I searched for the beach and a way out. My left leg vibrated and shook uncontrollably. I should have left the analysis of the computer printouts to the experts; I should have told Vice what I had found; I should have phoned Geoff as soon as I ended my conversation with Alfredo. I looked in the mirror, but all I saw were the portentous consequences of my naïve alliance. "What the fuck are you doing?" cut through Mahler's wasted efforts at diverting my attention. That innocent face, the carefree laughter and openness that was my memory of Jennifer brought it all back; she was lying in a hospital bed, my sister distraught and her faith disabled because of a sex fiend. Those targeted by Alfredo had inflicted even worse pain and suffering I reminded myself. It was thoughts about their victims that settled me, helped me keep my nerve. Revenge was a powerful antidote to fear and a weak backbone.

"Shit." The Healy's new tyres squealed in harmony with my scream. All thoughts of Alfredo vanished. The colour coded bumper of a dark green Toyota zoomed closer. My body was thrown hard left, anchored only by my seatbelt and my two hands that gripped the steering wheel as the car swerved to the right. I came to a stop unscathed. Through my passenger window I saw a snow white faced young girl peer at me in obvious terror. I signalled my apology to her and her angry father, sitting and fuming in front. Luck and the Healy's recently serviced brakes had saved us all. I settled the Healy meekly behind the truck in front and tried to ignore the gesticulating hand the Toyota driver was shaking at me to my far side. I was in a queue of standing traffic at junction 15 of the M6 near Walsall. A combination of heavy traffic and roadworks had brought all three lanes to a standstill outside the reflective blue glass building reminiscent of a ski slope that is the RAC Control Centre building and yet, I hadn't seen any of it until I was almost upon it. The shock of it all blew away thoughts of Alfredo. From there on, most of the journey was at a snail's pace until I got onto the M40. The extended journey time provided plenty of opportunity to revisit my plight and to change my position from vigilante to posse man back to vigilante often, and I did, at least a hundred times.

I can't remember what my final position was when I reached the children's hospital car park, but by the time I passed through the front doors to reception Alfredo slipped out of my consciousness and Jennifer took over.

A small head with bloated lips nestling in her mother's bosoms, her body tightly wrapped in her mother's arms. When Charlotte saw me her smile expressed joy, but as I got close I could see that her eyes were soft with sorrow. The message though was clear, we had to lie, we had to pretend that the nasty experience was over that everything was okey-dokey as though the attack was just a bad dream. When I last saw Jennifer she was withdrawn and her wired jaw kept her inner feelings locked inside. Less than a week had past and most of the bandages and plasters had been removed from her face, the heavy bruising had muted. The contrasting vermilion and deep purple replaced by a fine yellow ochre and mauve pastel. I was worried that as a man she would hate me. I smiled and to my relief Jennifer responded. She moved from the security of her mother and stretched her arms out towards me. I moved close and she gave me a hug that I will never forget.

"I'm okay," she said in her schoolgirl falsetto through her wired jaw. She had been part of nightmare, but not a dream. Charlotte knew it, but hadn't appreciated that Jennifer was resigned to it. I could see the difference in Jennifer. We had been close before and just then I sensed that she didn't despise all men and my fears for her eased, relieved she had come through it. With the ice broken, I tried to talk with her.

"How's the hospital food?" I asked.

"Whgat?" she said though her gripped teeth, pointing at her neat row of metal ties with a shrug that brought home the stupidity of my question. Charlotte stroked Jennifer's hair.

"She's stuck with this," Charlotte said holding up a plastic glass, its straw pointing accusingly. Jennifer patted her mother's hand.

The conversation was pretty restricted, even so, I spent most of the day with Jennifer and I was amazed by the normality of it all. There we were in unfamiliar surroundings, among doctors, nurses, patients and their parents, all of whom were strangers and yet Jennifer could put aside her experience, her injuries and enforced public intimacy and behave as normal. Though it wasn't normal. We didn't discuss the important things, how she felt, or her assault; instead, we spoke of the messages from school and her friends. Still, there was enough for me to know that Jennifer had made it through the trauma. I wasn't so certain about Charlotte. I noticed that Jennifer continually consoled her mother by stroking her hand. The usual roles of mother and daughter reversed. For Jennifer the ordeal was past, if not forgotten, whereas her mother, who hadn't been there, continued to relive every moment of it.

19. My instructions

Monday, 25th September – Day fifteen

With all that was going on I should have had an uncomfortable night, but I didn't, on the contrary I must have slept for ten hours straight through and for the first time in a week my recurring nightmares never materialised. There was no waking, shuddering in a sweat, no memories, no flashbacks, nothing. Just sleep. It wasn't my adherence to Pete's advice to give the alcohol a miss that allowed me the first restful sleep in four weeks, no it was that the previous night I had removed the yolk of liberal reasonableness from my spirit and embraced freewill. I had decided to be a righter of wrongs, a disciple of revenge. When I awoke, instead of pacing like an expectant father turning over the events of recent days, I sprung out of bed, dressed quickly and had breakfast in the hotel.

When I arrived at Chester House empowered and fresh after my 'full English' the Chief Constable was already outside addressing the media. He had obviously returned from holiday, his skin bronzed and shining. I couldn't hear what he was saying, but he looked solemn and serious, yet when he stopped to answer questions each of his responses was prefaced by an enormous smile. He was a happy man and beside him Bob Ulis was standing almost coyly like a school prize winner. Just then I had one of my crazy moments – There was a bang and then the noise of a drill hitting bone. I was looking down into the funnel of a steam train, at its smoke ring rising, I dropped through as it powdered me with soot and then deep black wine, tarry and clotting, spilled out from beneath my feet and formed the face of Ulis. When I came too one of the hand held TV cameras was smoking and there was a momentary pause in the proceedings. Ulis was undeterred by the minor commotion and continued to milk the moment. I turned away and walked through the entrance leaving the 'celebrities' to their three minutes of fame. Geoff caught up with me in the hallway.

"We need to talk."

"Morning Geoff."

"In my office in ten minutes?"

"Okay."

I dumped my stuff checked for messages – all four of them were from Audrey.

I called Pete. His message kicked in and switched me to his secretary.

"BPST."

"Hello, this is Rob Ahearn I have an appointment with Pete at 11, but I have to cancel."

"Can he contact you?"

"I'll be out all day, but tell him I'll call him tomorrow to explain."

"That's fine. I shall let Dr Whelan know. Thank you for calling."

I was ready for Geoff.

"Rob take a seat."

I sat in front of his broad desk.

"The Chief Constable has asked me to tell you that he has spoken to Sir Anthony and they have agreed that as Cerboni has been identified, your work here is finished. I have been asked by the Chief Constable and Assistant Chief Constable to thank you for your contribution to the investigation. From my own point of view, your help was invaluable. It was you who led us to Cerboni; thanks for your help."

"No, it was Dawn and Steve who uncovered him."

"I think we know differently. I don't know how you operate, I don't pretend to understand it, but I know that those visions or whatever they are, drew us towards Cerboni and when we find him you will have played a big part in his capture. I for one am deeply grateful, which is why I'm not going to ask what you were doing at Vice. I do, however, want to know what you were doing sending an e-mail to Cerboni. What the hell was that about?"

"Quite simple, I had a theory and I sent a message to a name in the chat room that I thought might be his offering to help him."

"And did he reply?"

"No. I don't even know if it was him." This was difficult; lying to a Detective Chief Superintendent wasn't easy, and downright uncomfortable when it was Geoff. One look into his eyes told you that he didn't need a lie detector.

"I don't believe you."

"What?"

"I don't know what you are up to, but don't try to conceal Cerboni's whereabouts from me. If you know where he is, tell me now."

"I promise you, I don't know where he is." At last I could speak the truth.

He studied my face.

"Okay, we understand each other. I guess you will be going back to Glasgow now."

"I have a few things to tidy up here and then I will head south to see my sister."

"Of course, I'm sorry, good luck Rob." He shot up from his chair and held out his hand. That was it, a handshake and it was over. On my way to my office I met Steve.

"Steve."

"Are you coming to the briefing this morning?"

"No, can't make it. What's been happening?"

"No sign of Cerboni yet. It looks as though your theory about twins could be right. A search of the city records for births registered in 1962 identified Cerboni's birth mother and you'll not believe it."

"What?"

"She came from Pozzuoli near Naples."

"I knew it. Anything else?"

"Plenty. A record at the charity hospital showed that his mother had delivered twin boys. One was Cerboni, the other was recorded as dead at birth, but we suspect otherwise. We are trying to trace the midwives and nurses who worked there."

"What 40 years ago, are you joking?"

"I know, it's a long shot. Some more good news?"

"What's that?"

"Vice has identified both Colson and Reglen in the videos taken from Muche's flat. It looks like that's the source because Zochten and Conran were in some too. Shields was the only one not there."

"Quite a cosy club."

"They have identified a few of the others on our list and a couple of others we don't know."

"Are you keeping them under surveillance?"

"Those whom we can trace; since Reglen and Colson many of them have gone underground."

I couldn't believe the change in me. A few days ago I had felt so depressed and unappreciated, but the telephone conversation with Cerboni had changed all that. Cerboni wanted my help and I wanted his. I knew that with his support the fire of hatred that I was stoking up against Jennifer's assailant would be fashioned into a white-hot spear to be released with deadly accuracy – I would have my revenge. I had work to do – there was no retreating now.

My mobile buzzed and foolishly I picked it up without checking.

"Rob, it's Pete."

"Hi.

"Are we still meeting today?"

"I'm sorry I can't make it."

"What's the problem?"

"You said to cut back, I've finished with the case. I'm just tying up the loose ends. And Liz's gone, so now I don't have any pressures. I slept, so I don't think we need to meet up again." I wanted to tell him that for once the night had separated from the day and the dream had gone. I had slept for ten hours – it was a miracle – but before I got it out he put some doubts in my mind.

"Have you seen or spoken to Liz."

"Yes, it's over."

"I am sorry about that. How do you feel about it?"

"Difficult to say."

"I think it might be helpful if we still meet."

"Okay, what about Thursday."

"At 11?"

"Sure."

"Bye Rob."

I put my mobile down, glad that I had finished that conversation. It hadn't been therapeutic, but I ignored it. I had already resigned myself to the fact that Liz wasn't coming back. With my new plan there could be no happy ever after with Liz. Anyway, I was determined that there would be no more wringing of my hands; I was going to get on with it.

At about 12 I went to Harry's to collect my watch. When I got there it was déjà vu, the shop was empty and there was no sign of him, but then I heard the shuffling feet and eventually his crumpled face appeared at the service hatch.

"Ah, you're back."

"Is it ready?"

"Of course." He turned away, but carried on speaking. "A fine watch mister, a wonderful timepiece."

"It was a present from my wife."

"She must love you very much."

I gave that one a miss.

"Not many watches would have survived that impact. Ah, here we are." He wheeled back slowly, dangling my watch between his index finger and thumb."

The new glass and face were gleaming.

"It looks great."

"As good as new, mister."

"Thanks how much do I owe you?"

"Forget about it. That's one that you owe me."

"I'd rather pay. Is £20 okay?"

"More than generous, more than generous, would you like a box for it?"

"No, I'll just wear it." I fastened its leather strap and checked the time – 12.20. I thanked him and left. I walked to the barbers next door and got my hair cut, nothing fancy just a number three. A short while later I was out of there and heading back to my office for what I thought would be the last time; one last tuna sandwich for my lunch with coffee, but no George. There were to be no grand farewells just a final comprehensive report, as requested by Audrey for Sir Anthony, to include my assessment of Cerboni and his motives.

By 5.50pm I had sent my report by e-mail to Sir Anthony and tidied up my office ready to leave. I went straight to the car park and got into the Healey. I felt conspicuous sitting there, not moving, but I didn't want to drive off in case I lost my mobile's signal just as he tried to call, so I sat there, checking my watch every minute or so, peering at the reception on my mobile. Those ten minutes seemed like hours, but bang on six I got the call.

"Go to your hotel room." The phone went dead.

I left the car park immediately. It was odd, even though I was possibly about to meet a serial killer I wasn't concerned for my safety, just excited, spurred on by a strange inner confidence. Despite the traffic, it was as though I was touring the Scottish Highlands without a care in the world. I was smiling, relaxed and keen to get on with it.

When I opened my bedroom door I half expected him to be there waiting, but there was no one. I settled on my bed closed my eyes and waited.

When I got up there was a small white envelope lying at my door. I picked it up and ran it lightly between my thumb and forefinger. There was something hard inside. I moved across to the desk and sat down. I opened it carefully. Inside there was a ticket with the number 203 on it and a tiny key. That was all, no note and no message. The ticket was for the left luggage at Piccadilly Station. I was charged with anticipation; it was going to happen and soon I was to meet The Sawman. I was to collect something and I needed to find out what, so I left for the station.

The drive this time was very different. As I drove through the centre of town my head buzzed with what I might find and played versions of the forthcoming scene over and over my in my head. My mood though was, if anything, even more positive.

I left the Healey in the car park at Fairfield Street at the south side of the station and entered the main complex. I dodged the late commuters pouring out of the station and made my way straight to the main information office. As I waited my turn I started to have doubts. I could feel the nervous tension build, but it wasn't long before I was on my way with directions to the left luggage office on platform ten.

It had just gone seven, yet there was quite a long queue of people waiting at the left luggage office. I joined the end of the line behind a short fat man. My hands began to sweat as I looked around for The Sawman. I stared at the many faces around me, but not one of them looked remotely like him. As I shuffled along the queue, new fears dogged me. The key had to be for a bag, but what if I was asked the colour or the size, I knew nothing about it. I was reassured after I saw that the people in front of me were simply handing over their tickets to the clerks without being asked any questions. The process looked simple enough; each person just handed over the ticket, the assistant disappeared and a minute or so later returned with a bag. It had to be a bag; everyone collected a bag.

I passed through the queue quickly. Soon it was the fat man's turn. I watched him check in his briefcase and then it was mine. I gave over my ticket. The clerk smiled, turned and disappeared. My heart was beating at full gallop; what was it; what was inside, another message perhaps or (my stomach cramped) it might be one of his trophies. He seemed to be gone a long time and I became even more agitated. When he came back he apologised for the delay and placed a small black leather bag on the counter. I paid him his fee and grabbed its handles. It was like a million other old holdalls, maybe a little smaller than most, but nothing special. I checked the tag to make certain it was The Sawman's. It was numbered 203. I calmed myself. All I had to do was open it. It wasn't heavy, but it wasn't light either. I shook it, nothing moved. I looked around for Cerboni. He had to be watching me, but there was no sign of him. I walked quickly towards an empty bench about 20 yards away. As I approached, a woman stopped beside it and sat down. There was enough room for us both, but I didn't feel like opening the bag in front of a stranger. There could have been anything inside and a picture of Shields' grotesque head filled my mind, so I changed direction and headed back to my car.

I unlocked the Healey's passenger door and placed the bag on the seat. I closed the door and hurriedly went round to the driver's door, unlocked it and slid inside. I closed the door and stared at the bag. I gripped the lock at the end of the fastener, put in the key and turned it. The lock opened easily and I unzipped the bag.

Inside, I could see something black and woollen. I took it out and held up a ski cap with eye slits cut into it – his mask I assumed. Next, I pulled out a scabbard and belt. I flicked off the leather retaining-strap on the scabbard and withdrew the hunting knife. It had a long steel blade with a serrated edge; a fearsome weapon. I was mindful that I was in a public car park and quickly pushed the knife back into its holder. Next I lifted out a small plastic bag containing black latex gloves. Then a new A-Z. At the bottom of the bag there was one other thing; a soft blue cloth wrapped around something small and hard. I set the cap, knife and gloves aside. I took out the parcel and slowly unwrapped it. Inside was a black mobile phone. There was a note attached that had a short message printed on it – 'Switch it on at ten'. That was all there was. I immediately checked my watch – it was only 7.20. I examined the phone carefully. Judging from the scratches it was old. I switched it on and it registered with BT. I checked the menu and looked up the message function; it was empty, neither stored calls nor telephone numbers. I switched it off. I looked at the note again. It was a small page pulled from a writing pad. The message was in black ballpoint in neat print.

I sat in the car and considered what I had been given. The phone was old, the gloves and A-Z new. I wondered whether the knife and the cap were the ones he had used to murder his victims. The knife looked too new. I placed them back in the bag with the gloves and put the note, A-Z and the phone in my pocket. I considered my position. The bag was evidence of his involvement, but irrelevant since we already knew that Cerboni was The Sawman; I was aware that he was going to make contact in a few hours, that in itself didn't mean that we would meet. I knew that I should contact Geoff. I knew that by not calling him I was putting my job at risk. None of that mattered. The old me would have simply called Wheaten and explained what I found and let him get on with it, but I wasn't the old me. I desperately wanted to seek The Sawman's help. I stored the bag in the boot, locked the car and went back inside the concourse. I bought some cigarettes and found a bar where I could smoke. I ordered a double malt and sat at an empty table in the corner.

I wanted revenge but not in the way The Sawman had planned. In truth I hadn't worked out the detail of my plan, but it didn't include murder. I had, of course, imagined myself as his accomplice, but that had been when I was fuelled by anger. I knew I couldn't murder anyone, even in my confused state I hadn't changed that much. I needed his help and I wanted to get him treatment but I was no vigilante. Still in my car I knew that I had the tools for murder. I wondered who he planned to kill and what they had done to deserve it. Whoever they were and whatever they had done, I might loathe them, but I'd never be capable of killing them, I took a slug of the Lagavulin and lit up my cigarette. I had some thinking to do and time on my hands to do it.

I knew that if I spent the rest of the evening sitting in the bar I would simply sink into an alcoholic stupor so I decided that I would go for a walk.

I had just left the main entrance when I remembered that I had parked the Healey in the short stay car park. I couldn't risk it being towed away so I transferred it to the long stay. The walking helped clear my head and get my thinking straight. I briefly reconsidered calling Geoff, but came to the conclusion that wouldn't help me get my revenge for Jennifer. If I was to have it, I had to meet Cerboni on my own. My head was pulsating with choices. I had to stop the killings. I had to help Cerboni. I needed his help with my plan. I didn't call Geoff.

I wandered along towards the city centre past more bars and clubs. The night had hardly got going, but there was already a buzz about the place. I didn't take much of it in as my mind was fully occupied with what might lay ahead. I stopped at a café bar. No alcohol, just a frothy cappuccino accompanied by a cigarette. I thought about a sandwich, but somehow I didn't feel like eating. The café was surprisingly empty and apart from some irritating music it was very peaceful. I played with the chocolate marbling on my coffee with my spoon and mulled things over. I reflected on the murderers that I had come across and pondered how many had sipped cappuccino in a café before they had slain their victim. I was sure by then that Cerboni had planned for me to assist him with murder. I recalled the autopsies that I had witnessed and Cerboni's handiwork. I speculated whether he had in mind me passing him his saw or whether I would be wielding it myself. At that point I was interrupted by the young waiter who served me my coffee. When I declined his offer of a refill I could sense that he was keen to enter into some banal conversation about the weather, so I pushed my empty coffee cup towards him, put three pound coins on the table and left. I carried on walking into the centre, stopping at Piccadilly Park where I sat down on a bench and watched the fountains spray their patterns in the wind.

Time passed slowly. After countless checking of my watch it was time to head back to the car. I was still too early. I waited out the final 45 minutes at the wheel drumming my fingers as I hummed some Teleman piece or other.

At ten o'clock precisely the phone rang.

"Hello."

"Yes Alfredo it's me."

"I'm sorry to keep you out so late, but you'll understand my work means I keep late hours."

I didn't comment.

"You have been sitting there a long time."

"You have been watching me."

"You have never been out of my sight."

I said nothing.

"It seems that I can trust you. Are you still prepared to help me."

"Yes."

"It is good that they have caught the animal that assaulted your niece, Jennifer. I suppose it was her assault that persuaded you to help me get rid of the scumbags like the pervert who attacked her. The ones who plague our children and ruin their lives."

"Where are you?"

"Oh, I'm not far. You'll see me soon if you agree to join me."

"Join you in what?"

"Our duty Dr Ahearn. We have work to do or are you going to let them carry on with their evil abuse?"

"What do I have to do?"

"In the bag is everything you need. I want you to go to a place where you will find Maffers and Kant. You remember them Dr Ahearn don't you? Raymond and Mark, you know, the men who murdered the mother, buggered her little five year old boy and beat and raped her seven year old daughter in a park. The little girl still doesn't talk. You remember; they got off with it, but you and I know they were guilty. Are you going to help me sort them this time?"

"Yes." I had to meet with him, but I would never do what he was asking.

"*Good, I will see you there. You will find the address on the back of the flyer stuck behind your bumper. Do you have your A-Z with you?*"

"Yes."

"*Good. May God be with you.*"

The phone went dead.

I got out of the car and went to the bumper. I could see the white paper. When I pulled it free I could see it was a cutting from a newspaper. On the front was a photograph of Raymond Maffers and Mark Kant pictured leaving the court-house as free men. I turned it over, on the back was written '*The Commel Commercial Zone in Salford, number 14, a grey breeze blocked building with a flat roof. Wait there.*' I looked around me to see if I could spot Cerboni – nothing.

I took the bag from the boot and got into the car. I studied the A-Z and found the location on the newspaper cutting. I put the cutting in my pocket and set off. It was probably my last chance to phone Geoff or Steve, but I was certain that Cerboni was watching. I had to maintain his trust if I was going to persuade him to seek treatment and get what I wanted.

I didn't know that area of Salford but I found the estate easily. I parked the Healey outside number 14 which was painted in large numbers on an up and over door, which was just as well as all the street lights in the estate were out. It was, however, as he had noted, a grey breeze blocked building with a flat roof, one of many among other larger steel panelled commercial buildings that made up the rest of the industrial estate. I switched off and waited.

After only a few minutes the mobile rang again.

"Listen carefully. I want you to put on the gloves and ski-cap, then walk behind number 14, take the path to the road, turn right and walk five blocks until you reach the back entrance to number 24. Do you understand?"

"Yes."

"Tell me."

"I put on the gloves and hat, take the path behind, turn right at the end and walk five blocks to number 24."

"Good."

"Do I pull the mask down?"

"No, wait until you reach the back entrance."

"Okay."

"When you get there, you will see an open window. Climb inside. Do not shout out. Do you understand?"

"Yes, when I get there I enter an open window."

"Good. Remember keep quiet and bring the knife and torch with you." The phone went dead.

I discarded my jacket in the trunk, put on the belt, gloves and the ski cap. I picked up the torch and locked the Healey. The scabbard against my leg felt unnatural and for the first time I was in fear of my life. I switched on the torch and made my way behind number 14.

I followed the overgrown path behind the building until it reached a road. I shone the torch on the buildings until I had counted five blocks. Number 24 was just the same as 14, only much shabbier. I walked gingerly along the gravelled road that led to a small car park outside the one storey building. All the windows were in darkness and there was no sign of life anywhere except for a Ford Transit van that was parked hard against the building's rear wall. It was covered in dirt and someone had wittily scrawled 'also available in white' across its back doors. I pulled the front of the Balaclava and rolled it over my face. As soon as I put on the mask my fears intensified, my muscles tensed and my grip tightened. I shone the torch over the gravel and walked across the rear courtyard to the van. I laid my hand on the bonnet. It was cold. It was impossible to tell whether it had been there a couple of hours or a couple of days.

I scanned the building, as would a burglar, slowly and deliberately. I found the open window on the far off corner on the ground floor. Spiders' webs laced the edges of the frame, but I could see that it would have been easy for Cerboni to break in. A metal grill of wiremesh, a cheap and pathetic disguise at security had been pulled or levered clear. The old window was split into three, a hinged top section, a smaller window that opened out and a fixed main section. From the top Cerboni, would have been able to reach the inner handle on the smaller window. My job was relatively simple. I grasped the frame stretched to my full height and pulled myself up until my head was inside. After that it was an undignified wriggle and a drop head first into the room.

I landed with a soft thud. I sat for a few seconds, listened and waited, half expecting Cerboni to be standing there in the gloom. When my eyes adjusted I could see he wasn't. I stood upright. Even with my torch it was difficult to see where I was. The air was heavy and dank. The beam shone on the walls, revealing painted concrete blocks, a water closet and sink. I had come through a toilet block window. The smell was not of human waste, but dampness and decay, but it made me want to pee. I relieved myself. The porcelain was cracked and crazed like mosaic. I was careful to keep the gushing as quiet as possible by aiming for the sides to diffuse the sound, only slightly disturbing the placid water as I splashed the age old brown stains that lay like coral just underneath the surface.

I instinctively went to wash, but drew back my latexed hand before I reached the tap. I wasn't sure what to do next, whether to wait for Cerboni, shout for him or go looking for him. I chose the latter.

The adrenaline rush spurred me on. With the hunting knife already drawn, I opened the door and surveyed the large open space in front of me. In the far off corner, the walls were sooty black, scorched by an old fire. The place smelled like wet potato peelings and damp newspaper. Long brown stains from the rusting window frames streaked down the walls like mascara on a tear soaked face. An old fluorescent light fitting, mapped by a rusty conduit pipe, dangled from the ceiling, the tube long gone. The only signs of life were the spider webs, the dead flies and beetles that lay naked in their open cemetery.

In the gloomy light I spied the stairs to my right and started to climb the concrete treads, my long steel blade scouting ahead of me. At the top I stopped and listened, but I could hear nothing other than my own breathing. The three doors along the corridor were all open or missing. I peered in the first opening. Even in the dark I could see that it was empty apart from a rusted metal office desk and a filing cabinet missing most of its drawers. The next room was also empty apart from a dirty double mattress and bundled bedding. I carried on towards the last. In that room there was a small wooden table and three plastic chairs. Behind those were two jackets hanging on hooks. The rest of the room was bare. I flicked on my flashlight, walked over to the jackets and inspected them. A rifle through the pocket revealed a few odd receipts, a set of Honda car keys and a few pound coins. Jacket sleeves, but no arms, car keys but no Honda and no Cerboni. I was puzzled. I put the contents of the pockets back and went back to the stairs.

When I got to the bottom I ignored the door to the toilet block and walked gingerly into the main open space. Again the place looked deserted. There was nothing except papers that looked like old invoices strewn across the floor. I rubbed my head and turned to go back the way I came when I heard a muffled scream. It was dull yet high pitched. I swivelled my body around following my knife in the general direction of the noise, but saw nothing. That was when I heard the whacking sound, faint, but unmistakable, then another and another. I waved the torch around the room. There was nothing. Then I saw it. It was the outline of a trap door in the floor at the far side of the room. A trap door, a no hiding place door, a here-I-am-to-be-caught trap door. I wasn't certain what to do. I decided it was best to play it safe.

I crossed the floor, walked around the grooved outline and then took a few steps backwards until I rested my back against the wall. I switched off the flashlight and cloaked myself in darkness. There I faced the trap door and waited, but not for long. I heard footsteps, then the door hinged up, yawning light into the room, lighting half the ceiling and the wall furthest from me. With the light came noises: whimpering, sniffling and sobbing sounds, rustling of clothing and padding of feet. I pushed back into the skin of the darkness gripping my knife tightly. A thin scruffy, sweaty man appeared in the light. In the same instance someone from behind sent me flying to the floor, knocking the knife from my hand. As I fell to the floor, I saw the black shape plunge a knife into the emerging body. The face was Maffers and the black clothed man could only have been Cerboni.

In the same move Cerboni had one hand over Maffers' mouth cutting his scream while his other hand thrust the blade into his victim's belly. I watched him twist the blade upwards spilling Maffers' guts. As he did so the trap door fell from Maffers hands and banged shut. Almost immediately a bass voice rumbled through the floor: "What are you doing, do you want to wake the whole fucking neighbourhood?"

Cerboni lowered the limp body to the floor and signalled for me to be quiet.

I lay there in silence while Cerboni, using Maffers' arms as handles, dragged his limp body towards the toilets. Maffers' head lolled from side to side and his legs made a hissing sound like a snake as he was pulled into the dark. Cerboni stooped to lower the head and upper torso gently to the floor and then started to walk back in the direction of the trapdoor. He had only taken a few paces when the trap-door began to rise and the light from below reached out.

Out of the yellow light a head appeared and looked straight at me, but for the moment, as the head's eyes adjusted to the dark, I was invisible to the stare. The door opened to its full height and I identified the face – it was Mark Kant.

"Who the fuck..." Kant shouted.

Cerboni dived at the head and upper body and they tumbled down through the floor entwined. I got up and rushed to the opening. At the bottom of half a dozen steps I could see them grappling with each other and then separate. The knife had been knocked from Cerboni's hand and his advantage of surprise gone. Kant was quick to take in his predicament. He reached for an iron bar nearby as Cerboni searched for his knife. Kant's back was to me, but I could see him get ready to wield his strike. I picked up my knife and ran down the stairs, but before I got close Kant had turned and I was thumped by the swinging bar across my left shoulder. My body in freefall dropped on Kant sending him backwards. That was the last thing I remembered.

Kant gets to his feet quickly and prepares to swing again this time at Cerboni, as he does so, Alfredo lunges. Kant sees the knife and tries to sidestep its blade causing it to miss its destined target, his heart. Cerboni's thrust takes him past Kant and his head cracks against the stone wall, sending him to the floor. Kant stands stiff, his body is in shock, but feels no pain even though the razor sharp steel of Cerboni's knife has sliced open a deep wound at the base of his neck when it was deflected over his shoulder. Cerboni staggers to his feet and brings his hand with the knife up to support his throbbing head. Kant sways, drops his weapon and covers his weeping neck with his hands. Kant's face contorts and blood from the neck wound spurts between his fingers and hands. As Kant gurgles and spits blood, seemingly unable to fall, Cerboni watches and gets ready for another attack. Kant teeters and then crashes against the steps. His head comes to rest against a tread where his blood pumping rhythmically in crimson plumes, spills across its surface and cascades to the step below.

Cerboni approaches Ahearn's prostrate body and crouches down beside it. He rolls back the mask, pulls it clear and studies Ahearn's unconsciousness. His gloved fingers feel for a pulse on his neck. The slight sensation of pumping blood convinces him that he is alive, but out cold. He pulls him clear of the steps. He hears the whimper. He follows the sound and advances further into the basement.

The walls of the basement are those of a modern day dungeon; instead of grey stone there is grey breeze block; no windows anywhere, just a single suspended light bulb. Instruments of torture lay all around. As he turns the corner he sees that he has company. In the full glare of the light, two young women, one sobbing and the other dead or unconscious, are hanging manacled by their hands against the wall. The face gags; their naked bodies; it takes a few seconds for him to understand what is happening. The heavy bruising makes it difficult for him to tell their age, but they are as thin as toothpicks, slender and youthful. These are not yet women, but young girls.

Slowly it dawns on him that the girls are the two who have been reported kidnapped. They are unexpected. He moves towards them still holding his arm and grasping the knife. As he reaches the first girl he sees the terror and fear in her red and tear soaked eyes. Sawman returns the knife to its sheaf and signals with his open palm and a hushing sound that he means her no harm. He walks to the other girl. He feels for a pulse; a tiny throb, but that apart she remains lifeless. He reaches up to the manacles. He uselessly tugs at them, then returns to Kant's body and flips it over. He puts his hand in Kant's trouser pocket and pulls out a set of keys for the van. He puts them in his pocket. He can hear the muffled screams behind him. He checks Kant's other pocket and finds what he is looking for; it's another set of keys.

He returns to the first girl and pulls off his masked Balaclava. Sawman looks deeply into the soft blue irises and tries to convey reassurance, but they manage only pity. He breathes heavily as he unlocks her manacles, catching the girl in one arm as she falls towards the floor. Her head falls against his shoulder and he lowers her gently to the ground. He wraps his coat around her shoulders, loosens her gag and tells her: "You're safe. Your friend needs your help."

She nods and confirms obedience with her eyes. Then he moves over to the other girl who throughout has remained unconscious.

He loosens her manacles and falls with her as her dead weight slips on top of him.

"Don't leave her, I will get help and be back." He gets up and heads for the stairs.

He walks to the stairs, passes the corpse and climbs. He crosses the room and picks up his rucksack. He carries it to where Maffers lays, drops to one knee and opens the bag. He takes out the saw and takes a huge breath. He works quickly. He walks to the washbasin where he rinses his latex- gloved hands. He takes a sheaf of paper towels and returns to Maffers. He wraps his work in the paper and carries it upstairs to the bedroom. With one hand he pulls the blanket and the dirty blue sheet from the bed and then drops the paper package onto the mattress. He trails the blanket and sheet behind him as he retraces his steps to the basement, stopping to collect the saw.

He lays the saw beside Kant and then walks towards the girls. He covers the unconscious girl with the blanket. Takes back his coat and passes the sheet around the other who stares back at him.

"Keep your eyes closed until the police arrive. Okay?"

She nods compliance.

"It will be over soon I promise," he says.

He returns to Kant and begins his work. He takes only a few minutes.

The Sawman walks to his rucksack and puts the saw inside. He looks around the room. A bloody headless body on the stairs, a young naked girl in a foetal position and another lies prostrate. He collects his bag and crosses to Rob Ahearn. He reaches inside his bag and removes his cellphone and a small bottle. He unscrews the top and holds the bottle under Ahearn's nose. "Rob. Rob."

I saw the outline of a face.

"Rob." My face was slapped hard. My breathing was slow and deliberate like a dirty telephone call. I didn't know where I was.

"Rob, it is Alfredo. You are okay."

"Alfredo?" I looked at the face staring at me. It was the face in my painting.

"I am sorry to disturb… your sleep."

"What's going on? What are you doing here?" My voice was a noisy whisper rising and falling.

"Just God's work."

At his side was something large wrapped in paper.

"What, what's happening?" I asked and immediately felt an excruciating pain shoot though my left shoulder. My head felt crushed.

"I think that you might have broken your collarbone when you fell. Here, sit up."

He helped me sit up and I rested my back against the wall and tried to think.

"You're not cut out for this are you?" His eyes looked deep into mine as he smiled. "There isn't much time."

Cerboni punched 999 into his cellphone.

"Hello. I need the police and ambulance. Hello, my name is Alfredo Cerboni I am in Salford and I have found your two young girls."

I could hear a mumbled voice.

"The two… the two who were abducted. The schoolgirls, Fern and Alice."

There were more mumbled questions.

"I think so."

"I am in the Commel Commercial Zone number … 14. These girls need help bad. They have been messed up by a couple of evil bastards. They need a couple of ambulances here quick. And Dr Ahearn is here too. I am afraid he got in my way. I had to hit him." There was another mumbled question.

"He's alright, just his collarbone," he switched off his phone and turned to me.

"An ambulance is on its way."

"What have I done?"

"Nothing. And don't worry about me, I have immediate remission of these sins."

"What?"

"Listen, there isn't much time. I called you to meet me here and when you got here you saw the body, disturbed me and then I hit you with a bar. I am sorry but I had no choice."

"Did I kill them?"

"What? No, I killed them. You were trying to stop me."

"I can't…"

"Rob, I killed them. Okay? It is a little complicated, there are two girls back there. I have to go now."

"Wait… give yourself up."

"That is not possible."

"Rob, are you okay?" I felt my face being slapped.

"Steve?" I could hear sirens screaming. "What's happening?"

"We know all about it. We have just had Cerboni on the phone. He called 999 to tell us he found the missing schoolgirls in a depot in Commel Commercial Zone. 14. He has killed at least two men who I think were the girls' abductors and he said he laid you out. I got here just ahead of the ambulances."

"Wait, wait just a minute. Say that again."

"The Sawman, remember him? He has found the two missing schoolgirls, Fern and Alice. He has also killed their abductors. He's the one that banged you on the head. Rob, what are you doing here? Never mind, we'll talk in a minute."

He left me with a paramedic. I had failed. My plan for revenge was no further forward.

The place was crawling with policemen and paramedics. I was helped to my feet and escorted through the broken front doors to a waiting ambulance. From my perch on the back I saw the stretchers carrying the girls emerge from the building followed by Steve and Dawn. The girls disappeared inside their ambulance and then Dawn jumped in with them before the doors closed and it sped off.

I was given a thorough checkover. My collarbone was okay. My shoulder was just badly bruised. I was told that my blood pressure was low and they wanted to take me to the hospital to have it checked out. I was still in the back when Steve came to see me.

"Rob, are you alright?"

"I'm fine. How are those poor girls?"

"I don't know, they have taken them to the hospital. What the hell happened here?"

"I don't know. I got a call from Cerboni to meet him and …" I shook my head. Lies welled up in my throat and constricted my voice to a squeak. Also, my stomach turned over at the thought that I could have committed premeditated murder.

As the paramedic bandaged my shoulder and placed my arm in a sling, Steve told me what he thought had happened. He thought that Cerboni had come in through the back window sometime before I arrived, killed Maffers as he came out of the trap door, pulled his body clear and then fought with Kant on the stairway to the basement. Kant had been knifed in the neck and had probably died immediately. Cerboni had found the girls, released them and then had removed Kant and Maffers' heads and penis. He had left those parts in a bedroom upstairs from where he had taken some bedding with which he had covered the girls. He surmised that I had disturbed him around then. As I lay unconscious Sawman had dialled 999. Steve wasn't sure whether Cerboni had been injured in the fights, but he had been fit enough to call the police and make his escape.

I was badly shaken up and my and recollection of events was unclear, Steve's theory made sense, but somewhere in my head I remembered it differently.

"Rob." Geoff appeared behind Steve. "Are you okay?"

I nodded.

"Good, then maybe you can tell me what you were doing here. Why did he ring you?" Geoff asked.

"I can't remember. I think he wanted me to help him, maybe he wanted to turn himself in. I know. I should have called."

"Why the hell didn't you?"

"I don't know. Maybe there wasn't time. Maybe he said come alone. I can't remember." And it was true I couldn't remember. "I wanted him to give himself up."

"You are in the middle of a police investigation, what were you thinking about? Are you stupid or just crazy? I want to know why you didn't call me or Steve when Cerboni contacted you."

"I don't know, I can't remember," I said.

"Well you better start to remember." His face was red with anger. "Where are the girls?" he shouted at Steve.

"The girls are on their way to hospital escorted by Dawn and Paul Casson," he replied.

"I have to get over there," Geoff responded. "And you," he said pointing at me. "You'd better get your thinking cap on. You've got a lot of explaining to do."

"What about his victims?" I asked, pathetically trying to change the subject.

"Victims? Those were scum. He probably saved the girls. That's what this crowd are saying already." Geoff glanced over his shoulder at a bank of reporters.

"Well that's true, although I am not so sure he planned to. I think he found them when he was going about his usual work," Steve said.

"Where is he?" I asked; my head throbbed.

"I think he will make a bolt for Scotland or a ferry to Ireland or France," Steve answered.

"Then let's catch him and put an end to this. With the girls back safe this could be a pretty good week if we catch The Sawman. And as for you," Geoff said threateningly, back on my case, "when you are all finished here I want a full statement. After, take him back to his hotel," he said to Steve, then to me, "but I want to see you again at seven sharp. We have a press conference tomorrow at nine and you will clear this matter up for me before then. I want you in my office by seven with a full explanation for all this."

I dropped my head and wished him to go.

"And another thing," Geoff said. I looked up.

"If he rings you again you put him on hold and call me straightaway." He said sarcastically.

Sore head or not, I was interviewed by Steve in the back of his car and as far as possible I stuck to the truth. I think. There were two versions in my head. I recounted the one that Steve suggested. It was shorter than the other one in my head because of a number of omissions: the note, the key, the first cellphone conversation, the locker, the message, the photographs, the mask, the knife, the entry, the murders and my meeting with Alfredo. I told them about the call at the hotel and climbing in the rear window. After that I only recalled being shaken by Steve. He seemed happy with it.

When my statement was recorded Steve called through to Dawn. She was at the hospital waiting to speak to the girls who were being examined by the doctors. Dawn told him that one of the girls, Alice Thimmel had been unconscious during the ambulance ride, but her vitals had been good. The other girl, Fern Johnson, wouldn't say much except that she had repeated that Cerboni had saved them. I was relieved.

My shoulder was aching and my head was thumping, but I had to have another look. Steve agreed to show me around. There was a cadre of media hounds at the perimeter, but the police were doing a good job keeping them out. I ignored their shouts and questions as I went back inside. We could hardly move for forensic people, but there was no sign of my friends from Special Branch. Ulis had arrived and was stomping all over the place as though he had personally freed the girls. Lights had been rigged up and a bloody body was lying flat out. The head was missing, as were his hands and penis, but I knew it was Raymond Maffers. His body was positioned like a bloody sacrifice, a beast not a lamb. In the basement was another mutilated body, Mark Kant; his head, hands and penis were missing too. The paint on the walls in the basement had long since faded, there were vertical seams of damp every foot or so. I could see the gruesome hanging chains and manacles. There were filthy bloody blankets on the floor and several torture instruments. The smell of sex, blood and sweat was overpowering.

We walked upstairs. In the second of the rooms I saw the missing heads. On the dirty double mattress and bundled bedding. They were lying cheek to cheek. Maffers' eyes were missing, but Kant's brown eyes were still there although they looked a little pronounced. The two shrivelled bloody penises were tucked under their chins.

20. Premeditated murder

Tuesday, 26th September – Day sixteen

Thanks to painkillers I managed a good night's sleep, no flash-backs, no nightmares, just sleep, but during the taxi ride to Chester House I started to worry. If the other version in my head was right, they were sure to find my footprints in the basement, they must have been all over the place and the girl was bound to mention that there were two Sawmen. I got there just before seven and Steve met me at the front door.

"Morning, you look good. How's the shoulder?" Steve asked as we walked towards Geoff's office.

"Sore, but okay. I guess it was a late night."

"I haven't been home."

"Was there that much to do?"

"You haven't heard?" I looked blank. "We fished Melnar out of the river. His throat had been cut, so he won't be talking."

"Not Cerboni?"

"No, the head was still in place. He had been dead for a few days. The post mortem report should be available in an hour or so."

We got into the lift.

"What are your thoughts?"

"Well, with the water it's difficult to say, but it looks like the same MO as the Rogerson killing."

"Beale?"

"Possibly."

"At least it's one less scumbag to worry about."

"Anyway, do you want the good news or the better news?"

"Let's have the good first," I said.

"Well, we have already figured out how he got out of there," (I was tempted to say a dirty white Ford Transit van but I didn't). "DVLA records showed that a white transit van was registered to Kant, but we didn't find any car keys on Maffers or Kant. The manager from the company from across the way told us that the transit van had been parked there for about a week. He thought that it had been abandoned."

"And the better news?"

"We found Cerboni's car and Forensics have identified a blood stain on the side of the brake pedal of Cerboni's car."

"And …"

"It matches Shields'."

He brought me up to speed. The police believed that the girls had been holed up in the basement from the day that they had been abducted. They found newspapers from the very next day in the upstairs room. They also found a lot of take away empties and lots of crushed beer and soda cans, which suggested that they had been there quite some time.

There was no mention of two Sawmen. I felt relieved; my only worry was Cerboni. He was on the loose and I wasn't sure what he would do when the police found him. My naïve hopes of revenge had gone, but I had to find him and have him certified before any trial.

When we arrived at Geoff's office, he wasn't there. Relieved, I waited with Steve outside. A few minutes later we were joined by Dawn.

"Hi, waiting to see Geoff?" she said. I nodded. "I'm just back from the hospital."

"How are the schoolgirls?" I asked.

"The Thimmel girl has come around. Not saying much, they are keeping her sedated. The Johnson girl identified Cerboni, but that was about all. She claims that he had saved her. She saw Cerboni fight with Kant and thought that he might be injured."

"Nothing new then?" Steve asked.

"Got some good news. I've heard from Tommy Lee. He says that Cerboni was Sega and that he left messages on the 'Sweet Dreams' site using his *nom de plume*." It wasn't news to me of course.

"Great," I said.

My new found confidence disappeared when Geoff arrived. The interview turned out to be a nightmare.

It was clear that the abbreviated version of the events had left doubts, so I provided more detail such as being confused at first when I got the call, and I freely admitted that I wasn't thinking straight, which was true. Also, I told them about the pee and the walk up the stairs – I had no choice they had already identified my footprints, but the main omissions from the night before were again left out.

"This doesn't make sense. You had your mobile with you, yet you never called us; you must have just about climbed over Kant's transit, yet you didn't mention it last night; you searched the place and you didn't hear or see Maffers or Kant."

"I told you, I can't remember. Christ, I had my head banged up remember."

"I have no difficulty remembering, it's you who has the memory lapse," he said accusingly. "What about Maffers' body?"

"What about it?"

"You must have seen it when you came out of the toilet."

"I think I went straight up the stairs."

"If you didn't fall over it going up you must have when you came back down."

"I've told you I didn't see it. I remember hearing the noise of the trapdoor being lifted up and then I was hit by someone." I rubbed my shoulder seeking sympathy, but Geoff's eyes never flinched.

"Was it Cerboni?" he asked, his jaw thrusting towards me.

"I don't know," I squirmed.

"So you don't remember Cerboni slugging you?" Geoff asked.

"No." Not in that version I didn't.

"But you said to Steve last night that as soon you looked in the trapdoor you were hit by someone, you didn't see Cerboni, you didn't see Maffers you hadn't seen the girls, what did you see?" His voice was loud and his tone hissed in exasperation.

"Kant with his head cut off. Is that enough? What is this, what are you trying to prove here?" I shouted.

"I want to know why you didn't call me and what you were doing there." He was deadly serious. His eyes pierced me and his voice trembled with anger.

"I told you. I thought if I met him on his own I could talk him into giving up."

"What do you take me for Ahearn? You are supposed to be an intelligent man. You knew how dangerous he was; what

315

did you think might happen when you met this psychopath? Are you expecting me to believe that you were simply going to have a coffee and convince him over a cosy chat to give himself up? Do me a favour."

"I thought that I might. Look, I'm not stupid and neither is Cerboni. He would spot any police presence before we got near him and scamper. I admit I wanted to have a word with him, before you spoke to him, to try and get him to seek psychiatric help before it was too late."

"I think that's bullshit and you know it. I don't know what foolhardy scheme you had in mind, but I know you had one and it wasn't getting Cerboni to give himself up. I warn you, if my lads turn up any evidence that suggests that you were involved in some way with these killings I'll do everything I can to see that you are charged as an accomplice and you'll spend a long time remembering who it was that brought you into this case. Right, that's all for now, but if anything else comes to mind, you better let me know. In the meantime, I want your mobile phone. You wouldn't want your personal number to be used by a murderer would you?"

"What if he calls?"

"If your story is right, I don't think that's likely, do you? After all, he could have killed you with that crowbar. I want the phone under constant tap if a call from him comes for you we will route it to you after we are certain the call is both recorded and traced."

When I came out of Geoff's room I was shaking, some of it was anger, but most of it was fear. I followed Geoff to the Chief Constable's office. The Chief Constable, his Assistant Ulis and Chester were already deep in conversation when we arrived. The Chief Constable shook me by the hand and welcomed me to the meeting. He thanked me for turning up so promptly after my ordeal. Just then I wasn't sure whether he was referring to the murders or my interview with Geoff. He told us that Ulis was to lead the conference although he would make himself available to answer any questions that contained any criticism of Greater Manchester Police's role in the investigation. I wasn't asked to play a part. Ulis had already decided that Geoff was to handle everything, apart from a brief introduction by the Chief Constable. The presentation was to be short and to the point. We were seeking the arrest of Alfredo Cerboni in connection with the murders of Kant and Maffers whom we suspected were involved in the abduction of the two schoolgirls, Fern Johnson and Alice Thimmel. Both girls were now with their parents and being cared for by hospital staff. Ulis was going to handle questions about the girls and Geoff was to field those about the murders and Cerboni. Geoff was also to explain the assistance I had provided to his officers under my role as a representative of the Home Office, which would, by necessity, be confined to my input to the broad strategy of the investigation. I was not to answer any specific questions concerning Kant's or Maffers' murder on the grounds that the matter was subjudice. Chester was quiet throughout, seemingly happy to take a back seat in The Sawman case and at Ulis' direction concentrate on Beale who was to be taken in for questioning about the Melnar murder. For once we all agreed on something, Beale was the most likely suspect.

There was already a sizeable crowd waiting in the conference room and outside I could hear the chants.

"Sawman, Sawman, Sawman."

I looked out the window and saw what looked like a huge gospel gathering. They were waving banners with 'The Sawman Saves' or 'Save the Sawman'. I pitied the officer that had to arrest him.

The media had already painted Sawman as a brave hero and a compassionate crusader. They had him risking his life to save the girls from a couple of depraved monsters armed with guns while he only had a hunting knife. The emotions were turned up with heart-rending accounts from victims of rape and sexual abuse, their tales of misery emphasising his beneficence and the perilous nature of his mission. Each paid tribute to Cerboni's courage in mounting a one-man vigilante force to punish the perpetrators of perversion and abuse. The news reports stopped short of glorifying his murders, but you were left with the impression that they would have liked him to receive the freedom of the city or a medal.

I wore a new shirt and tie and had shaved. It wasn't for the cameras; it was for Sawman. I wanted to get a message to him that strengthened our mutual empathy. I had learned that he was always immaculately turned out with a fresh shirt and a different suit each day. I didn't know where he was, but I was confident, that wherever he was, he would see me.

We took our places behind a long table: the Chief Constable flanked by Chester and Ulis. The Chief Constable spoke first.

"Good morning, thank you for waiting. Last night at 2.30 our officers responded to a mobile telephone call traced to a redundant unit in the Commel Commercial Zone in Salford where I am pleased to say we found the two missing school-girls, Alice Thimmel and Fern Johnson, both of whom are now in the safe custody of their parents under the watchful care of hospital staff."

There was a barrage of questions from the reporters.

"Please allow me to finish. I have allowed for questions at the end." There was quiet. "Now, I can advise that the latest bulletin from the hospital confirms that, although both girls have suffered a traumatic experience, they are making good progress towards recovery. I can add that each is receiving treatment for serious physical injuries, but both are expected to make a full recovery. The hospital administrator will issue a full progress report after this conference. I will now ask Assistant Chief Constable Ulis to provide you with details of the operation carried out at Salford."

The Chief Constable sat down and Bob Ulis rose to his feet.

"At the unit in Commel, our detectives under the direction of Detective Chief Superintendent Geoff Wheaton and supported by Dr Rob Ahearn of the Home Office, discovered the bodies of two men, Raymond Maffers and Mark Kant. We have evidence linking these two men with the abduction of the two schoolgirls, Fern Johnson and Alice Thimmel. I would now like to hand over to Detective Chief Superintendent Wheaton."

Geoff took over the podium.

"Good morning. As Chief Ulis mentioned, a squad of my detectives under my direction responded to a call for assistance from a caller at unit 14 of the Commel Commercial Zone. On arrival, we found the bodies of two white males, 32 years old Raymond Maffers and 36 years old Mark Kant."

The questions blasted.

"Please ladies and gentlemen allow me to finish. We believe that both men were the victims of the serial killer responsible for seven previous murders. Unfortunately, Cerboni had fled the scene before he could be apprehended. I will be pleased to take questions now."

"Tracey Steadman, BBC. Are you certain that the kidnappers were the two men murdered."

"Our investigations are continuing, but at this moment we believe that both men were responsible for the kidnapping of Miss Thimmel and Miss Johnson."

"John Bilsen, ITV News. Assistant Chief Constable Ulis issued an arrest warrant for Alfredo Cerboni at the last press conference. Was there any response to his public appeal for knowledge of Cerboni's whereabouts?"

"Our Control Centre has taken a huge number of calls from the public reporting sightings but at this stage I am not prepared to comment on any specific leads, which we are following as part of our operation."

"What about the DNA match with Luis Beale?" Geoff ignored the follow on question and took another.

"Chris Channing of GMTV. Is Cerboni the murderer?"

"If you are referring to Raymond Maffers and Mark Kant we have issued an arrest warrant for Alfredo Cerboni for the murder of both of these men. We also wish to interview Mr Cerboni in connection with the murders of Alexi Zochten, John Conran, Ernst Muche, Luis Shields, Charles Reglen, Elliot Colson and Maria Cerboni. Alfredo Cerboni is a white male aged 42. You are being circulated a recent photograph of Alfredo Cerboni together with a press release detailing last night's operation. We would also like to hear from anyone who knows the whereabouts of a 1996 white Ford Transit van license NY 98GH. There will be a further press conference at five o'clock when I will update you on our progress and allow more questions."

"One last question Chief Superintendent." It was Chris Channing of GMTV again.

"The call you received for assistance, was this a 999 call?"

"Yes."

"Was it Mr Cerboni who called?"

"Yes." There was a barrage of questions again. But Channing managed to get his next one over.

"Is it true that Mr Cerboni contacted Dr Ahearn directly on his mobile?"

"I am afraid this part of the conference is over, I'll hand you back to Chief Ulis."

"As you will appreciate our officers are still investigating these crimes therefore please excuse Detective Chief Superintendent Wheaton and Dr Ahearn. I will be pleased to answer questions on the safe return of the schoolgirls."

I wasn't allowed to take a single question. I got back to my office checked with Dawn and there was still no sign of Cerboni despite the fact that his face had been splashed on all the TV news bulletins. I was given my mobile back and a new handset. I was assured that any calls to my old mobile would be recorded and traced. Any callers other than Cerboni to that handset were to be referred to the other mobile. I wondered if he would call again.

Most of the afternoon was spent hanging around the incident desk in the communication centre, exciting for the first hour as calls came in detailing sightings of Cerboni, but when these turned out to be a postman, a dentist and an elderly woman who worked as a lollipop lady, my early enthusiasm blunted. Still it was difficult to believe with all the publicity that Cerboni hadn't been found.

I returned to my hotel around seven feeling a little despondent. As I plodded up the stairs the less than charming receptionist shouted me back. She had a face that would have suited a Vietnamese pot bellied pig. She pointed to a small envelope with my name scribbled on it. I took it upstairs.

There was something square and hard inside. I opened it. It was a package of CDs with the message 'cast them out'. I set up my laptop and loaded the first disc: it contained a list of names from A-D including, Conran and Colson. I selected Conran. I was staggered by the amount of detailed information. It was all there, his police file, his arrest file, description, address and a diary of his movements. It included where he went, who he saw and what he did. Each name I entered provided similar comprehensive information. Most importantly, each had details of their membership of 'Sweet Dreams' including the pseudonym used to access the site. I selected another name among the scores of others on the list. James Crasteine was a 55 year old councillor for Blackburn, married, no children. His pseudonym was Lugosi. I entered it on the 'Sweet Dreams' site putting in the password noted on his file when prompted – 31257Bela. After a few minutes I was provided with a list of categories including stimulation, voyeurism, sadism, torture, carnivores and bestiality. When I clicked on 'torture' I was provided with another list of pseudonyms. I clicked on 'just William' and a photograph of a boy appeared. It was difficult to gauge his age, but most certainly he was under 15. Below his photograph was the heading availability and when pressed a calendar like those used on hotel booking sites came up. Most of the dates were already booked.

Many of the members had attachments to their file. Those showed video clips of sexual abuse, many clearly identified the face of the victim and the perpetrator. There was also an index of references in each member's file, which I couldn't fathom.

I was shocked by this cesspit of depravity. I had witnessed some horrible sights in my time but my ten minutes spent reading was in a different world to the one that I inhabited. The horror of this club for voracious perverts gripped me like absinthe. How Cerboni had accessed the information I could only hazard a guess. If it was accurate, I was confident that the police could arrest many more paedophiles, rapists and possibly even murderers.

He had it all: the who, where, what and when. I contacted Geoff. No answer. I tried Steve again no answer. Dawn responded immediately. I told her what I had and she said that she would contact Geoff and come to my hotel. Very soon after, Dawn collected me and the discs. We went straight to Chester House where we were met by Geoff and a squad of detectives.

There was much looking over of shoulders as computer analysts from Vice reviewed copies of the discs. Two teams analysed and sorted the data, one looking at the members' list and the other identifying victims. There were shouts of 'yes' as the files revealed evidence to prosecute, although the atmosphere remained subdued; the horrific images too unsettling to allow exuberance to take hold. I gave up at three in the morning. My plan had been to work with Cerboni to unearth such a list and find evidence of their paedophilia. I thought that it would have taken all my skills as a psychologist to unearth it, as it turned out all I had to do was open an envelope. Still, I had my revenge.

I returned to the office about nine. They were all still there. They had worked through the night. Geoff brought me up to speed with what they had found and told me that they expected to make over 200 arrests, starting that morning. There was still no sign of Cerboni and I wondered where he was and what he was up to, but not for long, ten minutes later my cellphone buzzed.

"Rob Ahearn."

"Dr Ahearn, you got my present."

"Alfredo."

"I hope it was what you wanted."

"Yes, thank you. Alfredo where are you?"

"Not far, but I got to go now. I wanted to wish you well. You looked very smart on television. I am glad it will be you who tidies up after me. Removes the creeps that abuse our women and children. Our streets should be a little bit safer now don't you agree?" I didn't answer. "We couldn't let them carry on could we?" Again I said nothing. Steve came into my office and signalled that they were taping the call. To protect him I had to take control of the call, but before I did Alfredo unburdened himself.

"You understand I had no choice about the killings. I tried to keep my anger and grief locked up. They called me a sissy, and a queer. When they read about me now they will see me differently. The reporters said I did a good job. Our Lord knows what I did and will forgive what I have to do. I am sorry that your young officers had to witness their disgusting sex parlours.

324

I wish it hadn't been necessary. I had tried to do it differently, but you wouldn't let me."

"What do you mean?"

"Not you Dr Ahearn, Greater Manchester Police. I applied to them, but they wouldn't take me."

I should have guessed as much; I knew that the most coveted role of roaming psychopaths was a position of authority. "You know it's funny, we could have made a great team, you and me. We could have stopped them together. It's up to you now. My work is finished."

"Alfredo, I need to see you."

"There is nothing I would like better, but it is too late. I've got to go. Chio."

"Fuck. Fuck. Fuck," I shouted.

Steve and Dawn were on the other side of the window.

Steve mouthed "We've got him." Steve wasn't to know that wasn't what I wanted. I was worried for Cerboni and wanted him to get help.

Steve burst in. "We've got a location. He's still in the city. In the GMex."

My stomach churned and lungs pumped hard as we dashed to Steve's car. Dawn took the wheel while Steve busied himself with the radio.

"Cordon off the GMex and MICC complex" – the combined exhibition and international convention centres in the heart of the city – he shouted. "Seal every entrance and exit."

Ulis and Geoff were in the Jaguar that closed up behind us.

We sped towards Deansgate along Chester Road. Our car slid in and out of the traffic, causing a few drivers to check their pacemakers. Dawn drove at breathtaking speed, slipping the steering wheel through her palms without touching the steering spokes. Steve was on his mobile.

"Shit, all three halls are being used. There must be thousands of people on the site," Steve shouted as he slammed his hand on the dashboard. Adrenaline painting his face purple. "He's not getting away. No one gets in or out," he commanded and ended the call. "They'll be no more 'God's work,'" he said to us.

Just then I wasn't concerned with 'God's work', I already knew it was over, Steve, however, didn't understand. Steve had missed the significance of Cerboni's statement 'Lord will forgive what I have to do,' I hadn't.

Steve was screaming orders into the radio and putting on a flack jacket. When he had it on, he pulled down the glove compartment and took out a pistol.

"What are going to do with that?" I shouted. I grabbed the handrail as we slued into Whitworth Street.

"I'm not taking any chances," he called back over his shoulder.

Before I could say anything else, we screeched to a halt at the main entrance to GMex. The place was full of men and women in suits. I jumped out of the car fast, but I was still yards behind Steve who raced ahead like an Olympic runner. My years of cigarettes made certain that I was a spectator. Dawn passed me before we reached the entrance to the main hall. My eyes scanned the cathedral-like roof with its maze of metal and glass; finding one person there wasn't going to be easy. Steve, still at full speed, screamed at the visitors to get out of his way. It took less than a minute to get to the MICC Auditorium where Cerboni was last sighted. A throng of business people packed the thoroughfare to the main entry points. We were redirected on the run to the side where we entered a large door that led directly to an enormous stage. Our growing group of trackers slowed to a halt in the middle of the elevated conference platform as we spilled onto the stage in front of a sea of faces occupying plush red seats that rose all the way to the roof. There must have been over 500 of them staring at our amateurish performance. The hubbub ceased; the uneasy quiet broken by a loud shout from behind me that came from Geoff Wheaton who was issuing commands and instructions. The noise resumed again as we divided into two at his direction. One half dashed stage right, the other left as we filed into the auditorium via the side stairs.

The pace slowed as the lines of officers climbed the passages between the rows of seats. The police were shouting to everyone to sit down as they scanned the audience for one face – The Sawman.

We swept from the bottom to the top gallery, but there was no sign of him. A shout from Steve told us that he had been spotted on the upper terrace and the race was on again only this time there were new pacemakers, two conference security men. Our guides took us back out of the auditorium and through the concourse. As we neared the terrace an elderly man shouted that he had seen The Sawman run out the exit onto the terrace, how he knew it was The Sawman no one stopped to ask, we just followed in the direction of his pointing finger. We dashed through the doors onto the outside terrace. There were only three people on the terrace, a man and two women, one of whom was being comforted by the other two, but I still didn't spot Sawman. The man raised a hand and pointed over the barrier. I looked over. The race was over.

I had seen jumpers before, but never any that had landed in a tree. A sycamore cradled Alfredo's body, his limbs hanging limply like a scarecrow, peaceful and still. The green and yellow-brown leaves garlanded his head and shone his face towards the onlookers. His very dark, weary and dejected eyes were wide, just like those in the profile. He looked older than I remembered from our brief meeting, but that apart he was just as I had painted him; the high forehead, the black hair going grey at the edges. Alfredo lay there, the spitting image of Luis Beale, confirmation at last that those two strangers were indeed identical twins.

I knew what he was planning when he warned me that he had to go and I was saddened that I hadn't reached him in time to stop him. I reconciled that at least his end was more fitting than handcuffs and prison. He had suffered enough and I only wished that he could remain where he lay in a place of peace with comforting shade in summer and shelter from winter winds, but even that couldn't be. I had my plan for revenge, but had done nothing for him.

I don't recall much immediately after we found Alfredo I was told later that I fainted.

21. The score

I spoke to Jennifer last night, you'll be glad to hear that she is making great progress now she's home. She'll miss the rest of this term, but the doctors are confident that she will make a full recovery. Her attacker pleaded guilty and is due to be sentenced in a few weeks, it's a pity Alfredo can't be there to meet him.

Looking back I can't explain why I continued in the manhunt for Alfredo. I knew it would consume all my energy and turn my life upside down. I suppose I wanted to know whether he had crossed the fine line between good and evil in the name of goodness or malevolence. I believe he thought he was doing good, though I'm not now sure what good means. As a scientist I used to be driven by reasoned logic and as an atheist I had a problem with freewill, but through Cerboni I embraced it. It enabled me to extract justice where none was accessible. He helped me muster the courage and conviction I needed to exact justice for Jennifer. I freely admit that he was my inspiration for executing my revenge, but I also accept that the motives and the pathway I took were mine. He has changed me. I see things more sharply and I have put out the flame for the things that once burned bright within. The intellectual reasoning that weighed heavily on my decision making has been lifted and replaced by intuition. Now I decide and do it. The respect of the liberal intellectuals that was once so important to me is now a barb and I revel in the contempt that has replaced it. For these I owe a debt to Alfredo, I am just sorry that I couldn't repay him. I had hoped to persuade him to give himself up; to have an MRI scan confirm there were scars to his frontal lobe caused by a blow – most probably by his step-father when he was a boy – to identify neurological damage, deeming him unfit to plead and thereby ensure that he would be sent for treatment rather than prison. I suppose I knew all along that it would never have worked out like that. The Home Office and the police would never have allowed it. They would have brought in their experts, dismissed the mitigating factors and pronounced him fit to stand trial. Maybe Alfredo's way was best, but I am struggling to get over it.

I am not sure what I should do now. I am not sure that this is the time to be making life-changing decisions, but today is the day when I find out who I really am. That is why I am waiting and watching for Pete Whelan. Pete is taking me to his adult residential treatment centre for psychiatric and chemical dependency disorders. I've been there before. There aren't bare walls or padded cells, yet there is no mistaking that its architect wanted you to know that you are in the loony bin.

Anyway, by the end of today, I will know whether my score on the 40-point psychopathy checklist is above the 26 that merits the psychopath label. I will be happy if I only score 25, a borderline, somewhere between neurotic and psychotic. I wonder what Alfredo's score would have been. Whatever happens with my tests, I don't plan to stay there long. Just long enough to allow Pete to help me develop some coping strategies. After all, my visit is entirely voluntary. I've decided no matter what, I'm not going back to my old life. Maybe, I'll open a private agency. There's a lot of demand for my extra sensory perception. Then there's the painting. Sarah Bosanne told me that I could ask for £10,000 for my painting of Alfredo and I will, as soon as I'm free of this.

No sign of Pete yet. This view was the reason we bought the apartment; on the top floor, on the corner. Not a penthouse, a home with views and light, not big, but big enough as long as we stayed childless and we did. Below I can see that the chlorophyll is decomposing. The green leaves on the sycamore and chestnuts are rusting bright red and spotting with yellow. I was looking forward to watching them break free. Soon, they'll be falling and spinning onto the strolling shoppers and commuters as they take the air on the path below. Not yet, September hasn't ended, but in a couple of weeks they will. That's when the leaves will be at their peak; it will be different then, the crackle and crunch underfoot will be their wake up call and no one will pass without stopping to admire them. Yes, I'm good at noticing things that others ignore, that's why it came as such a shock when Liz left; I had no idea that Liz had reached the end of her tether. And now my marriage, like the leaves that will be swept up by the council's street cleaners, will be dead and buried. I know now that Liz has gone for good, but that this will be my home for a very long time.